AN AMISH COUNTRY LULLABY

PATRICIA JOHNS

Recycling programs for this product may not exist in your area.

ISBN-13: 978-1-335-46034-9

An Amish Country Lullaby

For questions and comments about the quality of this book, please contact us at CustomerService@Harlequin.com.

Harlequin Enterprises ULC
22 Adelaide St. West, 41st Floor
Toronto, Ontario M5H 4E3, Canada
www.Harlequin.com

HarperCollins Publishers
Macken House, 39/40 Mayor Street Upper,
Dublin 1, D01 C9W8, Ireland
www.HarperCollins.com

Printed in U.S.A.

"You should be a lawyer," Hope said.

He wasn't sure if she was impressed or not. "Do you see my point?" Curtis replied.

"I do..." She sighed. "But the Amish life out here is both unique and fragile."

"You're thinking about the Amish people," he said. "That's noble. But it doesn't have to be one or the other—Amish or English. We could all work together for everyone's good."

Hope didn't answer. He had a feeling they could argue about this until they were both blue in the face, and he didn't want to argue. He wanted her to see his vision, yes, but he didn't want to argue her into it.

"I've been told I'm very stubborn," Curtis said.

"Have you really?" Her tone said that was no surprise, but a smile touched her lips.

"Fine, I'm a stubborn guy," Curtis said, "but it's done well for me. When I get an idea and I know it's good, I find a way forward."

"Always?"

"Almost always."

Dear Reader,

If you enjoy my books about life in Amish country, I hope you'll come by my website and take a look at my other releases as well. My books all have strong, opinionated heroines, and noble men of integrity who fall for them. Add in a cherry pie and some cabbage rolls, and you've got a recipe for romance!

If you'd like to find me on social media, I always enjoy chatting with my readers. We have a lot of fun over there, and I'd love to have you join us.

If you'd like to sign up for my newsletter, there are monthly giveaways there, and it's a great way to keep up with my new releases, as well as hear about other terrific books written by authors you might know.

And lastly, if you enjoyed this book, would you do me a kindness and post a review? They really do make a difference, and I'd be eternally grateful!

Patricia

Patricia Johns is a *Publishers Weekly* bestselling author who writes from Alberta, Canada, where she lives with her husband and son. She writes romances and mysteries set in Amish country that will leave you yearning for a simpler life. You can find her at patriciajohns.com and on social media, where she loves to connect with her readers. Drop by her website and you might find your next read!

Books by Patricia Johns

Harlequin Heartwarming

An Amish Antiques Shop Romance

Her Amish Country Husband

An Amish Country Reunion

The Butternut Amish B&B

Her Amish Country Valentine
A Single Dad in Amish Country
A Boy's Amish Christmas

Amish Country Haven

A Deputy in Amish Country
A Cowboy in Amish Country

The Second Chance Club

Their Mountain Reunion
Mountain Mistletoe Christmas
Rocky Mountain Baby
Snowbound with Her Mountain Cowboy

Visit the Author Profile page
at Harlequin.com for more titles.

To my husband and son

When I look at my life and the things that matter most to me, you are the shining heart of it all. I love you!

CHAPTER ONE

IF THE AMISH ANTIQUES SHOP showed Hope Taylor anything, it was that people would pay good money to cling to the past.

Not that Hope blamed them. She was no different. She ran her hand over her domed belly, and her baby boy wriggled inside her and pushed a foot against her hand. She was seven months along. Her husband, the father of her baby, had passed away the same week she'd discovered she was pregnant. So she was doing some clinging, too, to the memories of her short but loving marriage and all the dreams they'd dreamed together.

The front door of Amish Antiques was propped open, a pool of sunlight spread over the wooden floor as a cool October breeze wound its way inside. The shop was perched on a corner in downtown Apfelkuchen, Pennsylvania—an inheritance from a great-aunt who had passed away and left the place to Hope and her two sisters jointly. The only caveat was that they run the shop together for a year, and then they could sell it or keep it as they saw fit.

The name *Apfelkuchen* sounded a little harsh to the English ear, but the meaning was a sweet one: apple pie. Hope, who had grown up here, had always liked that little detail. This was a unique little town, a melding of Amish businesses and English. That was what the Amish called everyone else—*Englishers*, because they spoke English. The Amish spoke Pennsylvania Dutch, which was a German dialect. It was as simple as that.

Elaine, Hope's younger sister, was teaching the second grade in Bluebird Elementary School, so she wouldn't come by until later that evening to pitch in at the store. Her older sister, Faith, stood on a step stool across the store, arranging an antique Amish-sewn quilt over a hanging rod to display it. It was made of deep, muted colors blocked together in a simple star pattern, and it spoke of the community that had created it. The Amish out here were serious people, devout and stalwart. Not a lot had changed in a hundred years. That was what made the Amish so peculiar—their refusal to adopt new advancements and their determination to continue living their lives the way they always had, with horses and buggies, woodstoves, and the pleasant rhythms of the past. They were like a cozy pocket of history.

The pat-pat-pat sound of little feet drew Hope's

attention, and she spotted a toddler in the doorway. Hope looked at the little girl in surprise. She trotted inside, looking around with big blue eyes and a somber expression. Her blond curls were mussed from the wind outside, and she wore a pair of pink leggings and a knit dress.

"Hi, there," Hope said, smiling down at the little girl.

"I tired…" the girl breathed. "Nap time."

"Is it?" Hope couldn't help but chuckle. "Where is Mommy?"

"Nap…" She toddled toward a pile of quilts that were waiting to be hung and tipped her little self over on top of them, shut her eyes and popped a thumb into her mouth. She looked serious about that nap.

Hope and Faith exchanged an amused look, and Hope headed over to the door and looked outside. There wasn't any sign of a panicked mother anywhere, but there would be soon, no doubt.

"Where did she come from?" Faith asked, climbing down her ladder. She bent and smoothed the little girl's curls where she lay on the quilt pile.

"We'll find out soon enough, I'm sure," Hope replied, glancing out the door again. "I wonder how often kids put themselves down for a nap."

"I don't think there are too many who do that. Tyke absolutely does not," Faith said. "Are you hoping your little guy will?"

"Well, it never occurred to me before now,"

Hope said, "but this is a whole new world of possibility, isn't it?"

Faith chuckled and rolled her eyes.

"Lucy? Lucy!" an anxious male voice shouted from the street. "Lucy, where are you?"

There he was—the panicked parent. But somehow, Hope hadn't expected a dad. She hurried to the door and waved. A tall, dark-haired man wearing chinos and a button-down shirt rolled up to the elbows spotted her. He looked comfortably tanned from the summer, or from a recent trip.

"Over here!" Hope called.

His attention swung in her direction, and she couldn't help but feel a little breathless when his gaze landed on her. He was fit and handsome—the kind of good looks that came from confidence. The word *chiseled* came to mind. She'd put him in his early thirties.

"A little girl? Two years old?" he called.

"About two feet tall and blonde!" she called back.

"That's her." He visibly deflated in relief.

An Amish horse and buggy clattered down the road, the horse stepping high and horseshoes ringing against pavement. It was a good thing that the little girl had come inside; streets could be dangerous places. The man impatiently waited for the buggy to pass before he jogged across the street. Hope gestured toward the shop door.

When he reached her, she found that he was a

few inches taller than her—a pleasant height—and he shot her another relieved smile.

"She came inside," Hope said. "She's a cutie."

"I'm sorry about that," he said, and he paused, blue eyes meeting hers with a slightly pointed look as if he was expecting something, then headed into the shop. He stopped when he spotted the toddler on the pile of quilts. She was already breathing deeply, still sucking on her thumb, her little legs akimbo.

"There she is..." he muttered. "That's a year off my life. She's my little Houdini." He turned back to Hope, giving her a quizzical look. "I'm Curtis Jespersen, by the way."

"Hope Taylor."

"Right. I thought that was you." He gave her a nod. "I was at the funeral. I'm a friend—I *was* a friend of Peter's."

"Oh, of course." Hope's heart fluttered to a stop. It was strange to meet one of her late husband's associates here in Apfelkuchen. But she didn't recognize this man. "It's nice to see you again."

"You don't remember me," he said with a small smile.

"Sorry." She pushed back the wave of sadness. "That was a hard day, and I don't remember a lot of the people I met."

"It's okay, I completely understand," he said. "Peter and I were both considering investing in some real estate, and that's how we got to know each other. How are you holding up?"

"I'm doing all right," she said.

"You look wonderful," he said, and his gaze flickered down to her belly. "I didn't know you two were expecting."

"We'd only found out a few days before the accident," she said. "He was ecstatic."

"I bet. You've got support?"

"Yeah, my sisters and I inherited this antiques shop, and we're running it together. It keeps me busy and keeps me close to family. Oh—" She gestured toward her sister. "This is my sister Faith Lantz."

"Pleasure." Curtis reached out and shook Faith's hand.

Then he crossed the room and squatted next to the slumbering toddler. He eased a hand underneath her and pulled her up and into his arms. She drooped onto his shoulder. "And you've both met Lucy."

"She's adorable," Hope said. "And ready for her nap, apparently."

"Yeah, she does that. She'll decide she's tired, and she'll just lay herself down wherever she happens to be. You know, in the grocery store, at the park, anywhere." He smiled ruefully. "And every once in a while she'll take off."

Hope chuckled. "She looked like she had a pretty good head start on you."

"Yeah… I've got to work on that." Some color touched his face.

"What brings you to Apfelkuchen?" Faith asked. "You aren't shopping for some antiques, by any chance?"

"I'm doing a bit of business here," Curtis replied. "I actually spent a few weeks every summer here at my grandfather's farm when I was a kid. So this town holds some really good memories for me. But I will make sure to come pick up some little piece of history before I leave."

Faith might be more interested in making a sale right now, but Hope's mind had caught on his mention of the summers spent in Apfelkuchen. Hope and her sisters would have been in the midst of growing up in Apfelkuchen when Curtis spent his summers here, but without going to school together, their paths wouldn't have crossed.

"Wait—" Hope said. "Jespersen Street, just a block south of here…is that your family, then?"

"Yep." He smiled a little self-consciously, adjusting his daughter in his arms. "Named after them, but I don't have any family here anymore. Actually… I'm actually going to need some childcare for Lucy for the next couple of weeks. Lucy's nanny was supposed to come with me on this trip, but her daughter is having a baby and she went for the birth, and I'm in the lurch. Do you know of any reputable day cares where I could leave Lucy during the day while I'm busy?"

Hope glanced over at her sister. "There are a couple of day homes in town. Faith and Trent's son goes to one."

"It's filled up, though," Faith confirmed. "There's a waiting list."

Apfelkuchen wasn't exactly a hopping town, but it did serve as a quaint little place for families to settle when the parents worked in larger towns nearby. There was always a demand for childcare.

"We don't have enough day cares available here. I'm planning on opening one here in town in a few months, in fact," Hope said.

That, and it was a business she could run that would allow her to care for her son at the same time. Plus, if her little boy was going to be an only child—and he very well might be—the companionship and socialization would be important for him before he started school.

"I guess I can't ask you to open your day care tomorrow, can I?" he said with a short laugh. "I'll figure something out."

"Where is your wife?" Hope asked.

"I'm single," he said. "There isn't a mom in the picture—Lucy is my biological niece. I adopted her when she was born. My sister wasn't able to care for her."

"Oh…" Hope sifted through the people she knew who might be able to lend a hand, but she hadn't been back in town all that long. There were a few Amish friends…

"If you need someone to watch her, I'd be happy to," Hope said. Was that too forward of her to offer?

"Would you really?" Curtis's eyebrows went up, and he looked down at his daughter's legs as if considering.

"I'm helping my sister with the shop," Hope said. "I live in the apartment upstairs right now, so if she got tired down here, I could take her up for something to eat or for a nap."

Hope cast her sister an inquiring look, and Faith just shrugged.

"Honestly, I don't want to put you out, but it would be a lifesaver for me. You can see how she can slip away from me if I'm distracted in any way. And having attended your wedding, I feel like I can trust you."

"You were at my wedding, too?" she asked feebly.

Curtis chuckled. "It's okay that you don't remember me. Don't worry about it."

That was nice of him to say, but as someone who'd been at the most important events of her adult life, she felt like she should try to get to know him just a little bit.

"I'm starting to feel bad about that," she admitted. "Were you the one who bought that little cottage in Italy?"

"Nope," he said. "I'm the guy who rustled up a band for your wedding when yours canceled last-minute, though."

"You're that Curtis!" Hope cast him an apologetic smile. "I do remember you now. Thank you for that. You were a good friend to Peter, and if we'd been married longer, I'm sure you and I would have gotten to know each other."

"I'm sure we would have," he agreed, and his warm gaze met hers. "I was really happy for Pete, for what it's worth. You were the best thing that happened to him."

Hope felt some heat touch her cheeks. He was just being nice to her—widows got the kid-glove treatment, it seemed—but she appreciated it all the same.

"Thank you," she said.

"Were you serious about taking care of Lucy for a few days?" he asked. "I mean, I can pay you whatever you'll be charging for your day care spots. I'll be in town for a week or two—two weeks being my maximum."

"Absolutely, I can help you out," she replied, and she smoothed a hand over her belly. "It'll give me some practice. But as for pay, don't worry about it."

"Hey, I don't want to take advantage here—"

"Tell you what," she interrupted. "Why don't you donate something to our local food bank? They're collecting monetary donations right now, and I know it would mean the world to them to get a cash gift."

"I can do that." He smiled, hitching Lucy up a

little bit higher on his shoulder. "But you should know that she will make a run for it if you turn your back. And I haven't gotten her allergy tested yet, but she gets a bit rashy when she gets strawberries, so I've been avoiding those."

"I've already seen how she can escape, and no strawberries—got it," Hope replied.

"She isn't potty trained yet, either," he said, patting her diapered rump. "I don't know when people tend to do that, but I figure she's still pretty little." He looked around as if his thoughts were to be found around the shop somewhere. "She naps twice a day, and she'll make it pretty clear when she's ready for a sleep… Um… She's pretty independent, but there comes a point when she wants me and nothing else will do. If that happens, you can call me, and I'll come right away."

"Sure," Hope said. "That's no problem. When do you want to start?"

"Tomorrow?" he asked.

"Sure," Hope replied.

"There's a town hall meeting tomorrow." Faith spoke up. "We were going to attend. Do you mind if Hope brings Lucy along for that? It's an important one—there is an agenda item about town growth."

"I'll be at that meeting, too," Curtis replied. "I'm presenting."

Hope snapped a look in her sister's direction.

"Do you mind me asking what you're presenting? They haven't told us much."

"I'd rather not discuss it until I've signed some papers," Curtis replied. "But I think it'll be good for Apfelkuchen—and for businesses like yours. I really do."

That sounded promising, and Curtis nodded toward the door. "I'll get going, then. But can I drop her off tomorrow morning around ten?"

"You bet." Hope shot him a smile.

"Great. I'll see you tomorrow, then." He gave Faith a smile and nod, and then turned back to Hope. "You really look wonderful, Hope. Motherhood looks good on you."

Hope felt herself blush, and Curtis held her gaze for a moment longer, then turned and headed for the door, Lucy drooling a little string onto his shoulder. He disappeared into the sunlight outside.

"Hmm…" Faith said softly.

"What?" Hope asked, tearing her gaze away from the doorway and feeling mildly embarrassed, although she wasn't sure why.

"I think Curtis Jespersen was flirting with you," Faith said.

"Curtis Jespersen is in desperate need of childcare," Hope replied, shaking her head. "That's all you're seeing."

Faith shrugged. "Maybe." Then she shot Hope

a teasing little smile. "And then again, maybe not. We'll see."

But that still felt wrong. Not now! She wasn't ready to move on or start dating. She was still reeling with complicated emotions surrounding her husband's passing.

"I'm a widow, Faith."

"I know." Her sister sobered. "And you'll always love Peter. Always. But that doesn't mean that other men aren't going to see what a catch you are. And Curtis noticed you. That's all I'm saying."

But that was more than Hope cared to think about right now. Her gaze trailed toward the window, and she spotted Curtis jogging across the street, his daughter gently jostling on his shoulder.

Curtis needed some help with his little girl for a few days—that was all this was. Wasn't it?

CHAPTER TWO

CURTIS WAS STAYING in the nicest room that Apfelkuchen had to offer, which was in the Apfelkuchen Motel along the highway on the edge of town. There were twelve rooms, all decorated with Amish flair—block quilts, wooden rocking chairs, white-painted walls and the wood-sheet floors that were so common in Amish homes in the area. They did have running water, though, along with electricity and even televisions in the rooms, so there was some modern comfort as well. These rooms were mostly enjoyed by truckers traveling through. Apfelkuchen desperately needed more lodging, and he'd been considering that very fact ever since his grandfather had passed away.

Curtis didn't need the inheritance. Five years ago, he would have laughed at that thought. But he'd bought and sold two small tech companies that had turned a very nice profit for him, and he was in a whole new position now. Wealthy—that was what people called him, but he didn't feel rich. He felt out of his element, mostly. Pete Taylor had been born into money, and he'd been the kind of friend who could show Curtis the next steps—how to take care of his investments, how to interview a nanny for his daughter and how to hire the help he needed to keep his life rolling.

This modest inheritance from Grandpa Jespersen wasn't the kind of thing that would turn his life around, but he did feel an obligation to use the money for the town, to build something here that would benefit the whole community. This money would be used to create something more lasting and remodel that street that held the family name.

Curtis had a cot set up next to his queen-size bed for Lucy, and she was still asleep from the nap that she'd started in the Amish Antiques Shop an hour earlier.

He stood at the window, looking outside at the sun dappling the lawn, his mind on Hope Taylor. It was so strange to have run into her here—he had no idea she'd grown up in Apfelkuchen, and it made his plans to help build up this town feel a little more serendipitous. He'd only said hello to Hope a couple of times when Peter had introduced her first as his fiancée and then as his wife a short time later. And Curtis had seen what Pete had seen in her. She was beautiful, sweet, engaging… Some people had thought the couple had gotten married too fast. There had been some whispers about gold-digging, but Curtis saw Pete's side of things, and with a woman like Hope, he'd have gotten married pretty quickly, too.

Well, before Lucy came into his life, at least.

Lucy had been an unexpected gift, one that had left him reeling for a while. When his sister, Lynn, had had her baby, social services had taken the infant right away. Lynn's drug addiction meant she couldn't be the mom Lucy needed. But social services had wanted to place Lucy with a family member, if possible. And when Curtis had gone to the hospital to see little Lucy, when the nurse had placed his tiny, premature niece into his arms, wires attached to her little body, a tube running up her tiny nose and a preemie diaper that had to be folded down to fit her…something inside him had just melted. He couldn't let anyone else take her in.

But his fiancée hadn't been on board. Somehow, he'd thought Samantha would melt, too, when she saw the pictures of Lucy, but she hadn't. They'd agreed years ago not to have children, and she had felt betrayed by his change of heart. Sam told him to choose—her or Lucy. That hadn't been fair. Lucy had needed a home, and at the very least, Curtis had wanted to discuss the option of them adopting her together. But Samantha had pointed out that Lynn was going to be in the picture and that would complicate their parenting. The bottom line was that Samantha simply hadn't wanted to do it. After a tough night of honest discussion, they'd called off the wedding and broken up. He understood, though. This situation was a difficult one, and asking a woman to step in as an adoptive mother to Lucy as well as have a relationship with Lynn, who he was sure would want to be in Lucy's life, was a lot to ask. Curtis came with a complicated family.

So the next morning, after he and Samantha broke up, Curtis called social services and asked what he needed to do to get custody of his newborn niece. She'd started out at three pounds and spent the next eight weeks in the NICU, but looking over at Lucy snoozing on her cot, healthy and snoring softly, he couldn't believe how far they'd come. They were a long way from that NICU unit with the wires and tubes and bustling nurses…

His cell phone pinged, and he looked down at a text from his lawyer.

The contract looks good. I've forwarded it along to his lawyer, and you can sign now. Congratulations on your purchase.

Curtis was buying all the buildings on Jespersen Street, the street that had been named after his family. This was a unique purchase, because while the street held several dilapidated buildings, all were owned by one man. Curtis had already gotten a preliminary approval for rezoning it, and he could see his plans in his mind's eye.

Grandpa Jespersen had been concerned about this old town. He'd said that it would die out one of these days if no one brought in any new business to the area. And now that Curtis had Lucy to raise, he'd started thinking about what he was leaving behind for her besides money.

An idea had occurred to him…an idea that would put Apfelkuchen back on the map. This one was for Grandpa Jespersen, and maybe it was for him, too. This town held the sweetest memories of his childhood, and he wanted to give back.

Lucy snuffled and blinked her eyes open. She lay there for a moment, then pushed herself up to a seated position.

"You're awake?" Curtis asked.

"Yeah." Lucy rubbed her eyes and tumbled off the cot. She shuffled in his direction, and he bent down and picked her up. She was the reason why he needed to leave something meaningful behind—something with their name on it that could last and bring joy. Lucy deserved that.

"You were tired, huh?" Curtis said.

Lucy rubbed her eyes again and looked around. "Snack?"

"Sure. Let's get you a snack."

LATER THAT AFTERNOON, Curtis and Lucy went to the Apfelkuchen business building—there was only one, and it had a doctor's office, a vet clinic that was only open two days a week, a dentist's office that was probably the busiest business in the strip and an office space shared by a few different law offices in the surrounding area when they needed it. He should have asked Hope to watch her this afternoon, but it had felt like too much of an imposition.

This lawyer was a young man, just out of law school by the looks of him. His suit didn't fit terribly well, but he had a sharp look in his eye that Curtis liked. Verne Fenton, the owner of those businesses on Jespersen Street, had also come to sign the last of the paperwork. He was a slim gentleman in his late seventies who wore a pair of jeans, a Western-style shirt and a bolo tie. Lucy was immediately fixated on that tie, and Curtis had to take a step away to keep her out of reach of it.

"I've got a great-granddaughter her age," Verne said with a grin. "And I knew your grandpa rather well. Bernie was a good man. I'm happy to get Jespersen Street back into the hands of a Jespersen. It feels right."

"To me, too," Curtis said. "I've got plans drawn up for the new housing complex, and I'm confident that this will work."

"It's always a bit of an educated guess, though," Verne replied.

"Are you trying to talk me out of it?" Curtis asked with a laugh.

"Not on your life!" Verne retorted. "But business is a gamble, as you well know. It always has been. I started up three restaurants in my lifetime, and I've had two go under. Who would have known that a pizza joint would be the one to succeed? And that's because the Amish folks like them some pizza. They don't want a roast beef dinner. They make that at home all the time. But pizza—that's the real treat."

"So the Amish are your main clientele?" Curtis asked.

"At least fifty percent," Verne replied. "This is an Amish area, and they're helpful and honest people. If you get Amish support, you'll do well."

And community support was an absolute necessity if he was going to get his business idea off the ground. Curtis's plan was going to bring people into town who'd be enthusiastic about buying Amish wares. And while Curtis couldn't see the Amish not liking that plan, Verne had a point. He'd do best if the Amish community was on board.

Lucy squirmed, and Curtis put her down and handed her the little rag doll she liked to play with.

"I'm sorry about bringing my daughter along," Curtis said. "I had a hang-up with childcare."

"Hey, this is for the next generation," Verne said. "What do we work so hard for, if it isn't for them?"

Curtis had to admit that since Lucy's birth, his projects had taken on new meaning…and a few of them had lost his interest for the same reason. Building up a small tech company and selling it for a profit was good money, but building something that would last had started to appeal a whole lot more.

"So, let's just go over what you're both signing here," the lawyer said. "Are you ready?"

The next half hour was spent going over the sales documents and signing in all the appropriate places. The buildings of Jespersen Street would now belong to Curtis in their clapboard, disintegrating entirety. They'd be torn down and Curtis would start laying a new foundation as quickly as possible. Of course, he would gather up some old photos of Jespersen Street back in its heyday and put up a plaque showing what used to be on this street, but it was time for a fresh start—for more than just Apfelkuchen, and for more than just their namesake street.

Curtis needed a fresh start, too. He needed a project to work on that would give back to his grandfather's community and that would make him feel like he was contributing to more than just the tech world, exciting as it was. He needed something with roots, bricks-and-mortar, and some heart and soul attached, too. When he walked down the streets of Apfelkuchen, he wanted to see more than just a town with his boyhood memories. He wanted to see a town that would be stronger and better because of his investment.

And maybe one day, Lucy would come back to Apfelkuchen when she was grown with a family of her own, and there would still be a flourishing town for them to enjoy. There was something Grandpa Jespersen used to say: "You're going to be remembered for something. Make it worthwhile."

"Congratulations to you both," the lawyer said as they initialed the last box and signed on the last line. "I'll submit the forms to public records, but your sale is final."

Curtis held out his hand to Verne, and the older man gave him a firm handshake. Lucy tugged at Verne's pant leg, and Verne bent down to give her a smile.

"You were very patient, little lady," Verne said.

Lucy reached up, whip fast, and snatched one string from his bolo tie. Curtis leaped forward and scooped up his daughter so she couldn't yank on it, and between the two of them, they got his tie out of her fist.

"Sorry about that," Curtis said.

Verne just laughed. "They remind us of the priorities, don't they? They grow up fast. I'm glad you're not missing out on this time with your daughter. Best of luck with your plans for Jespersen Street. I'm looking forward to seeing what you do with it."

CHAPTER THREE

THE AFTERNOON AT the Amish Antiques Shop had been surprisingly busy. Faith had been acquiring all sorts of antique books—some older than others. Really, it was the used book store Faith had once owned, transplanted into one side of the shop. An older gentleman had spent quite a bit of time with Faith in the book corner today, going through some of their older tomes.

The local high school drama teacher had come through looking for props for their musical that year. They were doing *My Fair Lady*, and they needed everything from costumes to bric-a-brac. A few customers had walked in off the street, and they'd sold some vintage kitchenware, a few silver teaspoons to a local artist who was making them into jewelry and a pair of old army boots.

Hope rummaged through a pile of flyers from their mailbox as she watched Faith discussing some antique gardening books with the older man who seemed to be a collector. Hope flipped through a grocery store flyer, a pizza shop ad, and then she spotted it—the flyer that had gone out last week to the whole town.

> Join with your neighbors in an interactive information session about some projected plans for town growth. Give feedback and get information. We want to hear from you!

That didn't tell them much, but in a place this size, it was about as much excitement as they got. Everyone would be there, if only out of curiosity. Curtis had said that he was going to be presenting at this town hall meeting… What could he possibly have in mind for Apfelkuchen? He was in the tech industry—that didn't exactly match with Amish Country. All the same, the town did need more jobs. Her interest was piqued.

A fan oscillated at the center of the store, moving the humid air around. In the first week of October, it was still quite warm, except for overnight when the temperature mercifully dropped. Hope plucked her dress away from her chest and flapped it around. Being seven months pregnant, the heat was getting to her.

She left the flyers where they were and pulled out her phone. Today, she'd been working on photographing the kitchenware items for their social media pages. There were hand-cranked eggbeaters, pastry cutters, graters, ladles, serving spoons, tongs, partial sets of silver cutlery, three cast-iron teapots of different sizes and different ages… Their most popular items these days were vintage Pyrex nesting bowls. They had one complete set and the rest were lone survivors from other people's sets, but a lot of customers came looking for a specific bowl of a specific size to replace in their own sets, and a surprising number of them spotted an item they wanted on social media. The only problem was enticing the customer to drive all the way out to Apfelkuchen to pay and pick it up.

Hope took photo after photo, careful to make sure each one was perfectly in focus. Elaine would put it all together on their social media and their simple website later on while the store was quiet in the evening.

The shop was a tangle of interesting items. Hope and her sisters had gone through most of the stock they had on the sales floor, but even they were surprised sometimes by a quilted table runner tucked into a pile, or a bag of nails, or horseshoes, or an unopened tin of shoe polish from the '50s. That was the satisfaction of this old store. It had its mysteries and almost seemed to have a soul of its own.

A young Amish woman came into the shop and cast Hope a smile. Sarah Yoder wore a pink cape dress and a white *kapp* over her blond hair that was pulled into a tight bun at the back of her head. She had a black cardigan draped over one arm. This late in the year, everyone was expecting cooler weather than they were getting today.

"Hi, Sarah!" Hope called.

Sarah was Faith's husband's cousin, so she was family…distantly. Sarah stopped at Hope's side and waited as she took one more photo of a little glass salt and pepper shaker set in the shape of windmills. They might seem out of place—after all, the Pennsylvania Dutch weren't Dutch at all. They were German-speaking Mennonites from Switzerland, but years ago the word *Deutche* had been misunderstood as "Dutch." So the people here just ran with the theme for tourists, and that included windmills and wooden shoes.

"How are you?" Hope asked. She arranged the last item on the shelf—a floral teacup and saucer. She centered it and took the photo. That shelf was done.

"I'm good," Sarah said. "How are you feeling?"

"Overheated," Hope said with a chuckle. "But I feel good."

"My sister is pregnant right now, too," Sarah said. "And everyone keeps telling her to put her feet up so that they'll stop aching."

"I try," Hope replied, but then she remembered her offer to watch Curtis's toddler. That was hardly putting her feet up.

She led the way over to the sales counter. "I know I'll have to start taking it easier soon, but when I do I'll have more time to think, and with my husband's passing, I don't think I'm ready to face my feelings without the cushion of hard work."

"That's almost Amish of you," Sarah said, giving her a gentle smile.

"Is it?"

"We believe that work is a gift from *Gott*. It unites us and keeps our hands busy and useful and…it's awfully useful to diverting our minds from sadder thoughts," Sarah replied.

"I can understand that."

The women exchanged a smile, and then Sarah looked down at the pile of flyers. She picked up the town hall meeting announcement that lay on top.

"Are you going to that?" Sarah asked.

"Sure am," Hope replied. "Are you?"

Sarah nodded. "We want to see what's being proposed. I don't know if it'll be good for our community or not. My *daet* is worried that it won't be."

It was interesting to see what the Amish were thinking in times of change. The Amish didn't change anything—that was what their *Ordnung*, or their rule book, was for. They did things the same way no matter what leaps the outside world took. The rest of America could be driving hover cars and the Amish would still be farming with big draft horses pulling the plow.

"Are people worried about it?" Hope asked.

Sarah pressed her lips together. "A little. If something is good for everyone without a doubt, they don't hold meetings to convince you of it."

"That's a good point," she admitted. "I think the idea is that we need to bring more jobs to Apfelkuchen and more people to shop at our stores."

Sarah angled her head to one side. "That's something. And I can appreciate that. We do need to make enough to pay the bills."

"It would be helpful for us here at the antiques shop, too," Hope said.

They were making sales, but it wasn't enough to pay Hope, Faith and Elaine full wages. This shop could only really support one owner.

"I suppose that applies to every single business in town," Sarah said. "But when changes are suggested, they aren't always something that's good for our Amish community. Like, if someone opened a bar, for example. Or if grocery stores stopped buying local produce. There are changes that can be detrimental to our way of life. I've been explaining all this to Eddie."

"How is your fiancé?" Hope asked.

Sarah's engagement had been shocking to just about everyone—to the Amish because he was an electrician, for crying out loud! And to the English because he was bound and determined to live Amish for the rest of his days—giving up his job, electricity, a motor vehicle…all the regular American comforts. He was now working on the

Yoder farm and learning the Amish ways before they could set a wedding date.

Sarah smiled, but there was a worried crinkle in her brow. "He's learning everything all at once, and sometimes I think his head might explode from all the information."

"Is he enjoying farming?" Hope asked.

If Eddie wanted to be Amish, he had to know how to farm. That was how the Amish supported themselves here. Other communities branched out a bit, especially when farmland was scarce, but here it was predominantly agriculture, and Eddie wasn't becoming Amish to reinvent the wheel. He needed to fit in, especially if he was going to get the blessing from Sarah's parents and the bishop to set that wedding date.

"*Yah*, he is enjoying it, but he's starting from scratch," Sarah said, her confidence seeming to slip. "*Daet* says he wouldn't dare leave him on his own for a week."

That sounded like gentle criticism from Albrecht Yoder.

"Everyone has to start somewhere," Hope replied. Expecting a town-raised man to have the same farming instincts as people born to it wasn't exactly fair. But this was why people didn't convert to an Amish lifestyle easily or often.

"I know, but he's tired. So tired." Tears suddenly misted Sarah's eyes. "I'm halfway scared he'll change his mind about turning Amish and give it up."

"And give *you* up?" Hope shook her head. "I saw him mooning over you. He's not giving you up."

"I hope not." Sarah sucked in a deep breath.

"Just give him your support," Hope said. "I have a feeling it means more than anyone else's."

"Oh, he wants my *daet*'s good opinion more than anything," Sarah said.

"Not more than yours," Hope countered.

Sarah blushed and nodded. "You're probably right."

Oh, to be back in those early days of being engaged and excited about the future. She almost envied Sarah, with her whole life ahead of her and a man who'd been willing to sacrifice every convenience just to be hers.

"Enjoy this," Hope said softly. "I know you can't wait until you're married already and all the uncertainty is gone, but you'll never have this time again when you're engaged and excited and just about drown in each other's eyes."

Sarah blushed again. "It's hard to wait for us to be officially married. I'm afraid at every turn something will ruin our happiness."

"It won't," Hope said. "I just means that your heart is on the line and you've got something worth protecting. It's the way it's supposed to be. Just believe in him."

All this was easier said than done, of course, but Hope knew what that kind of love felt like. The excitement and expectation… She knew what it felt like when a man loved her with all his heart. It was exciting, and it was scary.

In Hope's situation, marriage had turned out to be more challenging than she'd anticipated. Not an easy path of mutual support and affection but a struggle between two completely different people who loved each other deeply. Even with all that love, they'd had completely different needs, and there had been frustration on both sides. Marriage hadn't been what she'd expected.

Hope just wished that Sarah and Eddie were paying their dues now, and once they were married, they'd have clear sailing. Because after all their hardship, after Eddie and Sarah found a way forward, and after Eddie made the shocking decision to join the Amish in order to be her husband, the young couple deserved a break.

Marriage needed to be simpler for someone.

CHAPTER FOUR

THE NEXT MORNING, Curtis stood in the bathroom, holding Lucy up so the toothpaste dribbled into the sink and nowhere else. And he brushed her teeth. This was a feat. At home, they had a step stool, but here at the motel, he had to make do.

"Open wider," he said. "Don't chew the toothbrush, Lucy."

He wriggled the brush free of her clenched teeth and she giggled.

"No, I'm not playing," Curtis said. "You need clean teeth."

Lucy giggled again, and Curtis gave her a stern look, toothbrush aloft.

"Come on, Lucy," he said. "Let's finish up your teeth. When you're done, we're going to the restaurant for breakfast, and then we're going to visit our new friend."

Lucy sobered at that—whether it was for breakfast or Hope, he wasn't sure—but she opened her mouth to finish the brushing.

"Spit," he said, but she didn't. At this age, she

only ever swallowed toothpaste, but he tried all the same. Then he wiped her mouth with a towel and set her down on her feet. Lucy immediately took off out of the bathroom, and Curtis cleaned up, then grabbed his own toothbrush. As he brushed, he listened to the sound of his daughter chattering to herself.

Bringing Lucy with him on a business trip hadn't been ideal, but her nanny had needed personal time, and he didn't have anyone else to leave her with. His parents lived in an adults-only villa, and his dad needed a lot of his mother's help these days. His one cousin in Pittsburgh was a soft touch for Lynn. He was never sure what his sister would decide to do—sometimes she'd show up unannounced and she'd be high. He couldn't risk that when he wasn't there to defuse the situation.

So Lucy had come along with him, with the plan of figuring it out along the way. Somehow, Curtis found himself looking forward to seeing Hope again, and more than he probably should. He'd only met her twice, and seen her across a room a handful of times, but she'd left an impression. She'd been the best thing to ever happen to Peter, and he'd told himself if he ever found a woman like that, he'd marry her, too. It was incredibly sad that Peter hadn't gotten to see his wife's beautiful pregnancy, or meet his child, or grow old with Hope. Peter had just married the woman of his dreams when his life was cut short.

Curtis missed Pete a lot—there were still times when he reached for his phone to send a text, only to remember that Peter was dead. But Hope was still here, and while Curtis was grateful for her help with Lucy, he had an undeniable urge to somehow make her life easier while he could. She deserved that.

"Okay, Lucy," he said, coming out of the bathroom. "Let's go to breakfast."

There was a little Amish-owned-and-operated diner farther down the road that he remembered from his boyhood. Back then, they'd offered up a traditional Amish breakfast—eggs, bacon, sausage, pancakes, scrapple and a breakfast casserole that they'd served in little personal ramekins. And he was hankering for something comforting and familiar before he faced that town hall meeting.

The Peachy Diner was just as he remembered it, and still Amish-operated. The food was just as good as he remembered, too. And after he'd paid his bill and cleaned the sticky maple syrup off Lucy's fingers and face, they headed on down toward the center of town, with a quick detour to Jespersen Street first.

He slowed and scanned the dilapidated property—boarded-up windows, some graffiti spray-painted on the front of an old flower shop. He remembered that shop—run by an Amish family. The lady who ran it used to send a single bloom home with Curtis free of charge to give to his grandmother. And then there was the meat shop—but that had gone out of business because of the grocery store meat department that sold everything more cheaply. The Everything Shop's sign was still surprisingly crisp and clear. He remembered that store, and you truly couldn't narrow it down to one thing. You could buy rat traps, thread, sewing machine parts, flower seeds…and they'd had this delicious stick candy the owners made at home and sold wrapped in plastic, twisted at the ends and tied with ribbon. Curtis had loved that candy as a kid, and his grandfather used to chat with the owner and tell Curtis he could have only one stick of candy, so to choose very carefully. And Grandpa Jespersen would wait for as long as it took Curtis to choose. He used to appreciate that liberty, but now on this end of parenting, he suspected this had been his grandfather's chance to just chat with an adult. Whatever his reasoning, it was a sweet memory.

Back when he and Lynn were kids, all these places had been open for business, but they'd slowly shuttered over the years. Grandpa had kept him up to speed on every single closure, and it had been sad to hear about them. Curtis had had a personal memory of every single one of them. And every business represented a family that could no longer make a living there. What had they needed? More customers.

"Kitty cat," Lucy said from the back seat.

A cat slunk around the side of the building,

and another one licked itself on the boardwalk. These old buildings probably held a fair number of feral cats.

"Do you like kitties?" Curtis asked.

"Uh-huh."

Curtis smiled. Lucy was getting more articulate now, and it was fun to hold little conversations with her and figure out what she was thinking about. He put the SUV into gear and headed around the corner at the next stop sign, toward Main Street, where Amish Antiques was located. If his plan was successful, Hope's shop would do better, too. Everyone would benefit. No more shops dwindling down to nothing.

He parked on the street in front of the antiques shop. The trees in the park a block away were blazing orange and red, and the leaves had started to drop and had blown down the sidewalk this far. So when he got Lucy out of her car seat and put her backpack of snacks and toys over his shoulder, he picked up one of the leaves from the sidewalk and handed it to her.

"Pretty, huh?" Curtis said.

Lucy beamed up at him and sniffed the leaf.

"Come on," he said. "Let's go inside."

Curtis opened the shop door, a bell tinkling softly overhead. Lucy seemed to sense an opportunity for escape, because a dangerous glint twinkled in her blue eyes, and then she turned around and started up the sidewalk at a run. He muttered to himself and jogged after her, scooping her up after a few yards of freedom.

"No, you don't," he said, and he turned back toward the store. Hope stood in the door now, holding it open. She wore a vintage-style summer dress—the pattern looked floral—and she had a light wrap pulled over her arms, her belly poking out the front. Her cheeks were pink, and her dark hair was pulled into a messy bun on top of her head, and he couldn't put his finger on what he liked so much about that look, but he liked it on her.

"Morning!" Hope called.

"Good morning." He shot her a smile, and Hope stepped back to let him inside the shop.

Hope's sister was sorting through some papers at the front counter, and she smiled and nodded.

"Do you have a busy day?" Hope asked.

"Yeah, I do. I have meetings at the credit union and a few other things to do before the town hall meeting." He met her gaze. "I appreciate this."

"Of course." She turned her attention to Lucy. "How are you, Lucy?"

Lucy held out the leaf from the sidewalk, and when Hope's face broke into a stunning smile, Curtis's heart skipped a beat. But standing closer to her now, he noticed that the floral pattern on her dress included kittens mixed in. It was unexpectedly whimsical.

"This is Hope," Curtis told his daughter. "She's

our friend, and you're going to stay here with her today, okay?"

Lucy looked up at him dubiously.

"You know how you stay with Nanny Judy?" he asked.

"Nanny Judy," Lucy whispered.

"Well, this is Hope. She's like Nanny Judy. She is going to take care of you."

"We'll have fun today, Lucy," Hope said. "We can go for a walk to the park, and we can play in the leaves there. You might like that."

"She'd probably love it," Curtis said.

"And we'll be at the town hall, of course," Hope said.

"Of course." He met her smile. Would she support his vision? He hoped so. "Okay, so I have Lucy's bag. There are diapers, all her changing stuff, a change of clothes in case you need them, some snacks and a couple of board books she loves a lot. Like I said before, she's in this stage where she thinks running for it is hilarious, so be aware of that. Can you run after her? I mean…"

"You mean being as pregnant as I am?" Hope asked with a rueful smile. "Oh yes. Don't worry about that."

"Okay, well, she's used to being with me, or with her nanny. So she might not like it when I leave." He hated this part—walking away while Lucy wailed for him.

"We'll be okay," Hope said. "My nephew, Tyke,

is about a year older than Lucy is, so we've got lots of toddler experience here."

"Great," he said with a nod. "Okay, then." He glanced around the shop, not quite ready to leave yet. "Hope, can I ask you something?"

"Sure."

"What do people in Apfelkuchen want for their community?" he asked. "What do they need the most?"

Hope was silent for a moment, and she rested her slim, creamy hands on top of her belly. "Customers," she said at last.

"Yeah? Anything else?"

"Peace, quiet, calm…and customers." She shot him a rueful smile. "So easy to deliver on, right? Don't mess up any quiet comfort we enjoy, but provide an influx of customers."

"So easy," he said with a chuckle. "How's business on this street?"

"We've only been running the place for a few months, but we've needed a healthy online presence to make sales. We just don't get the foot traffic to keep ourselves afloat."

"What do you do online?" he asked.

"Well, I feel a bit foolish talking to a tech guru about our simple strategy," Hope said, "but we've got a website and some social media accounts. We're posting pictures of our day-to-day routines around here on social media, and of specific antiques with the stories behind them. So we try to make our social media accounts interesting. We're working on getting every single item in the store posted on our website so that customers can see what we've got."

"Smart," he murmured. She had a good business instinct.

"I guess Peter's work in sales rubbed off a bit," she said. "But we don't have a way for anyone to pay for an item from our website, so we're still limited to customers who can come to the shop to pay and pick up the order. So…we're still pretty local. But we're trying to grow."

Was that a request for help? Because this sort of thing was pretty simple for Curtis.

"Do you want a hand getting an online shop set up?" he asked.

Hope blinked at him. "Yes! I mean… Yes. We'd love that. I think it would help our sales." She turned around and beckoned to her sister. "Faith, Curtis has offered to help us get an online store set up!"

Faith straightened from where she stood at the counter. "Really? Curtis, that's really kind. What we need most is some advice. I don't want to monopolize your time, but we'd appreciate any guidance you can give us."

"Sure," he replied. "Give me your website address, and I'll take a look at what you've got and what platform you're working with. It's a place to start."

Faith picked up a business card and circled around the counter. Curtis put Lucy down and accepted the card.

"No touching things, okay?" Curtis said.

Lucy put her hands behind her back in a way that Nanny Judy had taught her and looked up innocently. Yeah, that innocent look was deceptive.

"Let me give you my cell phone number," Hope said, pulling her phone out of a pocket in her dress.

"Yeah, and I'll give you mine. If you need me, give me a call and I'll get back here as soon as I can."

They exchanged numbers, and Curtis pocketed his phone again.

"Okay, Lucy," he said, and he squatted down. "Daddy's going out for a bit, okay? You're going to be here with Hope. Remember, Hope is our friend." He looked up at Hope for a second. "We like her."

A smile touched Hope's lips.

"No, I come, too," Lucy said, heading for the door, and Curtis stretched to catch her.

"You've got to stay with Hope, Lucy. But I'll be back. Okay?"

"No." Lucy shook her head, and her lower lip started to quiver.

"Look at this—" Curtis reached out and caught the edge of Hope's dress. "Kittens!"

Lucy looked dubiously toward the dress, then her face lit up.

"Kitties!" Lucy said.

"Yes, kitties," Hope said, bending down. "Do you like kitties, Lucy? Do you want to see a cat? We have a cat here in the store. His name is Smokey."

"Do you really?" Curtis asked. He hadn't seen any sign of one.

"Yeah, he kind of adopted us," Hope replied. "He's really patient and sweet. He must have been someone's pet who got loose, but there were no tags, so now we have a cat."

"Kitty?" Lucy asked, looking up at Hope, her blue eyes wide.

"Let's see if we can find him," Hope said. "He likes to hide. Where would a kitty hide, do you think?"

Hope shot Curtis another one of those sunshiny smiles and fluttered her fingers at him. Yeah, this was his chance to go. Lucy trotted along at Hope's side, holding her hand and looking around for the promised cat.

Curtis headed out the front door. As it swung shut with a tinkle of bells, he heard Lucy's wail start up, and his heart yearned back toward his little girl.

"Daddy!" Lucy's cry followed him down the sidewalk, and he slowed, almost stopping once, but then he determinedly got back into his vehicle.

Lucy was in good hands. He knew that. She'd be safe and doted over. Call it gut instinct, but he trusted Hope with his little girl. If only walking away got easier as a dad.

It hadn't yet.

CHAPTER FIVE

LUCY STOOD BY the closed door, her mouth open in a square of anguish. Her blond curls stuck to her red, tearstained face as she reached fruitlessly for the doorknob. Hope's heart went out to the little girl.

"Oh, poor thing," Faith said from across the room. "It's hard on them."

"I know," Hope said, and she opened up a box of animal crackers. Her nephew, Tyke, would do just about anything for a fistful of these. "Do you want some animal crackers?"

"Daddy!" Lucy wailed, not even a glance spared for the treat. Well, maybe they would be a distraction for later.

"Oh, come here, sweetie," Hope said and bent down to pick her up. Bending at this stage in her pregnancy wasn't exactly graceful, but she managed to scoop Lucy up and pulled her into her arms. Lucy flailed and cried, and from inside her belly, the baby gave a little kick, bopping Lucy.

The little girl paused in her cry and looked down at Hope's belly in surprise.

"You felt that, did you?" Hope asked.

Lucy nodded and patted the top of Hope's belly. The baby gave another push and Lucy's tear-streaked face broke into a brilliant smile.

"There's a baby in there," Hope said. "I think he just woke up."

Lucy didn't seem to comprehend that, but she did look distracted from her earlier woes.

"Do you want to play with a baby dolly?" Faith asked, picking a faceless Amish doll from one of the shelves. It wore a little pink cape dress and a black bonnet, with white canvas arms, hands and feet peeking out. This one wasn't an antique, but Amish dolls were always a popular item in their shop.

Lucy reached for the doll.

"Baby…" she cooed. She understood that concept just fine, and Hope shot her sister a grateful smile.

"Thanks," she said.

Smokey chose that moment to saunter across the shop floor, tail held high. He was dark gray tomcat. Lucy squirmed to be put down, and Hope obliged.

"Kitty!" Lucy squealed in delight. Smokey looked over his shoulder, then hopped up onto the counter out of toddler reach and proceeded to groom himself. Lucy—having a cat to watch and a doll in her arms—settled onto the ground to play.

"You're going to be busy today," Faith said with a laugh.

"I know," Hope agreed. "But I'd best get used to it. When I'm running a day care, there will be more than just one toddler to chase. Which reminds me, I need to talk to Verne Fenton again about leasing the old schoolhouse. The last time we spoke, he said he couldn't guarantee it. He said it needed a lot of work."

"It's over a hundred years old," Faith said. "I imagine there are quite a few safety codes it would need to meet before you could use it."

"I know, but part of being left with Pete's estate is that I actually have the money to do the renovations. I'm not sure that people realize that. I have half a mind to buy it outright. It's such a gorgeous historical building. I could hire a company to renovate it myself—can't you imagine it with polished wood floors and that school bell clanging away at nine in the morning?"

"It would be beautiful," Faith agreed.

"I'll talk to Verne again," Hope said. "Let him know how serious I am about this."

And with any luck, she'd see Verne at the town hall meeting that day.

The morning sped by. Lucy took a midmorning nap on a couple of folded quilts on the floor by the cash register. She chose the time and place, popping her thumb into her mouth and curling up. Once she was asleep, Smokey joined her, curled up at her back. Having a purring little heater against her would only make for a better sleep.

After lunch, Faith wrote a sign that said, "At the town hall meeting—back shortly," and taped it on the window before she locked up the store after them.

The day was warm, but with that little bit of chill in the air that reminded them that summer was over and winter was on the way. Hope and Faith could have used Tyke's car seat for Lucy, but they decided to walk the two blocks to the town hall instead. It was on Fifth Street, across the street from the Presbyterian church.

"We have to hold hands, Lucy," Hope said. "Do you want to swing?"

Faith took her other hand and they swung the little girl between them, to her laughing delight, and when her shoes came down to the sidewalk again, Hope made a game of trying to have Lucy land on a leaf.

The whole street was lined with cars and pickup trucks on both sides, which made Hope all the more grateful that they weren't looking for parking. The buggy parking in the lot was full, and more buggies were parked on side streets. Hope's feet were tired now, and she was realizing that at this stage of her pregnancy just walking a few blocks wasn't as easy as it used to be.

The town hall was a redbrick building with white brick trim. It housed the mayor's office and a few of the other town magistrates, along with a large meeting area. Today, the meeting space was filled with folding chairs, and at the front, on a stage, a microphone was set up. A good number of people filled the seats already, and others milled around the sides of the room. About half the people there were Amish, and when an Amish man spotted Hope standing with Lucy's hand in hers, he quickly stood and beckoned her to take his seat.

"*Danke*," she said, using the Pennsylvania Dutch, and she gratefully sank into the folding chair.

His friend got up to let Faith have a seat, too, and the men moved to the back of the room to stand with a group of Amish men who stood with arms crossed over their chests, looking sober and thoughtful.

"Do you want to sit on my lap, Lucy?" Faith asked.

Lucy still had the Amish doll tucked under her arm, and she lifted her hands to be picked up. Faith pulled her up onto her lap, and they settled in as Mayor Michael Lantz got up to speak.

Mayor Lantz was distantly related to Faith's husband, but there were a lot of Lantz family lines in the area. He was a man in his forties who owned the local credit union and a few other businesses in town. Those sound investments in the community were the reason he'd been elected, and it had been a good choice. Everything ran smoothly under his leadership.

There was an introduction, some thank-yous to everyone for coming.

"Today, we are bringing forward a town expansion project," Mayor Lantz said. "As you all know, Jespersen Street has been falling apart for several years now. Jespersen Street is a historic street in Apfelkuchen, and it was named after one our founders, Augustine Jespersen. Many of our original families owned and operated shops on Jespersen Street. As many of you probably know, times have been tough, and our town population has been steadily decreasing. I'm pleased to announce that Jespersen Street is finally back in Jespersen hands. Curtis Jespersen, great-grandnephew of Augustine Jespersen, has just purchased the street's properties, and he has some ideas about bringing this iconic street back to life again. So without further ado, I'd like to introduce you to Curtis Jespersen."

There was a spattering of clapping, and Curtis took the microphone.

"Daddy!" Lucy said, her voice ringing over the murmurs.

Curtis grinned and shaded his eyes. Hope fluttered a wave at him, and she saw a smile touch his lips when he spotted them.

"Good afternoon, everyone," Curtis said. "It means a lot to me to finally have Jespersen Street back in the family. My grandfather, Bernie Jespersen, loved this community, and when I visited here as a boy, I learned why. Apfelkuchen is special. This is a place where people take care of each other, and where a handshake still means something. But let me tell you a little bit about my experience. My dad owned a string of laundromats in Pittsburgh, and when I graduated business school, he gifted me with my first laundromat. It might not sound like much. You make pocket change—literally! A quarter at a time. But I was able to build up that laundromat and sell it. The timing was right. I found the right buyer, and I made some money off it. I took that money and I bought my first tech investment—a little basement-run business that made some useful apps. And that's how things started for me. So I know I wasn't raised in this town. I know I don't understand all the challenges you folks face. But there's one thing I do understand very well, and that's business."

That was a rather prideful thing to say—at least that's how the Amish would describe it. *Kapp*-covered heads tipped together as Amish women passed along their opinions.

But Curtis did a rather beautiful job of introducing himself. He talked about his business experience in starting up tech companies and selling them. He talked about his desire to create something that would last longer than the next merger or the next piece of technology that took over.

"So I know how business works. I know what it takes to make money," Curtis continued. "This isn't me being crude. Money is a necessity—one we appreciate a whole lot more when we're struggling, right? And businesses need customers—*your* businesses need customers."

His gaze sought out Hope, and he smiled again.

"I have a plan that I believe will not only rejuvenate Jespersen Street and turn it into a beautiful attraction, but will also bring what our struggling businesses need most—customers who are eager to spend money here in this town, and who are eager to support the Amish businesses, especially."

The murmurs grew louder. This all seemed like an extravagant promise. Curtis pulled a sheet from a large display board, and he unveiled an artist's rendition of what looked like some row houses. They looked quite beautiful, but he wanted to build more housing for a town that was bleeding young people? Who was supposed to live there? Who was supposed to afford it?

"I would like to introduce you to Jespersen Row," Curtis said. "These will be short-term rental properties for people who want to come out to Amish Country to experience it for a week or more at a time. The units will be spacious, comfortable and will appeal to a higher-earning clientele. People in the city often talk about how they want to just get away from all the hustle and bustle for a while, and these short-term rentals will allow them to do just that. They'll bring their ready income into Apfelkuchen to spend in local shops and at roadside stands. Not only will we get a much-needed injection of money into the local economy, but we'll put Apfelkuchen on the map as a great place to let people experience the charm of the Amish countryside."

Customers with ready money, willing and eager to buy a little piece of local history. That was an appealing thought! Actual customers on the street, browsing the shop in person instead of looking at their wares on social media. That could do a lot for their bottom line, Hope thought.

"What do you think?" Hope whispered to her sister.

"It sounds like a good idea to me," Faith whispered back. "We could use some people looking to spend money here."

"I was thinking the same thing…"

But looking around, Hope saw that the Amish folks didn't seem quite so pleased.

"I'm sure there are questions and comments, and I want to hear them," Curtis said. "We're going to pass a microphone around so that we can all hear what you have to say."

The Amish man who'd given up his seat for

Hope walked forward to accept the microphone. He looked down at it uncomfortably, then cleared his throat.

"Well now..." he said slowly, his voice echoing. He cleared his throat again and moved the microphone farther away from his mouth. "I've got a brother in Bird-in-Hand, and I've visited him there. It's a different feel out there in the tourist areas. Amish folks aren't left alone to just live their lives. People are taking pictures and videos of them without even asking if they mind, and my three-year-old niece was followed around by tourists who kept taking her picture and trying to pose with her. It was an insult to our way of life, and a little dangerous, too. So, if you're wanting to bring in some *English* tourists to spend money out here, just how safe will this be for our *kinner*?"

And that kicked off the question-and-answer period, which went on for some time. Some people were excited at the prospect of bringing people into town who'd keep businesses afloat. But Hope had started to notice a distinct pattern—the English locals could see the bright side of bringing tourists to town, and Amish were warier. What about the road safety? What about children walking down country roads—would there be more speeding vehicles? What about the higher incidences of buggy crashes in tourist communities? What about bad influences on their young people?

There was a tap on Hope's shoulder, and she

turned to see that Sarah had snagged a seat behind them.

"Hi," she whispered.

"Have you heard all this?" Hope asked.

"*Yah*, I've been listening."

"What do you think?" Hope asked. "Is this a good idea, or a bad one?"

Sarah sucked in a slow breath. "My *daet* was saying that you can't unring a bell. If we start this, we can't go back again to the way things are now. And I think there's wisdom in that."

Hope had to agree. Some things, once started, couldn't be reversed. That was core of Amish caution. Some things could have ripple effects that no one even considered.

And looking up at Curtis standing there with his sleeves rolled up his forearms and that hopeful look on his face, she could feel the ripples in her own life already. Curtis Jespersen was the kind of man who made an impact...whether you were ready for it or not.

CHAPTER SIX

IT SEEMED LIKE everyone had a question or a comment, and Curtis was determined to hear them all. If people were willing to talk, then he was willing to listen. An hour passed, and with the lights shining down on him from the small stage, moisture beaded on his forehead. Curtis pointed across the room to the last person with their hand up to speak, an older woman who wore blue jeans and a tie-dyed shirt.

"Yes?" Curtis said.

The microphone made its way over to her.

"Hi, I'm Ellen," she said. "I just wanted to know about the old schoolhouse. That's a historic building that my own parents attended when they were young. Is it going to be torn down?"

"Not necessarily," Curtis said. "There are a few options for the schoolhouse, one of which is to transfer the building to a museum where it can be reassembled and kept for posterity."

Curtis was tired, and he didn't see any more hands raised right now with questions. He'd known this would be an intense presentation, but he hadn't anticipated quite so much division in the responses. He'd thought that most people would see the benefit of bringing tourists into the town. His grandfather would have. But his grandfather hadn't been Amish, either, and the biggest push-back he was getting was from the Amish locals.

"Thank you so much for your time this afternoon," Curtis said. "I appreciate all the feedback, and I appreciate you coming out."

The next half hour was spent shaking hands and answering a few more questions without microphones present. Mayor Lantz was answering questions, too, and Curtis was acutely aware that the man needed to keep his constituents happy. And if Mike Lantz had to choose between backing Curtis's plan or backing up the people who lived here, he'd choose his community.

As it should be.

Curtis looked up just as his daughter came smashing into his legs. Curtis laughed and leaned down to pick her up.

"Hey, princess," he said.

He looked over to find Hope and Faith standing there, Hope's warm gaze resting lightly on him.

"Sorry," Hope said. "I tried to hold her back as long as I could."

"That's okay," Curtis replied, and he gave Lucy a squeeze. "I'm all done with work for now."

"I need to get back to reopen the store," Faith

said, and then gave Hope a knowing little smile. "I also need to call my husband and tell him what happened in the meeting. He's busy on a construction site today, but I promised to fill him in."

"I can give Hope a ride back in a few minutes," Curtis said. "I mean, if that's okay with you, Hope. I just wanted to get your take on a few things."

"Sure," Hope replied. "Faith, say hi to Trent for me."

Faith gave them a wave and had her phone pulled out as she headed out of the auditorium. Curtis fell in next to Hope as they made their way out to the street.

"So, now you've heard the presentation," Curtis said, "what do you think?"

"I think…it's complicated," she replied. "I'm also rather concerned about that schoolhouse."

The schoolhouse again. He hadn't thought it would be a sticking point, but hearing it in Hope's soft voice, he really wanted to reassure her on that front.

"Like I said, we can relocate it," he replied. "I'm serious about that. I don't want to tear down local landmarks or mar the history around here. My grandfather went to that schoolhouse, too. It's local history."

She nodded, and he tried to read her expression.

"I'd hoped to lease that schoolhouse for my

day care," she said. "But I guess that's out of the question now."

His heart sank a little. The plans the architectural firm had drawn up for him used the entire street—including the land where the schoolhouse currently sat. If they scaled back, it wouldn't be as profitable. He'd done the math, as had his accountant.

"I'm sorry," he said.

"It is what it is," she replied. "I'll find another place. But it would have been really sweet to bring children's laughter back into that old schoolhouse."

"So…you're against this project, then," Curtis said.

"Does it matter?" she asked. "You've bought all the property on Jespersen Street. You can do whatever you like with it, so long as it passes town council."

She averted her gaze—upset with him? Somehow that possibility bothered him more than it should.

"I need community support," he said quietly. "How can I build this and advertise an authentic Amish Country experience out here if people hate it? It will flop without local support. That's a fact. But if we all work together—businesses supporting businesses—then we can all grow."

Hope angled her head to the side. "That sounds good, Curtis, but this community is made up of

Amish and English. And both communities have different needs."

"Let me ask you this," Curtis said. "How close am I to getting the Amish support around here?"

Hope shrugged. "I'm not sure. My friend made a good point. As she said it, you can't unring a bell. Once you start this, there is no coming back to the way things are now. If this ends up being a mistake, there will be no undoing it—not all the way, at least."

"And you?" he asked.

Hope pressed her lips together for a moment, then sighed. "For myself, this would be great for the antiques shop. It would bring the exact clientele we need right to our doorstep."

Curtis started to smile.

"But—" she raised a finger "—I can't look at this selfishly. Some of my sister's in-laws are Amish, so we know them better than most. And they have valid worries. The beautiful life that people are so intrigued with only works when these communities have space and aren't being pestered by Englishers trying to get their pictures or asking them intrusive questions. I understand why they're worried. I've got a baby coming, too. It's possible that what we stand to lose is greater than what we stand to gain."

"But what happens when this town shrinks even further and more businesses close? You know what they say—if a community isn't growing, it's shrinking. Nothing stays the same."

She eyed him for a moment. "How long has it been since you've spent a summer in Apfelkuchen?"

The last summer he'd spent here, his sister, Lynn, hadn't come along. She'd been getting into trouble, drinking a lot and partying. His parents were at their wits' end with her, and that summer she'd refused to go visit their grandparents.

"I was about thirteen, I suppose," he said. "But I kept up with my grandfather. We were very close."

"I believe you," she said. "I'm not saying that your heart is in the wrong place. I daresay a lot of people do support you, and like I said, if I was just thinking about myself, this would be an excellent plan. A brilliant one, really. But you don't know the Amish side. Bring in an honest business that can make money and draw in nonlocal customers, and you'll have everyone's support. But bringing in a bunch of lookie-loos to treat Amish people like tourist attractions?" She shook her head.

"I'm trying to bring in a business that will be a success, but it's not so easy," Curtis replied. "And when you see something that will sell well, you need to jump on it—be the first one there. Apfelkuchen could really benefit from this. I really believe that."

Lucy patted his shoulder, and for the first time,

he noticed the Amish doll in his daughter's arms. It was one of the little faceless dolls that Amish girls played with, and Lucy beamed up at him.

"Daddy!" Lucy said. "There's a kitty!"

He was frustrated. Somehow, he'd wanted Hope to see what he was trying to do. Yet why should hers matter over every other opinion he'd heard today? It shouldn't, but he'd wanted her to see it all the same.

"Is there a kitty? Did you find it?" he asked his daughter.

Lucy nodded exuberantly, and he noticed Hope relaxing a little bit when she looked at Lucy. Lucy seemed to have the same effect on Hope as she did on Curtis.

"You were married to Pete, so you understand the business world a little better than most, I think," Curtis said. "But I do need local support if this is going to work. If I don't get it, I won't be sinking money into a project doomed to fail. So you can rest easy there. But if I can get the local Amish support, I really think we can put this town on the map, and my grandfather would have really liked to see that."

"I can show you the Amish world," Hope said.

Curtis raised an eyebrow. "Can you?"

"Of course," Hope said. "But I'll level with you. I doubt you'll convince them. They're cautious people."

"What about your own business?" he asked.

"Will you be able to stay afloat with how things are going?"

She was silent for a moment, and he could see the conflict in her eyes.

"Oh, it would be good for us. Very good," she said at last. "But it's not right to just look at our situation and no one else's. We can get an online shop going. We can use the internet to spread our wings a bit. There are other solutions."

Hope was honorable—he couldn't deny that—and her heart was certainly in the right place. Curtis couldn't fault her for any of that. But all the same, she was wrong. She thought they could preserve this little corner of Amish Country without bringing in fresh customers to keep those businesses afloat. Business—and life—didn't work that way. Everything changed as time went on. They couldn't freeze time. But they could try to guide the river a little bit for their own benefit.

"Then do me a favor," Curtis said. "Give me some insight into Amish families and their concerns. I need to understand it."

"All right." A smile played at her lips, and his heart stuttered. She had no idea what effect she could have on people, did she?

"But—" he met her gaze "—stay open-minded. You might see it my way, after all."

"I will keep an open mind, if you will," she replied.

A chance to get a tour of the community from

a different perspective was priceless, but it wasn't just the information and new perspective that snagged at his attention. It was Hope. Was it terrible of him to want a few hours with her?

"Daddy!" Lucy said. "I got a dolly."

It was time to head out anyway. Lucy was wanting his attention now.

"I could take tomorrow morning away from the store and give you a little tour," Hope said.

"Okay," Curtis said, mentally going over his plans for the next day. He had a Zoom meeting in the afternoon, but his morning was flexible. Twist his arm and all that.

"Yeah, I can do that," Curtis said. "What time should I meet you?"

"Come by the shop at nine," Hope replied.

"We'll be there."

Curtis needed local support for his building project to get off the ground. So he'd start with Hope Taylor. She would be a unique ally in this if he could win her over. And right now, that challenge was an appealing thought.

CHAPTER SEVEN

"IT WAS A bit of a spontaneous plan," Hope said as she and Faith closed up the antiques shop for the evening. "You don't mind me taking the morning off to give Curtis a tour of Amish Country, do you?"

Hope flipped the sign to Closed, then flicked the lock on the door. Faith was already sweeping the other end of the store. Their younger sister, Elaine, stood at the counter counting up the cash, the bills flicking down in a blur.

"No, it's fine," Faith replied. "And this was your idea? Because I saw the way he was looking at you."

"Yes, it was my idea." Hope cast her older sister a glare. "Faith, stop reading more into this than is already there."

Faith laughed softly. "He's cute."

"How was he looking at her?" Elaine asked, jotting a number onto the deposit slip.

"Like she'd just dropped out of heaven," Faith replied.

"Ah, I know that look." Elaine chuckled. "And, Hope, you are going to get some romantic attention. It's going to happen. You might want to make your peace with it."

"He was Peter's good friend." Hope's throat tightened with emotion, and her sisters sobered immediately and exchanged a look.

"Sorry, Hope," Faith said. "I know—it's soon. I'm sorry. I shouldn't tease."

"I wasn't teasing," Elaine said. "I know it's soon, Hope, but…you're a widow. Which means you're technically available. And men are going to notice you, so if you don't want any romantic attention, you might want to make that clear."

"How?" Hope asked.

"Maybe don't go on spontaneous little day trips with them?" Elaine arched an eyebrow.

Smokey twined himself around Hope's legs, and she bent down to give him a pet.

"This is not a little day trip." Hope straightened again. "Curtis needs to see the Amish side of things. I'm doing this for the community."

"Hope does have a point. He's the first investor I've heard of who's wanted to inject some money into Apfelkuchen," Faith said. "It's not like opportunities come up every day. We don't want to scare him off, but he does need to understand what will work for this community and what won't."

At least Faith was on her side.

"I agree," Hope replied. "If we bring tourists into town promising them an Amish experience, what happens if the Amish people don't want to be part of that? I mean, none of this works if the Amish aren't sold on it, and from what I saw at the meeting, the Amish folks are wary."

Faith nodded. "But from the look of that presentation, he's already put a fair bit of money into building plans. And when a man puts his money somewhere, his heart tends to be there, too."

Elaine wrapped the deposit slip around the little stack of bills and tucked them into a bank bag.

"It is all very rational," Elaine said. "Do you two mind if I change the subject? I've got a problem with a student, and I could use some advice."

"Of course." Hope was relieved to have something else for them to focus on. "What's going on?"

"Tim Granger is back in town, and…his son is in my class."

Hope gasped. "What?"

Tim Granger had been one of Elaine's best friends when she was in high school, but they'd lost touch over the years. He'd become a state police trooper, if Hope remembered properly. He'd also gotten married—not invited Elaine to the wedding—and his wife had tragically passed away about a year ago.

"What do you mean, Tim Granger is back?" Faith asked. "Did he call you?"

"Nope. I met him when he dropped his son, Oliver, off for his first day of school on Monday."

"Monday!" Faith said. "And you tell us now?"

"You were busy," Elaine said. "Faith, you and Trent were helping his grandma with all those doctor appointments, and Hope, you and Mom were doing the ultrasound for the baby, and you were shopping for baby stuff… I didn't want to bother you."

That was a flimsy excuse, but Hope also knew her sister. Elaine could be private when her heart was involved, and Tim might not have been a romantic partner, but he'd still broken her heart and betrayed their friendship. This obviously stung for her. But she was talking to them about it now, and that counted for something.

"So what's he like?" Hope asked.

"The son or the father?" Elaine asked wryly. "Tim is a lot different. He's older, bigger and… sadder."

"Of course…" Hope murmured. Losing a spouse would do that, and she was now uniquely set up to understand that grief.

"I suppose that's to be expected after that kind of loss," Elaine agreed. "He's not the same guy who left. I don't know how to explain it, but he's different."

"What about his son?" Faith asked.

"Oliver's a sweet little guy. He's twig-thin like his dad was. And you can tell he really misses his mom a lot. He stayed inside at recess and just cried his little heart out."

Tears welled up in Hope's eyes at the thought of that poor little boy. She swallowed against a lump in her throat and smoothed a hand over her belly.

"Just…cried?" Hope asked.

Elaine's eyes welled, too, and she nodded. "When I asked what was making him so sad—trying to get him to put words to it—he couldn't. So I just held him. What could I do?"

They were all silent for a few beats, and Hope swallowed hard.

"Well, he's got an excellent teacher," she said. "He's lucky to have you, Elaine."

"I'm going to do my best," Elaine said. "The poor kid."

"What's Tim doing in Apfelkuchen?" Faith asked.

Elaine sucked in a deep breath. "Well, he's a Pennsylvania State Police detective now, if you recall. He said he transferred. I guess it's slower out here and easier for being a single dad."

"Understandable," Faith said, and Hope nodded her agreement.

"Anyway, you'd think that Oliver's heartbreak would be my biggest problem, but I'm pretty sure Oliver can't read."

"Really?" Faith frowned. "I mean, he's had a big set of changes, and he's new to the school, and…"

"When a student is placed in a classroom, it's the teacher's responsibility to find out where their skill level is. We need to know where to place them for learning groups, what reading books to give them, what math level they are at…so I've been working on that this week."

"And he can't read?" Hope asked.

"He has trouble with phonics and letter sounds. I got him to write his name and he was mixing up the letters. That happens with second graders, but when I sit down with him with a picture book with simple words, he can't sound them out or use the pictures to make a guess, either."

"Maybe he just doesn't care," Faith said. "He's got bigger things on his mind. I mean, his mommy died last year. Who knows how long he'll need to process that grief?"

"That's a possibility," Elaine agreed. "I'm not discounting that. For him, losing his mom is going to be a whole lot more important than school worksheets. But Oliver isn't the problem. It's his father."

"What about him?" Hope asked.

"Tim is convinced that Oliver reads just fine—and that he reads above grade level. I want Oliver to join a reading practice group, and Tim refuses. He says it's a waste of time and that Oliver will miss out on other learning."

"Have you talked to your principal?" Faith asked.

"Not yet." Elaine sighed. "I might need to if Tim won't listen to me, but I need to try and sort it out on my own first. We were really good friends, once upon a time. I should be able to talk to him."

"But you aren't talking as friends," Faith pointed out. "You're talking as a teacher to a parent. It's different. When kids become part of things, parents get super protective. It's…not going to be the same."

"I know," Elaine said. "But I have to try."

"Do you know why Tim disappeared on you?" Hope asked.

Elaine shook her head. "No idea. I'm not going to ask, either."

"Why not?"

"Because I don't care," Elaine said. "He didn't come back for me, obviously. Nor should he. He moved on from our friendship. He's back…and he'll very likely move on again. I've made my peace with that. This is about a little boy who needs support. And that's all."

A little boy without his mom. That stabbed a little deeper for Hope, because she was going to have a little boy who'd never meet his dad. He'd never know how much his daddy had loved him from the very moment he'd heard that Hope was pregnant. And Tim had lost a lot, too.

Elaine was right. This wasn't about old friendships anymore. Some heartbreaks were bigger than everything.

THE NEXT MORNING dawned chilly and overcast, a welcome drop in temperature from the day before. Hope pulled on a pair of maternity jeans with a soft band that pulled up over her bump. They were cuter than she'd thought they'd be when she looked at herself in the full-length mirror. She paired them with a loose, caramel-colored maternity sweater that felt a like a warm hug and added a wool shawl on top of it. Then she slid on some comfy shoes, grabbed her purse and headed down the stairs toward the shop below.

The Amish Antiques Shop opened at nine, and Faith was just unlocking the shop door when Hope came in through the side door.

"Curtis just got here," Faith said. She pushed open the door and waved, then turned back to Hope. "You look great, by the way."

Hope shot her sister a smile, but Elaine's warnings from yesterday were still ringing in her ears. If she didn't want Curtis to get the wrong idea, she'd need to be careful.

Curtis was standing outside his shiny black SUV as Hope came out the front door. He opened the passenger-side door for her, and when she got up into the leather seat, he closed it after her. All the outside noises melted into the velvet silence of the vehicle. She turned to see Lucy buckled into her car seat in the back, and Hope gave the toddler a smile.

"Hi, Lucy," she said.

Lucy gave her a shy smile. She had a rather love-worn rabbit clutched in her hands, and she looked around curiously.

"Smokey?" Lucy asked hopefully.

"Smokey is in the shop," Hope said. "We can't bring him with us. He hates car rides. What's your bunny's name?"

Curtis hopped into the driver's seat, and he cast her a smile.

"That's Bun-Bun," Curtis supplied. "Normally he's a night-night toy, but she wanted to bring him along today."

Hope did up her seat belt, and she turned back to give Lucy another smile. "Bun-Bun is a beautiful rabbit."

That seemed to be an appropriate assessment, because Lucy started to chatter about her stuffed toy, mostly to herself and sometimes to Bun-Bun, whom she held up in front of her to survey while she talked.

"All right," Curtis said. "Did you want to get a hot drink to go first? Or a pastry at the bakery?"

Hot drinks and pastries were starting to sound a little too date-like to Hope.

"I'm fine. You can grab something for yourself if you want, though."

Curtis's blue gaze clouded for a moment, then he nodded. Her point seemed to be made, because he said, "I'm in your hands. Where to first?"

"I wanted to show you some of the back roads

that take you past Amish farms. So head out to the highway and go west."

Curtis pulled away from the curb and signaled a turn. The baby stretched inside her, and she rubbed the spot where a little foot was poking her.

"You're going to see the real Amish area," Hope went on. "Here in town, Amish people will come do some shopping or maybe eat out for a treat, but if you want to see how the Amish really live, you have to see their homes."

"Do you know many Amish people personally?" he asked.

"A few. My sister Faith's husband has some Amish extended family, so they consider me family, too. They are very earnest, loving people."

"But he's not Amish? Was he born Amish? How does that work?"

"Trent's grandmother was Amish, but she left the faith when she married his grandfather. So their kids were all raised English. There's a lot of second and third cousins and great-aunts and great-uncles who are still Amish, though, and some of Trent's uncles even went back to being Amish after being raised English. But they had spent a lot of time with their Amish grandparents, so it wasn't exactly shocking."

"So, no shunnings or anything."

"No, nothing like that. Just two groups of people trying to live good lives."

Curtis turned onto the highway, and he stepped

on the gas. As he left Apfelkuchen behind them, the trees rolling out on either side of them were ablaze in autumn glory—deep gold, burnt orange, amber… A swirl of leaves spun across the road in front of them.

"Do you see that sign for pumpkins ahead?" Hope said. "You'll want to take a left there."

He nodded, then asked, "You used to live around here?"

"Oh, I was very much a town girl."

"Do your parents live in town still?"

"They do. Mom and Dad are in the same house where they raised us. They're both retired now."

"What about Pete's mom?" he asked. "Do you see her at all?"

Hope's mother-in-law was an energetic, opinionated woman. Hope thought she would have bonded with her eventually given time, but they'd never gotten that time. She hardly knew Catherine Taylor, although she knew that Peter's mother wanted to be in her grandson's life. There was no question about that. The thought made her pulse speed up a just a bit.

"We talk on the phone," she replied, trying to sound more relaxed about it than she felt.

Curtis made the turn onto a cracked road with a lower speed limit. "So that's why you came back to Apfelkuchen? For family support, I imagine?"

"In a way." Hope ran a hand over her belly. "Actually, I came because I jointly inherited the antiques shop with my sisters, and part of the deal was that we had to run it together for a year. That was before Peter died. He was traveling a lot, and I figured I could miss him from Pittsburgh or I could miss him from Apfelkuchen. Plus, I was bored out of my skull."

"Bored?"

It was impossible for a man to imagine that a well-off woman with no responsibilities besides her own entertainment could possibly be unhappy with the situation.

"I was in a gilded cage, Curtis," she said gently. "Peter provided very nicely for me, we had a luxury apartment in Pittsburgh where I could do whatever I wanted. But I had nothing to do, and with him traveling for work, I missed him so much. I thought that helping my sisters with the shop would give me something constructive to put my energy into."

She could still remember how her days had stretched out in front of her, long and lonely.

"Is it easier being here?" he asked, and he flicked his gaze at her in a direct look before returning his attention to the road.

Was it? Was coming home to Apfelkuchen the answer to her aching sense of loneliness? With her husband's death, having her family close had been a tremendous support. She wasn't sure how she would have gotten through this without them. But did it cure the problem at heart?

"Well, I'm happy here," she said. "As happy as can be expected."

"In a perfect world, what would you have to fill the gap?" he asked.

"A sense of purpose—something that roots me to this place, something that makes me indispensable."

"I think being someone's mom will do that," he said.

"I mean indispensable to Apfelkuchen."

He nodded slowly. "That's harder to do."

"It is," she agreed.

This conversation had swerved very easily into more personal domain, but she didn't get the sense that Curtis was trying to flirt. He just wanted to know.

"Okay, slow down up here," she said as they crested a hill.

And tumbling out below them was a vista of Amish Country—small family farms, fields stitched together like quilt blocks using barbed-wire fences. Copses of trees blushed red and orange, and cattle dotted the green pasture. The Amish schoolhouse was farther on, with children outside playing on the swings, seesaws and jungle gym equipment. A line of Amish girls walked down the center of the road in the direction of the schoolhouse, all wearing black bonnets and matching coats. Their tights were black, too, but fluttering out around their legs were brightly colored dresses—blue, pink and purple.

"Whoa." Curtis stepped on the brakes to slow down even more and finally pulled over to the side of the road and stopped. The girls didn't even turn around to look. "No thought of traffic, huh?"

"Not really. Everyone around here knows this is where the school is. They slow down."

The school-zone sign was farther on down the road, but most of the children walked to school. The practical school zone was much larger than Pennsylvania traffic law designated.

Curtis gave her a sober look. "And tourists wouldn't know."

He was a quick study, she'd give him that.

"No, tourists wouldn't. More than that, tourists would come to just gawk at the kids while they played at recess." She rubbed a hand over her belly. "Ever since I got pregnant, I've been seeing things a little bit differently. I don't know about you, but as a parent, I wouldn't like the idea of strangers coming to stare at my child while he was supposed to be at school. That's not safe."

Curtis nodded. "I get that. I wouldn't like it, either."

The girls walked on, those fluttering dresses making a splash of color across the gravel road. These kids grew up on Amish farms, with their own community and their own cultural expectations. And they were vulnerable.

"There's no saying who'd be coming to see the Amish life out here," Hope said. "Peter always said that his job was to make a sale, not to judge whether the boat was good for the guy or not. But out here, it has to be about more than a sale."

"It is about more than a sale," Curtis said. "Look, the point isn't to make a huge profit, it's to have a viable business."

"Then why bother?" she asked. "Without much profit, it doesn't sound like much of an investment for you."

"Because I've got a little girl, too," he said. "And I want to leave her something with our name on it that lasts. This isn't just for Grandpa's memory. It's for Lucy's future."

Maybe he understood better than she realized.

"It's not about the money, then," she said.

"It never was. But without some money coming into this town, it won't last. And I want this place to be alive and flourishing for generations."

CHAPTER EIGHT

CURTIS PUT HIS vehicle into Drive and pulled back onto the road. The Amish girls finally turned to look at him when he got closer, and they moved to the side while he drove carefully past. There were more families walking to school—one cluster of boys who were tussling with each other over one boy's hat, and farther on a group of older kids walking more sedately.

"I wonder if there's a solution," Curtis said.

"Don't bring in tourists," she replied.

"Or…could we close this road to everything but buggy traffic during school hours?"

"That's hard to enforce."

She was right. It would be incredibly hard to enforce. But he'd learned through the last few business sales that there were always problems, and those problems could be solved. Sometimes the solutions were creative. Sometimes they were incredibly easy! But just because there was a roadblock didn't mean there wasn't a way past it.

"People might be willing to find a workable

solution if they want more financial stability, though," he said. "The restaurants, the ice cream shop. Those places would do well, too, and there'd be more room to open up more stores—gift shops, a bookstore, craft shops. Everyone could do better. One of the problems people face out here is limited farmland. When you've got families having lots of kids, those kids can't stick close to home because there's no more land to buy and farm. So they have to move away. But what if there were other ways to make a living? What if there were Amish shops, Amish tourist attractions? Families could stay closer."

"You should be a lawyer," she said, and he wasn't sure if she was impressed or not.

"Do you see my point?"

"I do..." She sighed. "But the Amish life out here is both unique and fragile."

"You're thinking about the Amish people," he said. "That's noble. But it doesn't have to be one or the other—Amish or English. We could all work together for everyone's good. The English people could help protect the Amish way of life, and everyone could benefit together."

Hope didn't answer. He had a feeling they could argue about this until they were both blue in the face, and he didn't want to argue. He wanted her to see his vision, yes, but he didn't want to argue her into it.

"I've been told I'm very stubborn," Curtis said.

"Have you really?" Her tone said that was no surprise, but there was a twinkle in her eye.

"Fine, I'm a stubborn guy," Curtis said, "but it's done well for me. When I get an idea and I know it's good, I find a way forward."

"Always?"

"Almost always." What was she asking here?

You keep railroading me. That was what Samantha used to say, and he'd resented it. He'd done most things Sam's way.

"When it's important, I try to find solutions," he amended. "With Lucy—"

He looked over his shoulder at this daughter in the back seat. She was looking sleepy, but she was awake. He couldn't say anything sensitive in front of her. She might be young, but he couldn't take chances on how much she understood.

He came to a four-way stop then and braked.

"Which way do I go?" he asked.

"Take a right."

He flicked the signal light and then turned. A buggy came toward them at a fast trot, and he gave the horse as much room as he could and slowed down more until the vehicle had passed them.

"Where are we going?" he asked.

"Albrecht and Mary Yoder's farm. They're Trent's aunt and uncle, and they're really sweet people. We've known them for a long time, and they're a great place to start if you want to talk with actual Amish folks and hear their concerns."

It was smart—and it was a connection he couldn't make on his own.

"Thanks. That's kind of you," he said.

Hope glanced into the back seat. "It looks like Lucy nodded off back there. You stopped earlier when you mentioned her. You were talking about finding solutions."

"I was engaged," he said. There was something in the way she was looking at him that melted his reservations. "Samantha and I had been together for three years, and we were about ten months away from our wedding. My sister, Lynn, had given birth to Lucy prematurely. There were drugs in Lucy's system, and social services removed her from Lynn's care. Lynn is struggling with drug addiction, and she knew she couldn't pull herself together for her baby. They needed someone to step up, and there weren't a lot of options. I asked Sam what she thought, and she was against adopting her. Like, really against it. We were always pretty aligned in the past. We had the same values, the same money sense, the same hopes for our future. Taking in my sister's baby didn't fit in with any of that, and Sam couldn't pivot."

"So you broke up over it?" Hope asked.

"Yeah." It had been a gut punch for Curtis. He'd envisioned his future with Sam at his side, but she simply couldn't open her heart to one tiny, premature baby girl. She couldn't do it.

"There was no way to sort out a solution there?" Hope sounded genuinely sad.

"No. I tried everything. But she had a point. This wasn't just an adoption. This was adopting my sister's baby, and Lynn would know exactly where to find her again. It would be complicated. It *is* complicated."

"Is that why you brought Lucy with you on this trip?"

She was perceptive. Of course, he could have found someone to take Lucy for a few days. It would have been tough for both of them to be apart, but he could have done it.

"Pretty much. If I left her with someone else, my sister might try and come take her when she's not sober. Lynn won't push it with me, but she would with my cousins or my aunt. Even my parents. Lucy's safest with me."

His life had changed so much since he became a dad. Now, he was carting a two-year-old with him, planning for childcare, thinking ahead about nap times, meals, bedtime routines…

"Up there, you'll take another left," Hope said. "At the next stop sign."

Curtis followed her instructions and made the turn.

"Have either of you regretted the breakup?" Hope asked. "Has Sam ever wanted to meet

Lucy? I can't imagine anyone not falling for her on sight."

"I know I did." Curtis smiled sadly. "I went to the hospital when they told me that Lynn had given birth, and I couldn't hold her. She was too tiny, and she was in an incubator with all these tubes and wires. But the minute I laid eyes on her, I was smitten. She was just so little and she needed protecting. That night we broke up, I asked Sam to come to the hospital with me to see her, and she refused. I showed her pictures, but she was unmoved."

"Wow…" Hope murmured.

"I guess she couldn't change her mind about kids like I had. No room for Lucy. I guess it's a good thing that it came up before we got married," Curtis said.

Still, her words stayed in the back of his mind these days. *You keep railroading me.* Had he done that? But taking Lucy in had been the right thing to do. If he hadn't insisted, she might be in a foster home somewhere, deep in the child welfare system. All the same, he didn't want to be the kind of guy who just steamrolled over the woman he loved. That wasn't right, either.

Out the driver's-side window, cattle grazed on fall grass, still green but now supplemented by hay. A young Amish man stood on the back of a wagon, forking hay into the feeder. He looked up as they passed, his gaze following the vehicle.

"This is it," Hope said. "Up there on the left is Mary and Albrecht Yoder's home. And they normally have kittens around, so Lucy should be in her element."

Curtis glanced back, but Lucy was still asleep. She'd be excited when she woke up.

"So, you think they'll be okay with us just stopping by?" Curtis asked.

The last thing he needed was to inconvenience people by his presence.

"This is how the Amish visit. Remember, there are no telephones in the houses. Sometimes they'll leave voice messages for each other on answering services, but they have to go out and check those at the phone shanty—and that's a decent walk from the house. So if people want to go see each other, they just stop in. That's Amish hospitality."

"Okay, then." He signaled and turned down the drive. Some of the overhanging tree branches were bare of leaves, but others were still covered in bright yellow foliage. A two-story white farmhouse sat farther back on the property. A stable was off to the side, with a corral that held two horses, and an older Amish man with a bushy gray beard and a straw hat on his head was just coming out with a wheelbarrow.

"That's Albrecht," Hope said, and she waved at him. A smile appeared on his face as he recognized Hope, and he waved back.

These people really liked her, Curtis realized,

and it warmed his heart to know that. Of course, Hope was just a likable person, but it was nice to see people's warm reaction to her, all the same. Pete had been right about Hope being special.

"Come on," she said. "Let's go say hello."

Hope hopped out his vehicle first, and Curtis looked back at Lucy. His daughter was just waking up, and she blinked at him blearily.

"You ready to see some new friends?" he asked. "I hear there are kittens."

Lucy rubbed her eyes. "Kitties?"

"I'll get you unbuckled."

After Curtis got Lucy out of the back of the vehicle, he slammed the door shut and carried her over to where Hope was talking with Albrecht Yoder.

"This is Curtis," Hope said, turning toward him.

"I recognize you from that town hall meeting," Albrecht said.

"You were there?" Curtis asked.

"Of course." Albrecht gave Curtis a firm handshake. "We take our community seriously. So how do you know Hope?"

"He was one of Peter's good friends," Hope supplied. "And..." She glanced at him. "He's a good man."

The endorsement surprised Curtis, and he appreciated it, too. It was high praise, and coming from Hope, it landed differently.

"Thanks," he said, casting her a warm look. Then he jostled Lucy on his arm. "This is my daughter, Lucy."

"Hello, Lucy," Albrecht said, giving the toddler a smile.

"I like kitties!" Lucy announced.

"*Yah?* You do?" Albrecht put on an act of surprise. "For sure and for certain? Because we have plenty of kitties around here."

The side door of the house opened, and a young woman appeared on the step.

"Sarah!" Albrecht called. "We have a little girl who loves kittens here. Do you think you could catch one for her?"

Sarah laughed. "Of course, *Daet*. Where is Eddie?"

"Filling the feeder," Albrecht said.

"Hi, Hope!" She pulled on a coat and came outside. There was another round of introductions, and Sarah held her hands out for Lucy, who leaned delightedly toward her.

"Can I take her to the barn with me?" Sarah asked. "There is a new litter of kittens in there. I wouldn't be long."

Sarah had a bright, fresh look about her, and Curtis couldn't help but smile.

"Sure," he said. "Lucy, you go with Sarah to see the kittens, okay?"

"Kitties!" Lucy hollered, and Sarah popped

Lucy onto her hip. She was obviously used to little kids.

"They are so little and cute. You're going to love them..."

Sarah continued to chat with Lucy as they headed off in the direction of the barn, and when he looked at Hope, he saw a wistful smile on her face.

"So how are the wedding plans?" Hope asked Albrecht.

Curtis fell into step next to Hope as they followed the Amish man toward the house.

"First things first, Hope," Albrecht said, glancing back at them over his shoulder. "First things first."

"What wedding?" Curtis asked softly after Albrecht stepped ahead to lead them inside the house.

"Long story short?" Hope gave him a rueful little smile. "Sarah is marrying an English electrician."

CHAPTER NINE

INSIDE THE HOUSE, Hope gave Mary a quick hug, and then introduced her to Curtis. There were general hellos and an offer of pie, and a few minutes later, the women settled around the kitchen table, the men standing on the other side of the kitchen. This was the way the Amish tended to do business—the women gathered together to talk about personal, womanly matters, and the men took care of business and finance together.

"This is a gorgeous hutch," Curtis said, touching an intricately carved wooden display case. "Who made this?"

Mary had her good dishes there, and some piles of serving bowls, some pitchers. Hope had to agree that the hutch was beautiful.

"I did," Albrecht said.

"You carved this? Made the whole thing?"

"*Yah.*" Albrecht shrugged. "It gave me something to do one winter."

Curtis nodded in appreciation, and their conversation moved on. Hope watched as Curtis and

Albrecht got right down to business, arms crossed over their chests as they discussed the pros and cons of more tourists in the area. Mary was silent for a moment, listening to them, then sighed and pushed a piece of cherry pie toward Hope.

"You're eating for two, after all," Mary said.

The pie was done in a lattice crust, gooey red cherries peeking up from between the strips of flaky crust. Mary's pies would be award winning if she believed in competition. But the Amish believed very strongly in everyone being on the same level. Women didn't compete with their baking; they fed those they loved. Men didn't compete in their achievements, either; they provided for their families to the best of their abilities.

Hope smiled. "I do like that part of pregnancy."

"So did I." Mary met her smile. "So...you know this man?"

"Curtis?" Hope shrugged. "A little bit. But he was Peter's good friend, and if Peter had lived, I'm sure we would have gotten to know each other better. My husband had a very high opinion of him, and Peter was a good judge of character."

"He's not from around here, though."

"No, but he used to visit his grandfather who lived in the area. And he's a Jespersen."

"Hmm." Mary nodded slowly. "*Englishers* don't understand our way of life. It's not their fault."

They could discuss that for hours, but Hope didn't want to. She knew how things were between the Amish and the English. What she wanted to know about was the upcoming wedding. That was fuel for gossip in both communities.

"Speaking of Englishers, how is Eddie fitting in?" Hope asked.

"He's doing his best," Mary said. "And he's very kind and considerate of our daughter. He's working hard…"

Hope could feel Mary dancing around something. "But?"

"Albrecht says he doesn't have any instinct for farming," Mary said. "The other day he was helping to ear tag a calf and almost got himself trampled by the cow because he turned his back on her. He means well, he's just…not a farmer."

"How are his other lessons going?" Hope asked. "The religious lessons, and the language?"

"He's learning…" Mary nodded slowly. "The language will be difficult. He'll always have an accent, and he'll probably have trouble understanding people without Sarah there to fill in the blanks for him."

Becoming Amish was no easy feat, and Eddie was finding that out. When a man became Amish, he became the face of the household—the man who provided financially and who represented his family in community votes. How could he do that when he couldn't fully understand the language?

"It can't be easy for him," Hope said. "I can

only imagine. But he and Sarah can figure things out. She'll help teach him, and living with an Amish wife, speaking *Deutche* at home whenever possible...it'll come."

Mary didn't answer, just pressed her lips together.

"You do think the wedding will happen, don't you?"

"If he doesn't give up," Mary replied.

"You think he might?"

Hope's mind turned to Sarah in the shop the other day, the worry in her eyes. It was one thing for a man to declare his intentions and quite another for him to live them out. Being Amish was a tough life, and fitting in with the Amish was tougher still.

As if on cue, the side door opened and Sarah came inside with Lucy beside her. The toddler came skipping into the room and beelined for her father.

"Kitties! Daddy, there's kitties!" Lucy jabbered, and Curtis scooped her up.

"It looks like she enjoyed herself?" Curtis asked.

"Very much," Sarah replied. "If you want to bring a kitten home, we have plenty."

"No, no," Curtis laughed, and he glanced in Hope's direction, his warm gaze catching hers for one heart-stopping moment. "I don't think I could wrangle both a toddler and a kitten. My hands are full with just Lucy here."

Sarah pulled a chair up next to Hope and shot her a smile. "How are you doing, Hope? You look wonderful."

They chatted for a few minutes, but as Albrecht's voice grew louder, their attention was pulled toward the men's discussion. Albrecht was getting animated, and the women fell silent.

"We had to fight for our way of life, young man," Albrecht was saying. "In 1972, we got the right to educate our *kinner* in our own way. Before that, Amish men were being put in prison for refusing to enroll their *kinner* in public schools. The Amish life is one of hard work, but we are often misunderstood, too. And while public opinion is in our favor right now, it hasn't always been. And might not always be."

"Surely having more income will help your community, though," Curtis said.

"The Good Book says that the love of money is the root of all evil," Albrecht quoted.

"Doesn't it also say that if a man is poor he may be pressed into stealing and dishonor his faith?" Curtis asked.

"It also states laziness brings on poverty, and the Amish are nothing if not hardworking."

Curtis nodded slowly. "And I agree with that. I respect your way of life, Albrecht. Amish work ethic is known all over this country. Your handcrafts are second to none. And I would never be pompous enough to try and tell you how to be Amish, so please don't take my interest as disrespect. But money is a simple necessity. We need enough of it to provide for our families. When a town's population starts to go down, the effect tends to be like a broken dam. It starts with a few people leaving for greener pastures, and then more and more follow suit. That's starting to happen in Apfelkuchen. The official population has declined in the last five years. If we lose Apfelkuchen, it'll be hard on Amish families, too."

"And why does it concern you?" Albrecht asked curtly.

"It concerned my grandfather, and I'm finally in a position to be able to help. I want to do some good in his honor."

Lucy looked up at her father, a look of alarm on her little face, and Hope got up and held her hands out to the toddler.

"Come see me, Lucy?" Hope asked with a smile.

"Thanks, Hope," Curtis said, and he passed his daughter into her arms, then turned back to his discussion with Albrecht.

Lucy screwed up her face as if she'd cry, and Hope touched the tip of her nose with her finger.

"Boop," she whispered, and Lucy broke out into a smile. Hope felt a wave of relief. Lucy didn't need to be upset by an adult debate. She carried the toddler back over to the table.

"Your *Englisher* is rich, isn't he?" Sarah whispered to Hope, and there was a little bit of disapproval in her voice.

Hope startled at the question. In her short marriage, she'd gotten used to a certain level of comfort that Peter had provided, and after his death, all those bank accounts now belonged to her. So she would be considered rich in Sarah's eyes as well, even though her wealth was nothing compared to many others.

"Uh…yes," Hope admitted. "He is."

A wealthy Englisher who'd made his fortune buying and selling tech companies wasn't going to get the trust of the Amish people, though.

The side door opened again, and this time Eddie came inside. He looked almost Amish now—the clothes were in line with the Amish *Ordnung*, or their set of rules. But his hair was still growing out to the Amish hairstyle, and it was now rather bushy when he took off his straw hat and hung it on a peg.

"Hi, Eddie," Sarah said, and she sprang to her feet. "You must be thirsty. Let me get you some water."

Sarah's cheeks flushed and she hurried into the kitchen for a glass of water for her fiancé. When she brought it over to him, they stood by the door together talking quietly.

"She's certainly in love," Hope said softly.

"*Yah*, she is," Mary agreed. "Head over heels. I remember feeling that way twenty-some years ago, but my intended was an Amish man, not an electrician."

"And I don't suppose there is any way to let him continue working as an electrician?" Hope asked.

"Not if he wants to marry our daughter and be Amish."

Hope knew as much.

"Hope..." Mary leaned forward, keeping her voice quiet. "My husband will argue with Curtis, and it will do absolutely nothing. I know that, and even Albrecht knows that. But you might be able to convince him to stop this foolhardy plan of his."

"I'm not that close to him," Hope whispered back. "We're...friends, I suppose, but only through my late husband. I don't think I could stop him, either."

"You have a better chance of it," Mary said. "I've seen the way he looks at you. He cares what you think. We don't need more money if it brings other problems with it. *Gott* will provide."

Hope nodded. "I can try."

"*Danke.* I appreciate it."

When their visit wound down and they took their leave, Curtis buckled his daughter back into her car seat while Hope got into the passenger side. Sarah waved to them as she walked with

Eddie out toward the field, and Mary stood on the step with Albrecht.

"It was nice to meet you!" Curtis called to Mary and Albrecht, and then he got into the vehicle and shut the door.

For a moment, he just looked thoughtfully in the direction that Sarah and Eddie had gone, and then he started the engine.

"So Sarah is marrying Eddie," he said as they pulled up the drive.

"Hopefully. They're engaged at the very least, but settling into Amish life isn't turning out to be easy for Eddie."

They pulled onto the gravel road, and Curtis slowed and looked again at Sarah and Eddie, who had stopped by a fence.

"They're in love," Hope added.

"Sure are..." He sped up again. "Look, I know that there are tensions between the Amish lifestyle and the regular American ways, but if Sarah and Eddie can make it work, then why can't we do something that benefits everyone in Apfelkuchen and really make it work?"

"Eddie is becoming Amish," she pointed out.

"True."

"And Mary asked me to show you the light, so to speak, when it comes to Amish life around here."

"She did?"

Hope nodded. "Sorry."

Curtis sighed. “If Albrecht and Mary can accept Eddie—even if it’s a little grudging right now—I think there’s hope. I really do.”

And in any other circumstance, Hope would have appreciated his optimism. But with this plan of his to bring in the tourists, she wished he’d be a little more realistic.

Mary was right that money wasn’t always the answer. It hadn’t been enough for Hope’s marriage, and it wasn’t enough for Apfelkuchen, either, no matter how pure Curtis’s intentions. Reliance upon wealth was deceptive, and it could leave a person feeling utterly empty when it didn’t solve the deeper, heart-level issues.

That was something that Hope had learned the hard way in her very loving, but very lonesome marriage.

CHAPTER TEN

CURTIS DROVE SILENTLY as they made their way back toward town. The Amish weren't keen on his plans to bring tourists into the bosom of their community. It wasn't that he wanted to push this onto the Amish segment of Apfelkuchen's population, but he did believe that bringing paying customers into the town was the only way to keep it afloat. He took some comfort in the idea that they wouldn't have been keen on the idea of an Englisher electrician joining their ranks, either, but there Eddie was.

"They don't trust me," Curtis said, taking the turn onto the highway.

Hope cast him an apologetic look.

"It's okay," he said. "I even understand it. They don't know me. I'm not from their culture."

"I don't think I know you very well, either," she said, but her tone was conciliatory.

Curtis nodded. "True." He glanced at her and found her looking out the window, her profile hidden by her dark, wavy hair. "But you told him I'm a good man."

"I think you are. Peter trusted you."

Was that all? Just her late husband's good opinion? He'd rather her feeling about him come from a more personal place.

"What do you want to know about?" he asked.

"Anything?" He heard the smile in her voice.

"Absolutely anything. Shoot."

"Are you planning to stay here?" she asked.

He hadn't expected that. He thought he'd been pretty clear about why he'd come.

"No," he said. "I mean, I'll come back and check on things, but my life is in Pittsburgh. My parents need my help, and Lynn needs to know where to reach me. I need to be there for her."

"So you want to build these rentals, start up the business, put someone in charge of it and leave town."

"That's the idea," he said. "I realize that sounds a bit cold, but I can't be everywhere at once. It's not ideal, but it's the best I can do right now. For Apfelkuchen, for my grandfather's memory."

"You've mentioned wanting to put some roots down for Lucy," she said.

"Yeah. We've got family history here."

"But her personal history won't be," Hope said. "Roots only go down where you put your time. You can't buy them. It's about more than a name."

That stung, and he glanced over at Hope to see

how she'd meant it. Her expression was sad, not antagonistic.

"Have you changed your mind about me?" he asked.

"About you being a good man?" She shook her head. "No, I stand by that. I think you're fundamentally a good person. But you might be wanting something from this town that you can't get."

Maybe she was right. He wanted a soft place to fall, a community that knew his name and appreciated his contributions. He wanted the same for Lucy—a place with morals and character that could give her something the city couldn't.

"I want to give her what I had here," he admitted. "I want her to have a place to call home, somewhere that can catch her when life gets too busy and she needs a little perspective. I want to give her a place where she can find some deeper wisdom and get her balance back."

"Like a grandpa," Hope said softly.

An image of Grandpa Jespersen came back to him so forcefully that it brought tears to his eyes. Grandpa sitting at the kitchen table with a paring knife and an apple, carefully peeling it in one coiling ribbon. He'd had bushy eyebrows and a gentle way of listening that always made Curtis say more than he'd intended. Grandpa had always had advice, or just some hard-won wisdom. The last of which had been about his sister, Lynn. *You can't save her, Curtis. You want to, but you can't.*

Sometimes the hardest thing is to wait for someone to care enough to save themselves. She has to choose treatment.

"Maybe that's it," he admitted. Was that safety and security he wanted to give to her something of the past?

"What about your dad?" she asked. "He's her grandpa."

"He's got dementia now, and he's really struggling. Mom takes care of him, and I pay for a nurse to visit daily… Maybe you're right. Maybe what I'm looking for is already in the past."

If he couldn't give her the kind of grounding he'd had, how would she ever find her balance with her complicated life? Maybe it was his stubborn nature, but he wasn't ready to give up. Maybe the shine of Apfelkuchen was about his grandfather's love and presence, and maybe there was still more goodness here to be found.

As Curtis drove back into town, he glanced over at Hope. Her dark, glossy hair was tucked behind her ear, and her attention was fixed on her belly. Maybe the baby was moving. Something about her seemed to slow time down, like she was some of the goodness here in Apfelkuchen.

"How about some ice cream?" he asked.

"Right now?" Hope asked.

"Too cold of a day for that?" he asked.

"Oh, I can have ice cream anytime, Curtis."

He liked the way she said his name—she put some warmth into it. "Okay, then. My treat."

Hope turned and gave Lucy a big smile. "Lucy. Did you hear what your daddy says? We're getting ice cream."

"Ice cream?" Lucy's little toddler lisp made it sound more like "ice ceem," and he would never get tired of that.

Beiler Dairy Ice Cream was located in the heart of downtown, and while the shop was open, it wasn't busy. He parked out front and they all got out. Lucy was a bundle of energy, and he had to scoop her up to make sure she didn't take off on him.

"I've got good memories here," he said as they headed for the front door.

"Me, too," she said, and she paused, eyeing him for a moment. There was a handwritten sign on the door that read, "No soft serve ice cream due to electrical issues."

"What'll you have?"

"I normally get the soft serve," she said. "I wonder what's going on with it."

Hope stepped up to the counter, where an older Amish woman was waiting to help them. She wore a black Beiler's Dairy apron, and her hair was pulled back in a bun and covered with a white Amish *kapp*.

"Hi, Belinda," Hope said with a smile. "I saw

the sign on the door. What happened to your soft serve machine?"

"Oh, the machine is fine," Belinda replied. "It's the outlet where we plug it in. It's not working. In fact, all the outlets along this wall aren't working."

"I guess you'll need an electrician. My brother-in-law, Trent Lantz, does a good job, if you're looking."

"We'll get the work done," Belinda said, "but not quite yet. That will cost a fair bit, and just between you and me, we need to save up first."

Another business struggling. They had quality ice cream that could probably win awards, but that didn't do them any good when there simply wasn't enough traffic to keep them afloat.

They ordered—a chocolate waffle cone for Curtis, a salted caramel sundae for Hope and a cup of vanilla for Lucy. Then they headed over to a table and Belinda brought them a high chair.

"Thanks a lot," Curtis said, and he eased his daughter into the seat and pushed it up close to the table.

Lucy was excited to get her hands on the spoon and do it all herself. She'd be a sticky mess at the end of this, but she'd have fun, too. Curtis took a bite of his cone, and he watched as Hope swirled her plastic spoon through the whipped cream on top of her sundae.

"I didn't realize things were so tight here," Hope said quietly. "I thought of all the businesses in town, Beiler Dairy would be one of the busiest."

"It might have to do with overhead costs," he said.

"I could see that." She took a bite of her sundae, then shot out a hand to catch Lucy's little paper cup of ice cream before it went off the table.

"You're fast," he said. "Thanks."

She smiled in response, but her gaze moved toward the counter again, her expression thoughtful.

"At the antiques shop, we can get customers online—at least we can advertise there and take credit card payments over the phone. But an ice cream shop—you pretty much need to visit in person with a hankering for ice cream, don't you?"

"Pretty much," he agreed.

"I can see your point about bringing in more tourists with ready money to spend," she said. "English people experiencing Amish Country would enjoy some quality ice cream."

"They would," he said, and something inside him softened. She'd seen the problem, understood what he was getting at. "And for a lot of the Amish businesses, they need that foot traffic to make sales. Do you remember the stores on Jespersen Street?"

"Of course."

"My grandfather used to take me through those shops when I was a kid," he said. "And they couldn't stay afloat, either. I know that things change and that businesses come and go. I get that. But those were family businesses, and there were no fresh businesses to take over the space. Every shop that went under was a family that couldn't make it here."

"If only there was a solution that made everyone successful and didn't change a thing," Hope said with a sad little smile.

"Everything changes," he said.

"Don't I know it." She'd been through so much…

"How are you doing on your own now?" he asked.

"I'm getting used to it again," she said. "We were only married for four months."

"Yeah…"

"But I'd already started to rely on Peter. When you get married, something changes. It's hard to explain. When we were dating, I could handle his traveling and his busy schedule, but after we were married, I needed him around more. I missed him more."

"That's not a bad thing," he said. "I'd want my wife to want me around."

He meant it as a lighthearted observation, but she didn't smile.

"Curtis…if I hadn't asked him to come home early, he wouldn't have gotten into that accident."

Curtis's heart squeezed. "Hope…"

"You're going to say it's not my fault," she said.

"I know that I didn't do anything on purpose, but I learned something painful and true. I need to be more self-sufficient. I need to be able to stand on my own two feet."

"It wasn't your fault," he said. "I'm going to say that, and I'll repeat it if you need to hear it."

"It wasn't my intention," she said, and tears misted her eyes. "That's something different."

So this was where she was at in her grief—she was blaming herself. Somehow, that was even more heartbreaking than if she were simply missing her late husband. She thought she was the one who caused his accident.

"You are allowed to have needs, you know," he said.

"If I'd had fewer needs, Peter would be off on a sales trip right now, and he'd be coming back home again," she said. "I needed a more present husband, and Peter needed a stronger wife."

"I think you're strong," he said.

"Thank you. I'll get there."

But Curtis saw very clearly that while Hope thought she needed to be more self-sufficient, the very last thing she needed was a man who made her life more complicated. She had enough on her plate already.

Curtis picked up Lucy's tipped cup and helped her get more ice cream onto her spoon.

"Yum," Lucy said, her eyes bright with happiness.

Ice cream was enough to fill Lucy's heart with bliss at this age. But Curtis and Hope were adults—their hearts were a little more fragile and were harder to fill. He'd have to remember that, because while he was starting to feel tempted to steer this relationship in a more romantic direction, he wasn't her answer, either.

Hope had had her heart broken once already, and he wouldn't be the guy to break it again.

CHAPTER ELEVEN

THAT NIGHT, HOPE sat on the couch in her little apartment above the store, the TV on but muted. Her sisters had both gone home, Faith to her husband and son and Elaine to do some lesson planning for the next day. That left Hope standing by the window, listening to rain drumming down onto the roof overhead and pattering against the panes with every gust of wind. She looked down at the puddles illuminated in the glow of streetlights.

She held her cell phone in front of her, listening to Catherine Taylor, her mother-in-law, chatting on the other end.

"I wish I had more pregnancy advice," Catherine was saying. "But childbirth was really hard for me. I spent my pregnancy on bed rest, so I tend to assume that pregnant women are more fragile than most really are."

Hope smiled at that. Her mother-in-law had told her this a few times already over the last several months. Catherine wasn't one to meddle, and Hope appreciated that.

They lapsed into a silence for a few moments, and then Hope said, "I miss him a lot, Catherine."

"Me, too, Hope. Me, too."

This was one of the few things Hope and Catherine had in common—their grief over losing Peter.

"Do you know Peter's friend Curtis Jespersen?" Hope asked.

"Yes. He's a nice guy. He came to our place for Thanksgiving one year. He's charming, and far too handsome for his own good. Why?"

"He's in Apfelkuchen." She gave a quick rundown of what he was doing in town and about his toddler daughter.

"Is it nice to see him again?" Catherine asked.

"I honestly don't remember meeting him before," Hope said. "That just shows how little of Peter's life I really knew about."

"You weren't married very long…"

"I know, but still." Hope sighed. "He's been kind to me."

"Ah." Catherine's voice was knowing, but it wasn't resentful. "I understand."

"No, it's isn't like that," Hope said. "It's only been a few months since I lost Peter, and—"

"I'm not saying it is," Catherine cut in. "But I just want you to know that when you do decide to open yourself up to romance again, it's okay.

I'm not going to be upset with you. It doesn't take away anything that you shared with my son."

Tears misted Hope's eyes. She hadn't realized she needed to hear that. "Thank you, but I'm not ready."

"I've been there before," Catherine said. "Sometimes these things come up when you least expect them."

Catherine had lost Peter's father when Peter was a teenager. She'd married again, gotten divorced and then married a third time.

"Can I just give you a little piece of advice?" Catherine asked. "Tuck it away for when you're ready to start dating again."

"Okay…"

"A prenuptial agreement is an absolute necessity," Catherine said.

"For a marriage where I have more money than the man, you mean," Hope said.

"Yes, but… Oh, sweetheart…" Catherine sighed. "Men who are used to a certain lifestyle already are even harder to be married to. When I married Peter's dad, it was love in the truest sense. He was my everything. But then he died, and I was so lonely. I met my next husband and I thought it would be the same with him, but it wasn't. He had expectations I had no idea about. He didn't want me to age. He wanted me to nip and tuck and compete with women ten years younger than me. He ground me down, and when

I left him, it was an ugly divorce that our lawyers got rich off of. Now, with my current marriage… we signed prenups."

"He was okay with that?" Hope said.

"He understood," Catherine said. "Peter absolutely worshipped you. But there are guys out there who aren't so easy to live with as Peter. A prenup is your insurance. You've gotten married purely for love once…you don't get any more of those. Not with the money my son left to you. I'm sorry. I wish it were different, but you'll have to be smart from here on out and think ahead for the sake of your child. You will need a good lawyer and a solid prenup."

"How crazy was Peter for marrying me like he did?" Hope asked softly. They hadn't had a prenuptial agreement. Their romance had been a whirlwind, one that had sent his family into a tailspin. She was starting to understand why.

"Incredibly." There was a smile in Catherine's voice. "But it worked out. You were just as lovely as he told us you were."

"Thank you, Catherine."

"You let me know if I can help, okay?"

When Hope hung up, she watched the rain fall for a couple of minutes. So simple and soothing. But nothing was going to be simple again, was it? Catherine was right—the money Peter had left her was a gift, a cushion, a blessing…and a huge complication. She wasn't raised to run in those circles.

And as if on cue, her cell phone rang, showing Curtis's number. She felt an unexpected wave of relief. He felt like a friend now, and she could use a friend in her corner. She wasn't ready to think about dating, but even as a new friend, she didn't need to worry about what he was after. He didn't need her money.

"Hi, Curtis."

"Hi." His voice was low. "Lucy is asleep, so I'm trying to talk quietly."

"That's no problem. How are you doing?"

She sank into her armchair by the window.

"I just wanted to come by the shop and make good on my promise to get you set up with an online checkout for your website."

Hope straightened. "That would be really great."

"Good. I'm happy to help." There was a pause. "Hope, there's something I've been thinking about."

"Yeah?"

"I've been told in the past that I can just steamroll someone—never meaning to, just getting really fixated on my own stuff."

So had Peter, when he really thought he was onto something. Curtis and Peter weren't so different. Perhaps that was what had made them such good friends. They were both high-achieving men who made a lot of money. And they both had good hearts. But Peter had done some steamrolling of his own.

"Peter was like that, too. You're in good company," she said.

"Well, regardless, I don't want to do that to you," he said. "If I ever seem like I'm just rolling along blindly, you have my permission to give me a hard smack."

She laughed. "Really?"

"I mean it." There was warmth in his voice. "Look, I wanted you to show me around because I respect your opinion. Sometimes when I'm pushing back, I'm just trying to sort it all out in my head. It doesn't mean I'm not taking what you say to heart. Okay?"

"Understood."

"Thanks… So I'll drop Lucy off tomorrow morning, and I'll be back by say…one? And I can set you up with your online store then."

"Thank you, Curtis. We all appreciate this."

"It's no problem." And she wasn't sure if it was her imagination or not, but he sounded a little bit bashful. "See you then."

Hope ended the call and looked down at her phone thoughtfully for a moment. Curtis was part of the same world that Peter had occupied, and Catherine was right that life was going to be complicated going forward. Would prenups and lawyers really be such a big part of her life now?

She'd been adjusting to life without her husband, and to her pregnancy. What else was in store that she'd have to navigate now that Peter was gone?

The baby gave her a kick in the bladder, and she pocketed her phone and beelined for the washroom.

Right now, what she needed was some quiet and security. She might manage that by starting her own business and taking care of herself. Standing on her own two feet. Using her own two hands. Maybe that was the answer now.

THE NEXT MORNING, Curtis dropped Lucy off, and this time Lucy wasn't going to be distracted. She clung to her father's leg and utterly ignored Smokey. She had to be peeled off his pant leg to let Curtis leave, and Hope was surprised when he finally did march off, because by the look in his eyes, Lucy was breaking his heart.

But once he was out of sight, Lucy heaved a big sigh and tipped her head onto Hope's shoulder.

"Daddy will be back, Lucy," Hope said. "Right after lunch. Okay? He'll be back."

The day wasn't very busy, so Faith operated the store while Hope took Lucy for a walk around the block and then upstairs to watch some *Sesame Street*. While Lucy watched TV, Hope used her laptop to go through their social media page, marking items that had sold so that people wouldn't call asking for them.

After lunch, Lucy started getting sleepy, and Hope put her to her bed with the Amish doll to cuddle with. Smokey found his way upstairs to curl up at her back, too, and before long the little girl was fast asleep.

There was a knock on the apartment door at one o'clock sharp. Hope opened the door to see Curtis.

"Hey," he said. "Faith said that Lucy is sleeping?"

"She is," Hope said, stepping back to let him inside. "Come take a peek."

It was only then that Hope realized that she'd laid Lucy on her own bed, and Curtis was going to be looking into her bedroom in order to see his daughter. She smothered a grimace as she eased open the door for him to look inside.

Lucy was curled up, snoring softly, her cheeks rosy from the warm blanket. Hope had left her bedroom generally neat, but her toiletries were out on the top of her vanity, and there was an open hamper in one corner.

"I normally just let her sleep when she needs it," Curtis said quietly. "We can get started on the website."

Hope nodded and led the way back to the living room to her open laptop. She signed into the website back end and then passed it over to Curtis.

"We're going to need to change templates and

integrate an e-commerce plug-in," Curtis said. "But I can show you what you need…"

He looked around for a place to sit and moved toward the couch.

"I kind of sink into the couch a bit too much in my current…state," she said, and she felt some embarrassment touch her cheeks.

"Ah, gotcha." Curtis shot her a grin. "Kitchen table?"

"Might be better."

"For the record, I could help you get back up again," he said as they headed toward the kitchen.

"Don't count on it," she replied with a rueful little smile. "I'm a very pregnant lady."

"I'm stronger than I look." He met her gaze for a fleeting moment.

Was that flirting? She wasn't sure, but she found herself wondering if he'd truly be strong enough to hoist her to her feet with this basketball of a belly in front of her and a couch determined to swallow her. He was a rather muscular man, and the fact that he wasn't daunted by the prospect was endearing.

"Oh, you look plenty strong," she said, trying to push the mental image away.

"I'll take that as a compliment." He caught her gaze again, and when heat touched her cheeks, he chuckled.

He *was* flirting, wasn't he?

CHAPTER TWELVE

CURTIS SETTLED AT the kitchen table next to Hope, and he tried not to notice the way she smelled faintly of roses or the feeling of her soft arm brushing against his. They worked together until Lucy woke up and then got her set up with her dolls to keep her occupied while they changed website templates, set up a store and organized a customer receipt.

Today, he'd been planning on going to Grandpa Jespersen's farm for the first time. He'd been putting it off, and he couldn't explain why. This was why he was here, wasn't it? He was doing this in his grandfather's memory. But that farm held more than that. It held his adolescent optimism. It held the last pleasant memories he shared with his sister before her life fell apart with the drugs. It was like a time capsule in his heart, and he was half afraid that when he opened it, it would all just crumble to dust. And instead, he was sitting here helping Hope with her store.

That was part of why he'd offered. Yeah, he'd

wanted to help, but he'd also wanted to put off opening up that part of his heart. He'd kept a very heavy load on top of that lid—work, parenting, family and just plain busyness. And he needed to pry it up and look inside.

Tomorrow. Tomorrow would be soon enough.

The time slipped by, and Lucy began to get antsy. He needed to get her some supper and head back to the motel. This would be easier at home with her own bedroom and routines. It would be easier with Nanny Judy, too.

"I'd better get her fed," Curtis said. "But I think you're set."

"I really appreciate this, Curtis. It'll make a huge difference for us."

Footsteps sounded on the stairs and there was a knock on the door. Hope slipped past him and went to answer it, and her two sisters came inside, each carrying two pizza boxes. The aroma of pizza immediately filled the apartment.

All three women shared a family resemblance, although they were very different types. Faith was slim with dark hair and a ready smile. Elaine was petite and almost elfin, and Hope was more curvy, and, of course, pregnant. But there was something in their smiles that connected them—and maybe in the wolfish way they all stared at those pizza boxes.

"We closed up early," Faith said. "We figured

we needed some dinner. Trent is picking up Tyke and then he's on his way over."

Curtis had already spent most of the afternoon here, and it was time to give Hope some space.

"Sounds like a family night," Curtis said, and he gathered up his daughter from the couch. "Hope and I got your online store started. If you have any questions, Hope has my number."

"Why don't you stay?" Hope asked. "We've got an awful lot of pizza here."

"Yes, definitely stay, Curtis," Faith said. "My son is on his way, and I imagine he and Lucy will have fun playing."

"Besides, you're very welcome," Elaine added with a grin. "That's why we got extra pizza. Don't force us to eat all this ourselves."

Curtis looked over at Hope, and she raised her eyebrows invitingly. "Plus, I could probably use your help explaining everything when I show my sisters the online store."

"Pizza?" Lucy whispered, looking longingly toward the boxes, and that pretty much cinched it.

"Sure, I guess we could stay," he said. "Thanks."

"Tyke normally gets half a slice," Faith said. "The same for Lucy? They can share a piece."

Hope's sisters spread out over the kitchen, opening cupboards, setting the table and generally looking very much at home here. It was nice to see some of Hope's support system in action.

Elaine came walking past, and she put a fresh glass of milk in Hope's hand. Hope didn't say a word, but she looked down at the milk, then took a sip. Curtis smothered a grin. They were definitely taking care of her.

A few minutes later, Faith checked her phone and then went down to open the door. She came back up with a tall, lanky fellow in tow and a little boy with a plastic truck under his arm.

"Trent, this is Curtis," Faith said, and they shook hands. "And this is our son, Tyke."

"Hey, buddy," Curtis said. "That's my daughter over there, Lucy."

Lucy and Tyke stared at each other for a moment, then Tyke said, "Pizza?"

"I've got your piece right here, Tyke," Faith said, and she pulled out his half a slice. "Come sit with Lucy?"

The cozy little apartment was full of chatting, happy people now. Curtis got a slice of pepperoni, and Hope took a slice of vegetarian. Even though it wasn't technically his business, he'd remember that. Lucy and Tyke sat side by side with their pizza. Lucy tried to touch Tyke's plastic truck, and he pulled it away. He tried to touch her doll, and she did the same with a baleful look. They eyed each other uncertainly for a moment, and then Faith came by with a few potato chips each, and a brawl was averted.

The next hour passed with laughter, pizza and

cheer. Funny—he'd come to Apfelkuchen for some connection to his family history and found himself tangled up in Hope's family instead. But it was nice, too. They were good people.

When they'd finished eating, Hope's sisters and Faith's husband and son took their leave. A box with a quarter of a pizza was left on the table for Hope to put in the fridge for later. As the footsteps echoed down the stairs, he met Hope's gaze.

She was just so pretty… How inappropriate was it that he was thinking that about his late friend's wife?

"I'd better head out, too," Curtis said. "But it was nice to see your family. They're supportive."

"Even when I'd like some space from them," Hope said with a short laugh.

Had she wanted some time alone with him this evening? Or was he reading too much into that?

"I can walk you down," Hope said.

"Sure." He held out his arms for Lucy, and she lifted hers to be picked up. "You're looking sleepy, Lucy."

"Yeah…" Lucy tipped her head against his shoulder.

He took a moment to get her coat and her little shoes on, then Curtis grabbed his own coat, and Hope wrapped a warm-looking shawl around her shoulders. Curtis went down first, the soft tap of Hope's shoes echoing behind him, and he held the door open for her as she went into the fall evening. The sky was still twilit, a few stars pricking through the semidarkness. Streetlights illuminated the sidewalk.

He'd parked right in front of the store, and he opened the back door of his SUV and got his daughter settled in her car seat, her Amish doll clutched in her arms. He closed the door, and through the window, he saw her eyes drift shut.

"She's tuckered out," Hope said softly.

"Yeah. She had fun with Tyke."

Hope smoothed a hand over her belly, then something changed in her expression. She moved her hand from the top of her belly to the side, and her gaze turned inward.

"What?" he asked.

"He's kicking."

"Yeah?" He took an involuntary step toward her but stopped himself there. Her baby's movements weren't for him to share.

"Do you want to feel?" she asked, her bright gaze popping up to meet his, and she had a look of such serene wonder on her face.

"I actually do."

She reached for his hand and guided it to the firm dome of her belly. He felt a poke, then a ripple and another poke.

"Wow..." he murmured. "I can really feel that."

"Me, too," she said, and they both chuckled.

He put his other hand on the other side of her

belly and felt the baby poke at one hand and then the other, almost like a game.

"I guess he likes pizza," Hope said, looking up. Their eyes met suddenly, and his heart stuttered in his chest. Looking down into her eyes, he could almost lose himself. He realized that he was standing there on a street cradling her belly in his palms, and he cleared his throat and took a step back, pushing his hands into his pockets.

"Sorry," he said. "Thanks for letting me…feel that. It's really neat."

"It is, isn't it?" she asked. "I never get tired of it. Although they say by the time you give birth you're really done with being pregnant. I'm not feeling that way yet, though."

"Good," he said. "I'm glad you're enjoying this. You're going to be a good mom."

"I don't have anyone to share those moments with," she said, some color tingeing her cheeks. "Besides my family, I mean. I'm not exactly on my own. I'm making it sound worse than it is…"

"Pete," he said simply. She didn't have Pete to share this with.

"Yeah." She took a step back and ran a protective hand over her belly. "It's different."

She wrapped her shawl a little tighter around her shoulders.

"Hope, if you ever need anything," he said. "And I mean anything at all, tell me, okay? If you need a guy to have a talk with your son, or you need money for something, or—"

"Peter left me well provided for," she said, looking surprised.

Mentioning money had been crass, and he sighed.

"I guess I'm just trying to say that while you've got this big supportive family and I'm sure you'll be just fine, if I can make things easier for you, let me know."

If he could be the man who comforted her. If he could be the guy who held her hand, or who told her she was doing great. If hearing it from her family didn't convince her and she needed to hear it with a little bit of bass, he'd be her guy. Would he ever be brave enough to say that out loud?

She smiled then and nodded. "I will."

"I'd better get Lucy back to the hotel room," he said.

"Yeah, for sure." She took another step back, and it was time for him to leave. But looking at Hope standing there on the sidewalk, swathed in her shawl and her belly domed out in front of her, he wished he could stay longer. He wished he could find some excuse to spend a little more time together, but he had his toddler in her car seat and a bedtime routine waiting.

And then tomorrow, he'd head out to the Jespersen farm. It was time to just do it—face whatever was inside him. But Hope was just standing there, and before he could stop himself, he blurted out, "I don't know if this is too much to ask, but I was going to go by my grandfather's farm and just take a look at it. And I find that I don't want to do it alone."

It was the truth. He didn't want to face any of that alone. Not that it was her responsibility.

Hope stilled. "I can understand that."

"Any chance you'd come with me?"

She nodded. "I'd be happy to. Of course."

"Yeah?"

"I think we count as friends now, Curtis."

He smiled at that. Friends. That felt really nice. "Good. Okay, so maybe I can come by tomorrow afternoon and pick you up?"

Tomorrow was Saturday, and he only had one meeting in the morning, then he was free.

She nodded. "What time?"

"I can come by about noon."

"I'll see you then."

He didn't have a smooth exit or even anything terribly reassuring to say. He just hopped up into his vehicle. He turned to see that Lucy was already passed out in her car seat, and then he waited until Hope had gone back inside and the door closed solidly behind her.

Only then did Curtis start the vehicle and pull away from the curb. He was still a little surprised at himself for inviting her. Maybe he could blame it on the twilight, but there was a deep, lonely part of him that wanted her at his side.

CHAPTER THIRTEEN

"It's not a date," Hope said, folding a stack of hand-embroidered antique pillowcases. The designs were simple—a spattering of flowers, a vine with leaves, some evenly spaced diamond shapes. They had been made with love by Amish hands many years ago, and Hope had to wonder about the women who had so lovingly decorated their linens. Aunt Josephine had attached names and dates on little cards attached with straight pins to the corners. *Anne Beiler, 1956. Mary Stoltzfuz, 1942. Verna Weitz, 1970.*

She fingered the tiny pink flowers on the edge of a pillowcase.

"I mean, it sounds like a date," Faith replied. "And if Elaine were here, I think she'd agree with me."

"That's because you two gang up on me," Hope said with a laugh.

"No more than the two of you gang up on me." Faith grinned. "So…this nondate. Where are you going?"

"His grandfather's farm."

"Hmm." Faith nodded, but there was a twinkle in her eye that Hope found downright irritating.

Lucy was playing with a pile of toy soldiers and some plastic farm toys. The green toy soldiers were not Amish, but they'd come from a local home, and they were certainly antique. The combination of toys was an odd one, but they had been on the shelf and they seemed to amuse Lucy.

"He just doesn't want to go alone," Hope said. "We've gotten to be friends, and I think the farm is a little bit emotional for him."

"And he chose you."

It wasn't that Hope didn't see that Curtis was giving her special attention. She wasn't blind to it. And she could see why her sisters thought there might be more between them, too, but Peter's death had complicated some of these connections. Some friendships had distanced. Other people had drawn closer. Like Curtis.

"I know," Hope replied. She glanced toward Lucy and then lowered her voice a little more. "He's a really good guy, but he's a whole lot like Peter."

"And he's cute."

Hope laughed. "We're going to sidestep everything else and go right to his looks? Yes, he's cute, I'll give you that. I'm not blind to his charms. But he's not asking me out, or suggesting anything romantic. Honestly, I think he's just feeling protective of me because of his friendship with Peter. I'm pregnant and widowed, and he was really good friends with my husband. That's all."

"You think so?" Faith met her gaze then, looking thoughtful. "Maybe that's all it is."

"I think that's it," Hope said earnestly. "Don't worry, I won't be too long."

"I'm dropping by Mom and Dad's place tonight," Faith said. "I'll see what Mom thinks."

"That's not fair," Hope said, "because it's all about how you tell the story."

Faith shot her a grin. "Mom has a good instinct about these things—you know it. I'll tell it very fairly, and we'll see what she says."

When Curtis arrived, Lucy went dancing toward the door, holding a plastic cow and a little green soldier. Curtis had loosened his button-up shirt at the neck, and he scooped his daughter up and cast Hope a warm smile.

"Ready to go?" he asked.

"Just let me grab my purse."

There was a ping on Faith's phone. "Oh!"

"Oh, what?" Hope turned, hitched her purse over her shoulder, then wrapped her shawl over it.

"We've got our first online order." Faith beamed. "That washtub just sold!"

"Let me see—" Hope went over and peeked over her sister's shoulder at the emailed notice of the sale. It was so official, and so easy. The website even calculated shipping options for the customer to choose from.

"I'd better buy boxes and get that packaged up," Faith said a little breathlessly. "Thank you so much, Curtis, for helping us with this."

She was distracted by the sale...that was a good thing. Maybe she'd be so distracted that she wouldn't pull Mom into this, too. A sister could only hope.

Curtis touched Hope's back as she passed in front of him out the door, and that casual touch sent a little shiver down her spine that had nothing to do with the crisp fall air outside.

He was being a gentleman, and maybe it just showed that she was missing a man's attention, because this felt really nice. She liked him opening doors. She liked him being the one behind the wheel, too. It was familiar. She knew what marriage felt like, and she missed some of those comforts a whole lot.

A few minutes later, they were heading down the highway. Lucy was having an animated conversation between her toy soldier and the plastic cow from her seat in the back.

"How far is the farm?" Hope asked.

"It's about twenty minutes out of town," he said.

She leaned back in the leather seat, heat pumping comfortably onto her legs. Her feet were sore today from standing in the shop—something that was happening more and more as her pregnancy progressed.

"Can I ask if you hear from your sister much?" Hope asked. "How is she doing?"

Curtis startled. "Uh—" He looked toward her uncertainly. "People don't normally ask about her."

"Why not?"

"The news is seldom good." He smiled faintly. "She's not doing great. It's the same old thing. She's on social assistance off and on, and she keeps getting jobs and losing them. She didn't show up to work for a couple of weeks at her most recent gig, and she's obviously fired."

"That's too bad."

"It's the drugs," he said. "I keep asking her to quit when she calls me, and she gets mad at me and insists that she hasn't done drugs in years."

"Anything to protect her addiction," Hope said.

"Yep."

"Do you give her money?" she asked.

"I do help her as best I can, but I can't give her cash. It isn't safe for her. I pay for a week in a hotel once in a while to get her off the street. But the last time I did that, she trashed the room and I had to pay for the cleaning and repairs. She's called me a few times when she needed groceries or medical help. I need her to know she isn't alone, but it's still hard to keep a balance between helping her and not giving her something that will make things worse. I don't know if I've explained that very well."

Hope could feel her chest getting tighter just thinking about it, and she turned her attention out the window.

"Are you sorry you asked?"

She looked back at him. "No, of course not. It must be stressful."

"It can be."

"How do you balance it?" she asked.

"I make sure she doesn't get anywhere near my daughter when she's high, and I connect her with social services when needed. Sometimes she'll accept the help from other people better than she will from me, and other times she disappears for a while."

"How often does she see Lucy?" Hope asked.

"On average, once every four or five months, I'd say."

"Does Lucy know who she is?"

"She knows that she's Mommy, but I don't know what that means to her."

"You must worry about your sister a lot."

"Yeah..." He sighed. "She'll always be my big sister. I know it's too much to ask anyone else to see her the way I do. She's not their sister. And I know the addiction has a stranglehold on her, but deep inside, she's still Lynn."

They drove down a country road that started out paved and then melted into gravel. Farmland stretched out on either side of the road, cattle grazing in a pasture on Curtis's side of the vehicle and a combine moving through a field of wheat on Hope's.

They turned into a drive and stopped at a locked gate. Curtis hopped out, popped off the padlock and pushed open the creaky, rusted gate to let them in. Somehow, she hadn't expected an abandoned farm when he'd said he'd show her where he'd spent his summers. Had no one bought the place? Curtis hopped back into the driver's seat.

The property sprawled out in front of them—a little white farmhouse with a sagging porch, a barn with peeling red paint, overgrown gardens and fields that had almost gone back to nature.

"This is it," Curtis said quietly, and his gaze was fixed on the little farmhouse, his eyes filled with tumbling emotion. "My cousin and his wife were living with him up until he passed away. They were doing the farmwork, and my grandfather was paying them. But when Grandpa died, they moved out to the East Coast to be closer to her family. Grandpa left them some money, since he knew they weren't staying in the area."

"How long since you've been here?" she asked.

"My grandfather's funeral last year." He cleared his throat.

And somehow, Curtis's low voice stabbed right through all her defenses. It was much easier to push aside a man's offer of gallant support and a whole lot harder when he needed hers.

"Kitties?" Lucy asked hopefully from the back seat.

"Maybe," Curtis said softly, and Hope reached over and squeezed his hand.

CHAPTER FOURTEEN

THIS HAD BEEN a terrible idea. Curtis should have at least driven by the place before bringing Hope here—gotten the first flood of emotion out of his system. Seeing the house look so forlorn and empty hit him right in the gut.

Driving up to his grandfather's farm, he used to be greeted by a dog or two. His grandpa would normally be around somewhere, as would Jeff and Amy, and when Curtis honked the horn, Grandpa would come out from whatever outbuilding he'd been working in. There would be a freezer full of the old man's favorite foods—hot dogs, hamburgers, frozen French fries and pierogi. And toward the end there was Amy's cooking, too. There would be long talks, and jokes about the kind of work that didn't produce calluses, and everything would feel right in the world.

"This is it," Curtis said, and he forced some cheer into his voice. "We're at the farm, Lucy."

Curtis got his daughter out of the back seat and

she squirmed to be put down, her doll clasped in one arm, the plastic cow forgotten.

"When Grandpa died, I wasn't sure if I wanted to sell the farm or keep it. I just kept putting off the decision, and I guess it got away from me." He looked around at the overgrown garden, the long grass growing in clumps on the lawn.

"I think this farm is different," Hope said. "It's not just another project. It's more personal. You're grieving."

"Yeah, I suppose so." She was letting him off the hook, and maybe he appreciated that. "It would be hard to see someone else living here, and that's ridiculous, I know—we really should rent it out."

"It's not ridiculous," she countered. "It's normal. You're human, Curtis."

He cast her a sad smile. Maybe it was easier having her here with him, after all.

Lucy squatted down in the grass and bounced her doll up and down.

"Come on, Lucy," he called. "Let's go that way."

Lucy stood up and followed them, and he noticed that Hope was watching for Lucy, too, a tender look in her eye. Was it all children who softened her like this, or was Lucy special?

They headed through the shin-high grass, past the clothesline and the overgrown garden. There was a veritable wave of chives having taken over the garden and sprinkled through the grass nearby, too.

"There was a time when my sister wasn't the problem child," Curtis said. "She used to love this farm, too. She said she felt like she was in *Little House on the Prairie*."

They walked to the fence and looked out over the field—a combination of wheat and wild grass growing together, waving in the autumn wind. Something about the neglected garden and fields made this place feel more melancholy still.

"Up?" Lucy said, and Curtis looked down, expecting to see his daughter's upturned face, but instead Lucy was facing Hope, her little hands upstretched and her doll on the ground next to her.

"Hope can't carry you, Lucy," Curtis said.

"Nonsense." Hope bent down and scooped the little girl up. She balanced the toddler on her arm next to her belly, then arranged her shawl so it covered Lucy's legs, too. It felt like his daughter was intruding on Hope's personal space, but she just smiled at Lucy when the toddler put a hand on Hope's belly.

"Did you feel that?"

Lucy nodded. "The baby."

"That's right. That's the baby. He's moving around in there, isn't he?"

Curtis picked up the doll, and they ambled together along the fence.

"This place needs a family," Hope said. "Don't

you think? This field can be mown for hay and animal feed. And the garden could be set right in the spring. I'm no expert, but the barn over there looks pretty solid, and if you brought in an Amish carpenter, they'd rip out that porch and put in a new one in a day."

Curtis smiled. "It does look a little forlorn, doesn't it?"

"It just needs some TLC," she replied, and then she met his gaze and shrugged. "Okay, it's a bit sad. I just want to cheer the whole place up."

He liked that her solution for the farm was to fix it up and move a family in. Maybe he was ready to see someone else build a few new memories here, after all. She was right—it needed new life, like Jespersen Street.

"You see that tree over there, Lucy?" Curtis said, pointing at a big oak tree by the barn.

Lucy looked in the wrong direction. She wouldn't really understand anyway. She was too little still.

"Anyway, my sister and I used to climb it," Curtis said, more to Hope now than to Lucy.

"That looks like a good climber," she agreed.

"It was the best. We were town kids—tree climbing was as good as it got."

They circled around toward the barn, and Curtis scanned the roof. It looked solid enough—Hope had been right. But a farm could melt into the ground in a single generation if no one was taking care of the land and the buildings.

"Do you ever think of moving to Apfelkuchen?" Hope asked.

"That's never been the plan," he said. "Like I said before, I wanted to set up a manager for the short-term rentals, rent out the farm and then head back to the city." When she didn't answer him, he added, "My life is in the city."

"Your heart is in this land."

It was—but this hurt. Coming back hurt, facing those memories of optimistic days when his sister was still her beautiful, hopeful self and his grandparents were both alive.

"I don't know," he said. "This trip is turning out to be more complicated than I thought it would be."

Hope started back in the direction of the house again, and he fell into step beside her. She was limping slightly.

"You okay?" he asked.

"My feet are sore," she replied. "It must be this stage of pregnancy or something."

"Here—" He reached for his daughter and then caught Hope's hand in his, tugging her against him. "You can lean on me a bit."

She didn't pull away. Her hand in his, she leaned into his shoulder a little, and he liked the way it felt.

"Leafs!" Lucy hollered in delight as they came

upon a denuded tree next to the house, the yellow leaves scattered across the grass. He put his daughter down to play with the fallen leaves and then nodded toward the edge of the porch.

"Sit there," he said.

She didn't argue and sank down.

"Now, give me your foot." He sat on a step beneath her and tugged the shoe off her proffered foot.

She seemed a little uncertain. "Curtis—" she started, but when he rubbed his thumb into the arch of her foot, she let her head drop forward and sighed. "Okay, that feels good."

He wasn't sure what had made him decide to do this—just that she was in pain, and he knew what to do about sore feet. It was a pretty easy solution.

"A leaf!" Lucy said happily, bringing a big golden leaf over to Hope. She accepted it with a smile, and Lucy danced off again in search of another one to her liking.

Curtis rubbed her foot in slow, firm movements from her heel to her toes. When he'd finished with one foot, he pulled her shoe off her other and performed the same massage.

"I have never in my life wanted a foot rub before," Hope said. "But that is heavenly."

Curtis shot her an amused look. "Must be a pregnancy thing."

"Must be," she said. "Thank you."

Lucy came with another leaf and Hope accepted it with a smile.

"I meant it when I said if you needed anything you should let me know," he said.

"Should I call you for a foot massage?" she asked with a teasing little smile.

"Sure." Heck, if she called him up after he left and said her feet hurt, he'd drive the two hours for her.

"I'll be okay, Curtis," she said. "I know you're worrying about me, but many single mothers have soldiered on before now. I'll do the same."

Curtis looked up at her, her foot in his hand, and he felt a flood of tenderness so powerful that it nearly rocked him.

"I think I'll miss you," he said, and as the words came out, he knew he was saying too much.

"You will?" She met his gaze, her lips parted, and somehow sitting at her feet like this felt only appropriate.

"Yeah..." He wasn't sure how to explain himself.

"You'll be back, though," she said. "You'll have a building going up."

"Any chance you'd let me take you out to dinner a few times when I come back through town?" he asked.

"If I don't have a big, jealous boyfriend by then."

He smiled at that. "Okay. I guess I'll have to

take my chances on that. But let's say you don't have a big, jealous boyfriend. Maybe we could keep up."

Maybe he could keep her talking to him instead. Was that selfish? Probably, but the thought of her with another guy stung.

Curtis put her shoe back on for her, and Lucy arrived at the same time with another leaf.

"Do you want to go inside the house?" Hope asked.

"It's locked up tight," he replied. "I've seen what I needed to see."

Maybe it hadn't been the past that he'd needed to see in this old farm—maybe it was a path forward into the future, beyond the grief.

"You ready to head back?" he asked, and he handed Lucy her doll again.

"Sure." Hope eased back onto her feet, her movements careful. He held out his hand to take hers.

If he stuck around here any longer, he might start imagining a future with him and Hope and Lucy together on this farm, but that wasn't a possibility. Because no matter how much he liked holding her hand or rubbing her feet, he was still the guy who had a complicated family, and Hope was still the woman who'd had complication enough. He'd already experienced the fallout with Samantha and didn't want to repeat it.

Sometimes, if a guy really wanted to do right by a woman, he let her move on.

He should back off and let her find someone else in her own time. It would be the right thing to do.

CHAPTER FIFTEEN

THAT EVENING, HOPE sat on a stool behind the front counter with her laptop in front of her as she and Elaine worked on adding more items to the online shop. Smokey ambled past, and Hope looked in the direction he'd come from. Had he been in the basement? It was hard to figure out where the cat spent his time, but now he found a warm spot by a heating vent and lay down beside it.

"So Curtis brought you to the family farm today?" Elaine asked. "That's rather sweet."

"It was," Hope agreed. "You know where Sadie Mast used to live? Where she had that trampoline birthday party? It's down there—in that direction."

Elaine took a picture of one of the quilts hanging on the wall and looked at her phone. She deleted it and centered another shot.

"He wants to rent the place out," Hope went on. "It's empty right now—his grandfather only died a year ago, but it has that old, abandoned feeling to it."

"He's opening up with you."

"I suppose so."

"Are you opening up with him?" Elaine came back over to where Hope sat with the laptop.

"I mean…" Hope thought about that foot rub on the porch, and she felt some heat in her face. "I might be."

Elaine chuckled. "Good. It's not a bad thing to meet a nice guy."

"My husband just died, Elaine."

"It's not a bad thing to make a new friend, either," Elaine said. "You can get to know him. And if he's supportive and kind—well, you deserve to be treated well, don't you? And you are allowed to have friends."

"I had a chat with Catherine the other day—" Hope sucked in a breath. "She was basically warning me about dating now that I'm a widow and have the money Peter left to me."

"What did she say?"

Hope gave a quick rundown of the conversation, and then added, "Catherine's second husband was Peter's stepfather when he was a teenager, and he just hated him. The man was emotionally abusive, self-important… And Peter always said that his mom would have done better to just stand up on her two feet and face life on her own than try to find someone to take his dad's place so quickly."

"I understand Catherine's worry after that kind

of trauma, but a prenup?" Elaine winced. "Is that where you're at now—you'll need a prenup and a lawyer?"

"That's Catherine's advice," Hope said.

Elaine sighed. "That's a different world, isn't it?"

Hope met her sister's gaze, then nodded. "It sure is."

"How do you bring that sort of thing up?" Elaine asked.

"I have no idea," Hope said. "And I don't intend to. I'm going use the money my husband left me and open up my day care. And I'm going to do what Catherine should have done, stand on my own two feet."

"That makes sense." Elaine cast her a sympathetic look. "But it's possible to keep Curtis as a friend, you know. You don't have to chase people off just because they're kind to you."

"When did you get so wise?" Hope asked with a wry smile.

"To a classroom of second graders, I'm a genius," Elaine said with a laugh. "'Miss Fairchild, why does the sun go down? Miss Fairchild, how come Lenny's dad has no hair? Miss Fairchild, how come you don't have a husband?'"

Hope laughed. "Do they really ask personal questions?"

"All the time." Elaine held out her phone with

the photo of the quilt on the screen. "What do you think?"

Hope leaned forward to get a closer look. "That's a good one. Email it to me along with the measurements and I'll put it on the website."

Hope set to work getting the photo and uploading it to the store page on their website. As Curtis had showed her, she also included the measurements and a description of the provenance to go with the picture, and she included the estimated weight so the site could calculate shipping. After their last online sale, she was feeling optimistic.

"I had to send an email home today about Tim's son, Oliver," Elaine said.

"What did he do?"

"He refused to do his work, he disrupted the class… Oliver has stopped crying and now he's acting out." Elaine pressed her lips together.

"Is this about his mom's death?"

"I'm sure it factors in," she replied. "I'm just not sure if it's the only problem."

"What do you mean?"

"He's not able to spell his name properly, and he can't read at grade level," Elaine said. "I can't help but wonder if there is more that's frustrating him."

"Have you talked to Tim about it?"

"Like I said, I sent the email."

"You were good friends once upon a time. Can't you just have a heart-to-heart?"

"I'm his son's teacher. That changes the whole dynamic," Elaine replied. "I have to do this by the book or I could end up losing my job. Parents are protective of their kids, and right now Tim isn't my old friend. He's my student's dad."

The sisters exchanged a thoughtful look, but then the bell over the front door tinkled, and Hope looked over to see Tim Granger himself in his State Police uniform.

"Speak of the devil," Elaine murmured softly.

A little boy came in behind him, and Hope could immediately see that Oliver looked a lot like Tim. He had the same mop of dark blond hair, the big eyes, the same light skin tone. He was the spitting image of his father.

The timing couldn't have been worse, though. It would be terrible to be overheard discussing their situation.

"Hi there," Elaine said, looking surprised.

"Hi." Tim Granger had a grim look on his face, and he stood with that cop stance—arms a couple of inches away from his torso to make room for his belt and bulletproof vest. "I got your email."

Oliver looked away and dug the toe of his running shoe into the floor, and Hope watched the squirming youngster sympathetically.

"Good. Would you like to set up a meeting so we can speak in person?"

Hope was always impressed by Elaine's ability to transform into someone's teacher in the presence of kids from her class or their parents. It was like Hope's little sister suddenly aged before her eyes.

"No, no—" Tim cleared his throat. "You mentioned you weren't available tonight because you were working at the store, so I thought I'd just come by. I'm teaching my son to take responsibility for his actions, and he owes you an apology."

"We discussed it in the classroom, and once we've talked it through, we let it go," Elaine said. "So it's okay. I was just informing you about what happened so that you could talk with him about your family's values."

Hope tried to keep her face neutral, but the tension between Elaine and Tim was palpable.

"Yeah, well, these are my values," Tim replied. "Boys learn how to make things right by making them right. And if this were your first email about this sort of thing, maybe I'd go easier on him, but it isn't."

"Hi, Oliver," Elaine said, bending down. "How are you doing?"

"Fine." But he wouldn't look at Elaine.

"Oliver, did you have something to say?" Tim nudged.

Oliver sucked in a breath, and he gaze went right over Elaine's shoulder. "I'm sorry for being bad in class, Miss Fairchild. I won't do that again."

"Tomorrow's a whole new day, Oliver," Elaine said. "Everyone gets a fresh start every morning, okay? Thank you for coming by, kiddo. You're a good boy, you know that?"

Oliver squirmed a little bit, and then he finally looked up at Elaine mutely, and Hope's heart squeezed at the sight of the little boy who'd lost so much.

Hope wondered if she'd struggle, too, with her own son. Peter wouldn't be there to understand their son's way of thinking, or the things that would be tough for him. All those fatherly insights into their son's heart and mind had died with Peter before their baby had even arrived. Would anyone else love and understand their son like Peter would have?

She doubted it.

The baby stretched inside her, and she rubbed the spot where a heel landed. Hope would do her best and she'd be a good mom, but looking at Oliver over there, standing next to his father with that expression of misery on his face, she had to wonder if she'd ever be in Tim's shoes—doing her best but feeling like a failure. Because Tim looked just as miserable as his son did.

Elaine and Tim continued to chat, and Oliver wandered away. He went up one aisle and then stopped at the counter where Hope sat on a stool, her laptop in front of her.

"Hi," Oliver said.

"Hi." Hope closed her laptop.

"Can I ask you something?"

"Sure." She smiled down at the solemn, upturned face.

"How come my teacher works here?" he asked. "My dad said that my teacher works at this store."

"Your teacher is one of the owners of this store."

"She owns it?"

"Yup."

"She's the boss?"

Hope chuckled. How well would a six- or seven-year-old understand this? "Sure. She's the boss. One of them."

"Huh." He seemed to be digesting that piece of information. "Who are you?"

"I'm Miss Fairchild's sister. My name is Hope."

"I didn't know that teachers had sisters," he murmured.

"Are you enjoying school?" Hope asked.

"No."

"Why not?"

Oliver just stared at her. On the other side of the store, Elaine and Tim were talking, Elaine with her arms crossed over her chest and Tim with a rather softened look on his face as he listened to what it was Elaine was saying.

"Do you have any friends at school?" Hope asked.

"Some."

"Is it fun to see your friends?"

"I guess it's fun to see Cameron."

"Okay, so tell me this," Hope said, leaning over as much as her belly would allow. "If you could be doing anything you wanted right now—anything at all in the whole wide world—what would it be?"

"I'd go play with Cameron."

"That sounds nice." It was a bit of a relief to know that this small, fragile-looking boy had a friend at school.

"Oliver?" Tim called. The conversation with Elaine seemed to be over, and Oliver headed in his father's direction. Tim turned to say something to Elaine, and just as he turned, Hope saw Oliver's hand reach out, snatch up a saltshaker from a shelf and then disappear into his pocket.

Hope's jaw dropped. Had Oliver just shoplifted something right under all their noses? The boy followed his father out of the shop, and as he went out the door, he looked back once, his gaze meeting Hope's. He seemed to realize then that Hope had seen him, because his face flushed red and he pulled his hand out of pocket and put the saltshaker onto the window ledge before running out after his dad.

"Did you see that?" Hope asked.

"See what?"

"Oliver tried to steal this." Hope crossed the store and picked up the little cut-crystal saltshaker.

Elaine stared at Hope in surprise. "He didn't!"

"He did! I watched him do it! He put it back when he saw that I'd seen him."

Elaine rubbed her hands over her face and sighed. "What is going on with this kid?"

Hope had no answers, and there was no mystical mothering intuition inside her that could provide one, either.

"What did Tim say?" Hope asked.

"Just that he knows for a fact that his son can read, and reads well. And he thinks that his mother's death was particularly hard for him. I'm suggesting maybe having a chat with a counselor at school. It's free, and she can talk about what Oliver's going through with him. Maybe she can help him navigate his grief a little bit."

"That sounds good," Hope said quietly, and she looked back toward the door. "He's angry."

"Incredibly," Elaine agreed. "Poor little guy."

"Poor little guy," Hope echoed.

CHAPTER SIXTEEN

CURTIS SAT IN a chair, his feet up on the hotel room bed. Lucy was already tucked into her cot, snoring softly. All the exercise and fresh air she was getting on this trip was leaving her tired right out come bedtime, and he was seeing a difference in her out here in Amish Country. Lucy's cheeks were rosier, and she laughed more.

Curtis and Lynn used to love coming out here as kids. Food tasted better. They slept more soundly. Grandpa always let them stay up as long as they wanted, although Curtis couldn't remember ever staying up past ten. Grandpa got them up at dawn, and there was always something fun to do—collect eggs, milk the cows, feed the chickens, ride horses. He still remembered the year that Lynn refused to go to the farm. He'd been fourteen and Lynn was sixteen. She hadn't gotten her driver's license yet, and their parents were pushing her to get it. She was too busy with the wrong sorts of friends, though, and that summer she downright refused to go to the farm. She called it boring. Curtis had suspected the truth, though—drugs were a whole lot harder to get in Apfelkuchen. His parents were only starting to realize she had a problem at that point, but Curtis had seen her joints in her pencil case, and the pills in a baggie shoved in that pencil case, too.

So Curtis had gone to see Grandpa alone that summer, and the next one, too. Curtis had told his grandfather the truth about his sister, and Grandpa had been heartbroken.

"She can kick that habit, you know," Grandpa said repeatedly. "People before her have done it, and she can do it, too. She can get clean and sober, and she can have a story to tell. But she has to want it."

And that had been the problem ever after—Lynn had never wanted to get sober. It was like she was stuck. He was sure that a part of her wanted to stop the drugs for herself, and even for her daughter. But Curtis was inclined to agree with Grandpa about one thing—Lynn could do it, if she put her mind to her. She *could*. But when she'd signed Lucy over to him, he'd lost hope that she ever would.

Lucy's breath came slow and deep. She'd had a busy day while he'd had meetings. She and Hope had gone to the park, and when he'd picked her up again, she had a new collection of leaves that she just couldn't part with.

He thought about the time he'd spent with

Hope. Maybe he shouldn't have brought her out to the farm, but he was glad that he'd done it. She'd made him see something he hadn't noticed before—that farm needed a future. And he did, too. A man might be built from his past experiences, but he was more than the sum of them.

And somehow, whenever he thought about his future these days, Hope kept popping into his mind. Hope with her sparkling eyes and pretty smile… Hope with her baby on the way. He sighed and sank onto the edge of the bed. He was being ridiculous. Hope had her own life to arrange, and Peter had provided well for her. She'd be fine, and she didn't need him complicating her life.

His phone rang—it was Lynn. She hadn't called in a couple of months. She'd dropped off the map the last time he refused to give her money. But his heart jolted—she was reaching out to him now.

"Hi, Lynn," he said. "How are you doing?"

"Not good," she said. "I need money."

The warm feeling from a moment earlier slipped away, replaced by the wariness that was all too familiar now when it came to his sister. He loved her, of course, but she wasn't the same anymore.

"I can't give you money. What do you need—can I order something for you?" He couldn't just hand her cash. He knew what she'd do with it. Her addiction was too strong.

"I need to pay rent. I need to buy food. I need toothpaste."

"I can do that for you," he said. "I can get you food and toiletries. Where are you staying? Because I tried bringing groceries by your last place, and the super said you moved out."

The super actually had said she'd abandoned the apartment, hadn't paid her bills and had left an appalling mess behind. Curtis had had to pay for a professional cleaner to go in there. It had been that bad.

"I'm…somewhere else. I just need the money."

"Lynn, I can't do that."

"Why?"

"You know why."

She huffed irritably. "How is Lucy?"

"She's good. Growing and doing great."

"Can I talk to her?" Her voice was shaking. She was going through withdrawal.

"She's sleeping, Lynn."

"Wake her up."

He tried to push down his rising anger. He would not wake up his daughter, and he would not give Lynn money.

"Lynn, you sound like you're in rough shape," he said. "Go to an emergency room and tell them you're going through withdrawal and you want help getting clean."

"Just give me the money!" she shouted, and he

heard the crack of the phone hitting something hard a few times. “What is wrong with you?”

“Go to a hospital, Lynn. You don’t want to live like this.”

The call went dead, and Curtis dropped his phone onto the bed next to him. He didn’t understand why she kept refusing rehab. It felt like she’d forgotten what a normal, sober life even felt like. It had been a long time, he had to admit. She’d gone from teenager to adult while struggling with addiction. Maybe he couldn’t blame her for not remembering anymore. He’d talked to a therapist, who had explained that it wasn’t so simple for Lynn to choose the help. If he gave her the money, she’d only use it on drugs. But if she overdosed, he’d never forgive himself.

“Daddy?” He’d woken up Lucy, and he tried to push back that coursing anger and helplessness. Lucy needed calm and stability.

“It’s okay, sweetie,” he said. “It’s bedtime. Time to sleep.”

“Can you do the night-night song?”

All over again… He sighed. “Sure. Lay back down. We’ll do the night-night song.”

This was the very instability that he needed to protect Lucy from, and it was a life that Hope would never be able to handle, either. She wanted calm and reassurance, and Curtis came with complications that just wouldn’t quit.

Grandpa had insisted that Lynn could get clean,

but tonight that possibility felt very, very far away. He slid down to the floor next to his daughter's cot and took her soft little hand in his. It was time for the night-night song.

CHAPTER SEVENTEEN

"EDDIE'S FAMILY IS FURIOUS."

Hope sat in her parents' kitchen with her mother as Lucy picked at a little plate of cheese cubes and crackers. Her mother leaned her elbows on the kitchen table.

"I thought they were in support of this marriage," Hope said, leaning forward, too. This was a change from what she'd been hearing so far.

"They tried to be," her mother said. "I mean, Sarah Yoder is just such a sweet girl. They can see why he fell in love with her, but it seems like only Eddie is giving anything up for this marriage."

"I didn't realize they felt that way," Hope said. "I'd thought Eddie's family was okay with it."

"What would you say if Elaine decided to abandon her career and go marry an Amish guy?" her mother asked.

"I mean, if she really loved him..."

"And let's say that the Amish guy's family didn't see what a beautiful, sweet soul she is. Let's say they just sat back and judged her ability to can meat or sew clothes from scratch."

"I'd be pretty protective," Hope agreed.

"I'd turn into a mother bear," her mom said. "And Eddie's family is feeling the same way. Eddie's made a choice, but that doesn't mean his family thinks he's made the right one. He's giving up his career, his truck, his driver's license, electricity…everything." Her mother counted the items off on her fingers, then shrugged. "And Sarah gets to keep her culture, her way of life, her family, her friends and everything that has ever been comfortable for her. All of it."

"So his folks are angry."

"They're hoping to talk him out of this wedding," she said. "They're planning on sitting him down the next time he visits and telling him just that."

Sarah would be crushed. True, she was the sheltered one in all of this, but she did love Eddie with all her heart. And if she knew that his parents didn't want him to marry her, it would hurt her deeply.

"I do understand that he's giving up a lot," Hope said, "but that guy is in love with her. I mean, head over heels."

"Love is the foundation of a marriage, but it's not the wood and nails, is it?"

"Now you sound Amish," Hope chuckled.

"Maybe I do," her mother sighed. "But look at

Faith and Trent." It was true. They'd been so in love when they'd first gotten married, and then things had fallen apart and they divorced. Thank goodness they'd found each other again and given each other another shot. Her mother continued, "They had to rebuild their marriage and start over after their divorce, because marriage isn't the ending point—it's just the beginning! Look at the challenges in just understanding each other you had with Peter. Did you love him? Heart and soul! But marriage isn't only about love. It's about the hard work you put into building something together."

"Of course," Hope said.

"It's just too bad that the Amish don't allow for any compromise," her mother said. "Eddie has been working so hard to prove himself, and the last time he came to see his parents..." Her mother's voice cracked, and she swallowed. "The last time he came, he told them that Sarah's dad doesn't think he has what it takes to be a farmer. He was crushed. His mom said that he just about cried. He's given up all the comforts of a regular American life, and they don't seem to appreciate that."

"The Yoders are probably afraid he won't stay Amish," Hope said.

"Probably."

"And if he can't hack it, if he's already married Sarah, she'd have to choose again between staying with her shunned husband or having her family in her life. Eddie has to be really sure that this is the life he wants. I see what you mean, but a lot is riding on this for Sarah, too."

"I agree," her mother replied seriously. "And that's why his parents want him to look at this very seriously. He's not married yet. He can back out. Why should he want to dedicate his life to a group of people who won't help him to succeed?"

And that was a very good question. He was supposed to join this community and devote himself to their way of life. Besides Sarah, who was making that a worthwhile effort?

"What are his family going to do?" Hope asked. "Besides sit him down, I mean."

"Well, apparently there are quite a few of them who are refusing to attend the wedding when it happens, and his parents want him to move back into their home for a while instead of living in the in-law suite at Sarah's place. They want him to have some freedom to think and make choices without being pressured. His heart is at stake here, too."

"And as much as I'd hate to see Sarah and Eddie not make it, I do see the point," Hope agreed softly.

"We all know that Eddie loves Sarah, but is it wise to marry someone who isn't willing to sacrifice anything for you in return?"

Hope couldn't help but think of Catherine's second marriage to a man who'd wanted Catherine to do everything for him and felt no obligation to reciprocate. That wasn't love—that was an arrangement, a deal. It wasn't the love that both men and women craved.

"Although it is rather wonderful of Eddie to make sure she doesn't have to give up her family. Because for the Amish, it's all or nothing. If she chose him now that she's a part of the church, she'd be shunned and she'd lose everyone. At least Eddie can keep his family in his life."

Her mother nodded. "Very noble. Very romantic, but I'm thinking like the mother of adult children here. I want to see my children loved and appreciated. Eddie's mom is seeing him discouraged and feeling like a failure. It hurts, even when they're grown."

And this was the Amish community that Curtis wanted to convince to embrace a big change. Hope had had no idea that Eddie's family was less than supportive about the wedding. It looked like this couple had a lot more to contend with than just the Amish community's leadership.

Was love really going to be enough?

When Hope got back to the antiques shop, she brought Lucy inside. Lucy had a whole collection of acorns she'd gathered up on the sidewalk, and she chattered away about them as they came inside.

An older Amish man stood by the quilts, his

hands clasped behind his back as he perused. He had a bushy white beard, wore a straw hat and his shoulders had a stoop. He reached up and fingered the corner of a quilt. Hope watched him curiously. Sometimes the Amish came to the shop to sell some items from their attics, and sometimes the Amish women simply took the opportunity to pick up a flour sifter or some item that was hard to come across in the regular shops.

"That's Bishop Moses," Faith whispered as Hope brought Lucy up to a little box of toys they'd accumulated for her.

"Are you sure?" Hope whispered back.

"Of course, I'm sure."

Bishop Moses was the leader of the Apfelkuchen Amish community. He was the law, the final say in everything from Eddie and Sarah's wedding to whether or not the Amish would cooperate with tourist initiatives. If Bishop Moses disapproved of something, the Amish community would turn their backs on it. She should remind Curtis of this. Hope watched the older man move on to some antique farm equipment. They had a small but impressive collection. There were a few different styles of bull nose pliers, some ax heads, sheep castrators, a scythe and several different-size cowbells.

"Do you think it would be too forward of me to ask him about the tourist situation?" Hope whispered.

"I'm sure you could..." Faith lowered her voice more. "His opinion is the important one."

The bishop was a deeply respected man in these parts, and Hope could see his importance in the way he walked. He was thoughtful, seemed introspective, but he looked like a man who had seen things, too.

"He's here to shop," Hope said. "I don't want to bug him."

Bishop Moses wandered closer, then he looked up suddenly, catching Hope's eye with a twinkling blue gaze.

"It's definitely him," Bishop Moses said in a conspiratorial tone. "And I've heard he's quite pleasant. You could ask him whatever you wanted."

Hope burst out laughing. "I'm so sorry, Bishop," she said.

"Just Moses. We don't use titles here. If our position is worth remembering, people will remember it without a title."

That was Amish humility. One person was never above another, but his humble attitude didn't alter his influence.

"Well, I'm sorry all the same. We haven't formally met. My name is Hope Taylor. My sisters and I own this shop."

"I've heard of you," Moses replied, and he regarded her for a moment as if coming to a conclusion. "I actually came by to ask you a few questions of my own."

"Oh?" Hope sobered.

"I've been told that you know the *Englisher* who bought Jespersen Street."

"I do know him a little bit. He was a friend of my late husband."

Moses nodded slowly. His gaze softened, but he didn't offer condolences. Just seemed to silently acknowledge her loss.

"Is he trustworthy?" Moses inquired.

Hope blinked, then looked over at her sister for help. Faith just shrugged and took a step away—this was Hope's conversation, it would seem.

"Yes, I do believe he is," Hope said.

"We have a community event this evening—a corn roast at the Beiler Dairy farm. We're collecting some funds to support the Beiler family during a difficult time. It would be a good chance for Curtis to meet our community and talk with more of us. You'rc all welcome, of course." He nodded to Faith, too.

"This evening?" she asked.

"*Yah.* Do you know the place?"

"I do, and I think he'll really appreciate this opportunity. Thank you."

Lucy got up from her spot on the pillows and came trotting over with her doll tucked under her arm. From all the loving she'd been giving the toy, the neck was starting to get a little floppy. She looked up at Moses with her big blue eyes.

"I got a kitty," Lucy said. "See?"

She pointed back at Smokey, who was ignoring them.

"That is a wonderful cat," Moses said. "Very nice. I see you have a doll, too."

"It's a baby," Lucy said. "And that's a baby." She pointed at Hope's belly.

"Indeed." Moses looked a little embarrassed then. He gave Lucy a little bow, and then he looked up at Hope.

"I am sorry for your loss," he said gently. "And I am thankful for the good things that are still ahead of you. Don't lose sight of that."

It was such a simple, heartfelt sentiment that tears pricked her eyes. The bishop could break up a romance or dissuade his community from supporting a new business. He could make it nearly impossible for a young electrician to marry the woman he loved, or he could welcome him…if he chose. He could frustrate so much, but his support could build, too.

Titles weren't necessary with the Amish. Everyone knew who Bishop Moses was, and his influence could not be denied. The Amish man headed out of the shop, the bell tinkling overhead as the door swung shut. A finger of cold air whisked inside after him.

There were good things still ahead—he was

right about that. Her life was disrupted, but it was not over. Her heart might have broken, but it was healing. It was time to start thinking about the future.

And she dearly hoped that Sarah and Eddie would find a way together. True, honest love was rare enough in this old world that it deserved a fighting chance.

CHAPTER EIGHTEEN

CURTIS'S DAY WAS filled with septic service queries. A row of ten condos would add an extra burden on an already-overloaded septic system in downtown Apfelkuchen, one that had been due for expansion for some time now. But that meant dipping into reserve funds and possibly raising local property taxes for the work. Bringing business to a small town was not a cheap endeavor.

It had been a surprisingly complicated and exhausting day. But when he pushed open the door of Amish Antiques, Lucy came dancing over to him with a big smile on her face.

"I'm learning my ADC's!" Lucy announced.

"Your ABC's?" he asked.

"Yeah!" And Lucy started to sing the alphabet with letters repeated and all out of order. "A D C D S Q M!"

"Isn't she doing great?" Hope asked, giving him a pointed look.

"She's doing really great," he agreed and he laughed. "Come here, Lucy. Give me a hug."

Lucy put her arms up and he scooped her into his arms. She planted a sticky kiss on his cheek, then wriggled to be set down again.

"Bishop Moses came by the store today," Hope said, "and he invited us to a community corn roast happening tonight. He thought it might be a good chance for you to see the Amish community and talk with more people."

"Yeah? That's really nice. Does that mean I have Amish support?"

"I'm not sure I'd go that far, but you have an invitation to social gathering. It's being held at the Beiler Dairy. Bishop Moses is an important man. He has clout around here."

An invitation from the bishop to attend a community event…that was priceless. It did feel like a vote of confidence. It was definitely a step forward. He could feel the knot loosening. This was a gift, and he was grateful.

"Do you know where Beiler Dairy is?" he asked.

"Sure do."

"Any chance you'd come with me and Lucy?"

"I think I can make it." Hope's glittering gaze met his, and for just a moment, it was like his heart stopped in his chest. Then she turned to Faith. "Are you coming, too, Faith?"

Faith's gaze flicked toward Curtis, and in the split second when their eyes met, he saw some understanding. She quickly shook her head.

"No, no, Trent and I had plans to watch some Netflix and fall asleep by nine." She laughed. "You three enjoy."

That felt like a gift, too, in its own way.

THAT EVENING, CURTIS noticed the conservative outfit that Hope had chosen for the evening—a gray woolen skirt that went down to mid-calf, knee-high boots underneath and a lighter gray cowl-necked sweater. She wrapped a particularly thick-looking woolen shawl on top of it all, and while she didn't wear a stitch of bright color tonight, her cheeks were pink. Hope was pretty, whatever she wore. She was one of those women who just glowed. He'd thought that before she was pregnant, and it was even truer now.

He wasn't sure what to expect at the Amish gathering. Would he be welcomed? Grandpa Jespersen had had a deep respect for his Amish neighbors, but he'd also said, "Let the Amish do what the Amish do. That's how you get along."

Hope had both an address that Curtis's GPS didn't recognize and a little hand-drawn map that proved to be more useful. She gave him directions, squinting at the little drawing, and Curtis turned when she told him to.

"Where did you get the directions from?" he asked.

"Belinda Beiler. I stopped by the ice cream shop."

Hope had connections here, even if she hadn't lived here her whole adult life. She had friendships, acquaintances, people she'd known for years or who had known her family. So, no, he wouldn't call it something as businesslike as *connections*. Hope had roots. That was what she had in this community. She didn't have a street named for her family, but she had something more.

"Are you looking forward to this?" Curtis asked.

"You bet. The food will be terrific—whatever they serve. It's an honor to be invited, you know."

"Yeah, I can understand that." And he was honored, but he was also glad to have Hope at his side.

It took about twenty minutes of back-roads driving for them to finally close in on the place. The last mile or so they followed three buggies all going in the same direction, and it was a pretty safe bet that they were headed to the dairy farm, too.

When they finally turned down the long drive, the front pasture was filled with buggies, neatly lined up. Curtis wasn't sure where to go. There were a couple of Amish boys who were parking the buggies for people who were arriving, and Curtis waited while they took care of the two buggies ahead of him. Another couple of boys unhitched horses and led them to a picket line where there was food and water waiting.

"Do you know where I should park?" he said.

"I'm not sure."

The Amish people who left their buggies watched them cautiously, looking back over their shoulders and hurrying the kids on ahead of them. Then the boys turned their attention to them and Curtis rolled down his window.

"Good evening," Curtis said. "We were invited by Bishop Moses. Just wondering where to park."

"Oh, right," the bigger boy said. "Bishop Moses said you can park up by the house."

"Thanks," Curtis said, and he pulled a five-dollar bill out of his pocket. "Are you boys taking tips?"

"What?" The boy blinked.

"Normally the valet service gets a tip," Curtis said.

"Not us—" the younger boy started, but the first boy elbowed him in the ribs.

"Sure. *Danke!*"

Curtis handed over the bill with a smile, then rolled up his window and carried on toward the house.

"I hope I don't get him into trouble," Curtis said.

"I have a feeling it might be worth it to him," Hope replied.

The backyard had a firepit and some big, bubbling pots of water boiling over the flames. The men were the ones pitching corn into the water, black felt hats pushed back on their heads, and a couple of them in shirtsleeves and suspenders as they stood close to the heat. The sun was low, but there were a lot of Amish folks here this evening. There was the scent of bonfire in the air mingling with the earthy smell of cattle.

Beyond the milk barns, rolling pasture stretched out and cattle dotted the field. With the long, low rays of the sun splashing across the grass, Curtis could feel tension he didn't know he was holding on to start to melt out of his shoulders.

The side door to the house kept opening and shutting as women in different-colored cape dresses went in and out, loading the folding tables lined up in the yard with food. One woman came out holding a platter with mugs of some steaming beverage. Curtis hopped out of the vehicle and circled around to open Hope's door for her. He gave her a hand as she slid down to the ground, and then he opened the back door to get Lucy from her car seat. When he got his daughter out, he found Hope chatting with the young Amish woman from the Yoder farm. She wore a black shawl over a pink cape dress, and she looked a little pale.

"Curtis, you remember Sarah, don't you?" Hope said.

"Of course," Curtis replied, and Lucy's eyes lit up at the sight of her. A friendship had obviously been forged with that visit, because Lucy leaned out of his arms toward her, and a smile suddenly split Sarah's face. She reached for Lucy and popped her onto her hip.

"How are you, Lucy?" Sarah asked, then she smiled up at Curtis. "It's nice to see you. You know, we can watch Lucy for a while, if you want. Can't we, Hope?"

"We'd love to," Hope said, and she met his gaze just for a moment. Her offer felt so personal.

"I didn't want you with me for childcare," he said in Hope's ear, keeping his voice low. "That wasn't my goal here."

"Kitties?" Lucy asked Sarah hopefully.

"That's right. Last time I saw you, there were kittens, weren't there?" Sarah said. "This isn't my farm, sweetie, but I bet we can find a cat around somewhere."

As Sarah gave Lucy her undivided attention, Hope turned toward him.

"I know," she said, picking up on what he'd last said. "But she's very little, and someone needs to keep an eye on her. Besides, this is a good opportunity for you to talk to people about your project. The bishop invited you, so people know why you're here. You'll get their honest opinions."

His gaze slid toward his daughter, who was plucking at the *kapp* string that hung down from Sarah's gauzy white head covering. She was entranced by Sarah.

"You're right," he agreed. "Thank you. I'll come find you in a few minutes."

He felt better as Hope smiled at him and then followed Sarah. Lucy was a runner, but he trusted Hope.

For the next little while, he went around talking with the men about their concerns. They all seemed ready to discuss it, too, which was probably thanks to the bishop. The bishop found him almost immediately and introduced him to an elder and a deacon. They talked about their dislike of having people watch them for entertainment. A few fathers talked about the school and their worry about the children being gawked at and possibly even targeted. They explained that their children walked home from school and that giving children some independence was good for their development. If they had to start dropping them off and picking them up from school in order to protect them from looky-loo Englishers, the children would lose a lot of those independent experiences that helped them to grow up and gain confidence in their own abilities.

As a father himself, Curtis could see the problem there. He'd suggested a few solutions—giving Englishers somewhere else to get an Amish experience so that they wouldn't just wander around looking for one, for example. He suggested guided buggy tours as a good way to control the Amish experience for tourists. It would also provide some good income for yet another business. At that suggestion, a young man with a shaved face perked up at the idea of a buggy tour. After a moment, Curtis recognized him. It was Eddie, the Englisher electrician who was marrying Sarah.

The food smelled delicious. Corn on the cob—of course—and there was a meal called haystacks. It was a layered dish—starting with crackers or corn chips, then a layer of cooked ground pork, and lettuce, tomatoes, sour cream, grated cheese, olives, some sort of minced relish… People just formed a line and walked past the toppings, making their haystack to their liking.

"Hey, man," Eddie said, catching up to him.

"How are you?" Curtis asked.

"I'm… I'm okay." The younger man pulled off his hat and raked a hand through his half-grown-out hair, then replaced it again. "I like your idea about the guided tours. That's a business I could do. I need to find something."

"It would be pretty lucrative if there were tourists coming through," Curtis agreed. "Other Amish areas have had good success with tour businesses."

Since their trip to the Yoder farm, Curtis had been researching and talking to business owners and city councilors in other Amish areas, gathering information.

"I mean, the overhead cost is a buggy and a couple of horses, right?"

"That's about it. I thought I heard you were learning to farm."

"I am…but it's not coming easily. I wouldn't be able to make a plot of land profitable fast enough to get married. So I need to figure out something else that'll support a family."

The pressure was on, it seemed, and that was something Curtis could sympathize with.

"Hey, you're an electrician, right? The Beiler Dairy Ice Cream shop in town has some outlets along one wall that aren't working properly."

"That's part of why they're raising money tonight," Eddie replied.

"Right. I guess I shouldn't have worried."

"The Amish take care of their own," Eddie said, but his smile slipped. "I, um, I went by and fixed the main outlet for them already."

"That was really decent of you," Curtis said.

"No, it wasn't." Eddie sighed. "I'm trying to become Amish, and my skill set in electrical work is…problematic."

"I guess there aren't too many Amish electricians," Curtis agreed.

He shook his head. "I'm in trouble for doing it."

That seemed a little extreme. "Why? This was an Amish family who needed help."

"Because that part of my life is supposed to be in the past. Like you said, there are no Amish electricians. I'm supposed to forge a whole new life, a whole new career…everything."

"But the ice cream place is an Amish business," Curtis countered. "If they're allowed to use electricity in their business, surely you can fix it for them."

"You'd think, but no. That Amish business should be hiring an *Englisher* to fix it. There are some things we Amish just don't touch."

We Amish. Curtis noticed the phrasing there.

"So what does that mean, that you're in trouble?" he asked.

"I don't know yet. I'm finding out. I'm in the unique position of trying to prove that I'll live Amish and abide by the rules. And I will. I mean—I'm not playing a game here. I'm committed to the Amish life with Sarah."

"They don't believe you're serious?"

"Not exactly. They believe I want to make this work, that I love Sarah. But they need to see proof that I'm going to be able to do it. And honestly—I need to prove it to Sarah, too. She's taking a chance on me."

"Would you ever become Amish if it weren't for Sarah?" Curtis asked.

Eddie was silent for a moment, then he shook his head. "I'm supposed to say yes. That whether or not I married her, I'd be choosing this life."

"What's the truth?" Curtis asked.

"No, I wouldn't. Not that I don't admire their faith and their way of life. Not that I don't see the beauty in their devotion to tradition and clean living. But it's hard to join the community—really hard. I could live off-grid somewhere if I really wanted to and I wouldn't have to prove myself to anyone, learn a new language, all of it. But Sarah makes all that hard work worth it."

"She'll help you sort it out, then," Curtis said.

"Yeah, she will." Eddie's gaze moved toward a group of Amish women—Sarah must be with them. He didn't sound convinced, though. Maybe she couldn't help. Maybe this was one of those times a man just had to face the consequences on his own.

The Amish had a very specific way of seeing the world, and of seeing their obligations to their faith and to each other. It wasn't always logical to an outsider's way of thinking, either. Curtis would have to step carefully.

CHAPTER NINETEEN

THE WARMTH FROM the bonfire soaked into Hope's legs. Lucy leaned comfortably against Hope's belly, enjoying the warmth, too. Her eyes were looking heavy. There was something about the heat from a wood fire that couldn't be matched.

Curtis was talking with Eddie over in a line for food, looking serious. Hope had to wonder what they were talking about. She now knew Eddie's family's position on this wedding. Would Eddie change his mind?

With the Amish, the men ate first, and then once they'd gotten their plates filled, the women would gather around and get their food, too. Hope could wait for her turn, but she had to admit that she was hungry. The meat from the haystacks mingled with boiled corn smelled delicious.

Curtis looked back in her direction, and Hope dropped her gaze.

"Is he your boyfriend?" Sarah asked, slipping into a chair next to her.

"What? Curtis?"

Sarah looked back at her innocently enough, but she didn't repeat herself.

"Um, no. We're just friends."

"Oh… Right. I'm sorry, Hope, I didn't think you *Englishers* kept dating secrets like we Amish do. I shouldn't have asked. How silly of me."

"I'm not keeping a secret," Hope said with a low laugh. "We really are just friends. If we were dating, I'd tell you."

Sarah leaned forward and looked in Curtis's direction, then shrugged. "Does he know that?"

"Yes, he does. There's no confusion," Hope said. "I think all you're seeing is that I'm pregnant, so he's feeling a little protective. That's all."

"In my experience with men—" Sarah paused. "Well, it's not extensive, but still. In my experience of watching men, at the very least, I've found that pregnancy is more likely to make them run away."

Hope didn't have an answer for that, and Lucy decided it was time to wander around. That saved Hope from having to explain her chemistry with Curtis. Because the chemistry was there—she knew it. But that was all it was. Two people who found each other attractive and enjoyed each other's company. But when one of them was raising a toddler and the other was pregnant and still grieving her husband—even if she was starting to think that being married again sounded very sweet—there was nothing simple about it.

A few minutes later, Hope had Lucy back in the chair by the fire, and Curtis came over with one full plate of haystacks and a second one with a few crackers, chips, some shredded cheese and some cut cucumber for Lucy. Lucy slid off Hope's knee and went over to her father.

"This one's for you," Curtis said to Hope. "I'm sorry—I should have asked what you wanted. I just got a little bit of everything."

"In an Amish gathering, the men normally get their plates first," Hope said.

"I'm not Amish, am I?" He met her gaze meaningfully. "You need to eat. I'm not eating before you."

Hope accepted the food with a rumble in her stomach.

"This does look good," she said. "You should get yourself some."

Curtis grinned and sank into another chair next to her.

"I will once the line thins down," he said.

She'd had this dish before, but somehow, that plate of haystacks was the most delicious meal she could remember eating. There was something sweet about tucking into a plate of good Amish cooking with Curtis beside her, him holding Lucy's plate and letting her pick off it with her fingers.

When Hope looked over at Sarah, the young Amish woman gave her a wry little smile. Hope felt some heat touch her cheeks, and she laughed softly and dropped her gaze.

"What?" Curtis asked.

"Nothing."

He was a kind and decent man. She could do far worse, if she were ready to dive back into the dating scene. But she wasn't ready, and that was that.

THE EVENING WORE ON, and by eight, Lucy had fallen asleep on her father's shoulder. The sun had set, and the Amish folks had split between the younger people, who were playing board games in the house—Eddie and Sarah included—and the older folks, who had started singing hymns around the bonfires.

The elders had discreetly gone around the different groups of people with a hat, and they'd all put something into it—bills, coins, whatever they could, it seemed. When they came by the fire where Hope and Curtis sat, Hope put in a twenty, and Curtis put some bills in, too. He really was decent.

"We should head out," Curtis said softly once the elder had moved on.

"Yeah, I think it's time," she replied.

They said a few goodbyes to the people they knew, and the bishop gave them a solemn nod in farewell. When they got to the vehicle, Hope opened the door for Curtis so he could put Lucy into her car seat. She moaned a little bit as he buckled her in, but once he put a fuzzy blanket over her, her soft snores started up again.

"So…what did you think?" Hope asked once they were buckled in themselves.

"It's a unique way of life, isn't it?" he said.

"Very. A vulnerable one, too."

He nodded, and he pulled around and headed up the drive. The horses in the pasture looked up as the headlights swept over them. The moon was high, and the scent of bonfire clung to their clothes. Hope leaned her head back against the headrest and the heat pumped comfortably onto her legs.

"It's vulnerable in many ways, though," he said. "If a community can't support more farmers, for example, those young adults are going to have to move away and settle elsewhere."

Hope smoothed a hand over her belly. "Is it because of the hormones that that makes me feel a little weepy?"

Curtis chuckled and turned onto the main road. "Things hit differently as a parent. It makes me feel kind of sad, too, thinking of my daughter growing up, getting married, moving away from me."

"I feel like I owe my parents an apology," she said. She remembered how her mother had cried when they'd each moved out, and the joy of everyone getting together again for Thanksgiving and Christmas.

"I think we'll be ready once we get there," he said.

"You sure?" she asked.

"Nope, but I hope so." He shot her a smile.

"I'm glad you understand all this," she said. "I don't feel quite so alone in it."

"Faith has a son, though, right?"

"Tyke, her stepson. You're right, she understands, too, but she also has Trent. When Tyke grows up, they'll have each other to lean on. When my son grows up… I'll likely be alone."

Curtis pulled to a stop at an intersection. He looked over at her for a beat—the road empty.

"Alone? Why?"

"I'm not sure I'll get married again," she said.

"Why not?"

"Marriage can be complicated, and I'll have a son to worry about."

"What about you, though? Don't you want love and companionship?"

Hope looked out the window at the passing, moon-soaked fields. Shc knew her son would grow up. She knew she'd have to treasure ever stage and memory. But she'd also learned something about herself since her husband died.

"I actually have some regrets from my marriage," she admitted.

"Yeah?" Curtis's voice was quiet.

"I let go of my own ambitions when I married Peter. I thought that the amount of money he made meant that his career needed to be the priority and that I should make being his wife my job. And that…didn't work for me."

"Did he expect you to do that? To let go of your own stuff and focus on taking care of his?"

"I don't know. We weren't married long enough to even butt heads over it." She glanced over to find Curtis's attention on the road, but his expression had softened. Somehow this was easier to talk about without him looking at her.

"But you'd do it differently if you could go back?" he asked.

"Yeah, I would," she said. "I don't want to have a man taking care of everything for me."

Curtis's gaze flicked in her direction and a smile tickled at his lips. "How awful."

She smiled ruefully. "I'm serious, though. I let Peter take care of it all. And he did it because he loved me, but frankly, there wasn't anything else left for me to do. And even though he was by far the bigger earner, my ambitions mattered, too. I've got plans for a day care here in Apfelkuchen, and I'm going to get serious about that."

"After the baby is born?" he asked.

"No, I'm going to find a location I can lease sooner than that, get some children's toys and activity centers lined up. I'm going to get my business license and be ready to go by the time my baby is eight weeks old."

"And what if you had someone to take care of

things for you for a while," he asked. "Would that make things easier?"

Hope looked over at him and he shot her a serious look. He meant well—she knew that. He was being noble and valiant. But it was misplaced.

"I have money," she said.

"So this is because you want to, not because you need the income."

"I do need to start bringing in an income, don't get me wrong. But I need something that's mine, too," she said. "The baby will be mine, but he'll grow up. A career is something beyond motherhood. It's something where I can contribute to our community and something that I can grow—for myself. It's important to have that. Boredom can turn toxic. I think I was clingy with Peter because I was so bored, and I hate that."

They crested a hill, and beneath them the town of Apfelkuchen spread out in a glittery array of lights. She recognized streets, her old high school and the street where the antiques shop was located, although she couldn't make it out from up here.

Curtis pulled over into the parking lot of a little Amish fruit stand that was empty at this time of night. A tarp covered the front of the stand—the extent of the security. Curtis turned toward her.

"Can I just say something?" He reached out and caught her hand. "Hope, you don't ask for too much. I'm not saying that you wouldn't have sorted all that out with Pete. I think you would have. He was head over heels for you. But you weren't being clingy. You weren't asking for too much. Wanting to see your husband, to have him in the same bed as you at night, to share breakfast in the morning and dinner at night—that's just a normal level of togetherness in a relationship."

"Then why didn't he want that, too?" She heard the shake in her voice, and resented it. Her hand was still in his, and he ran his thumb over her knuckles.

"I don't know. He probably was focused on providing for you. I mean, a man gets married and he's thinking about doing right by you financially. We can be dense sometimes."

"Really?"

"Yeah."

"You, too?" She smiled faintly.

"Absolutely. Up until you told me you want to focus on your own career and really don't want a man diving in to rescue you… I was kind of imagining it a little bit."

"Rescuing me?"

"Why not?" He gave her a tender smile. "You're kind, beautiful, insightful, smart…and you're about to have a baby. In my head—as a bit of a Neanderthal—I want to step in and offer you all kinds of support."

"It's unnecessary…but sweet."

"Yeah…sorry."

"I really am okay."

"I know." He lifted her hand to his lips and kissed the top of her fingers. "You're going to be just fine, and your son is going to be one lucky boy to have you as his mother. It'll come together. I just don't want you think that you were messing things up with Pete. You weren't. You were amazing, and he knew it."

"Did he tell you that?"

"A few times. He was kind of obnoxious about it." He winked, and she couldn't help but smile back. "All he told me was how lucky he was to have you and the vacations he wanted to take you on. He had Caribbean hopes for your first anniversary."

Was it possible that she wasn't actually pushing for too much? Maybe all they'd needed was more time together—something they hadn't gotten because his life had been cut short.

"Thank you, Curtis. I needed to hear that."

He released her hand and pulled back onto the road, but she could feel the sensation of his soft lips pressing against her fingers. She looked over at him and his gaze flicked toward her. A smile touched his lips.

He'd wanted to be her hero… That was tempting. But she needed to get her life balanced so that she could feel fulfilled in her own pursuits.

Being rescued—no matter how sweet and handsome the rescuer—was not enough, and she now knew that better than anyone.

CHAPTER TWENTY

WHEN CURTIS PULLED to a stop in front of the Amish Antiques Shop, the street was silent and empty. Apfelkuchen's downtown stores were all closed by now. The only places in town open until ten were a couple of fast-food places and a single bar. Curtis didn't drink, and even if he did, the bar scene had never been for him.

A horse pulling an open buggy moved past them—a young Amish couple out on a date. The young man had his arm around the young woman's shoulders. Funny how dating wasn't all that different between cultures. Some things were universal.

He looked over at Hope as she undid her seat belt. She was beautiful in the soft light of the streetlamp. There was something about her that tugged at him. She'd made it clear that she had her own plans—and he had his—but she was still extraordinary. He'd never met a woman like her. She cast him a smile, then pushed open the door and slid to the ground without waiting for his assistance.

Curtis turned off the vehicle and got out. He met her on the other side, and he peeked in the window to make sure the Lucy was still asleep.

"She had a big night," Hope said.

"Yeah, she did." He turned his focus back to the woman in front of him. "Thank you for coming with me. It was easier having you there."

"Lucy is a sweetie," Hope said.

"No, I—" That wasn't what he'd meant at all, and he refused to let this night end with her thinking that he was glad she'd come for childcare. "Thank you for helping me keep an eye on her, but that's not what I meant. I mean having you there, with me, that helped. You."

"Oh…" She smiled. "You're welcome. I'm not sure what I did."

"People just like me more if you're around."

She laughed. "That's not true."

"In Apfelkuchen it is," he said, but he chuckled. "Your opinion of me matters around here."

"You'll settle in," she said. "You've got a whole street named after you."

"I've got a whole street named after my great-uncle." He smiled ruefully. "Let's keep that in perspective. Your good opinion matters to me, too. I feel like I do better with you in the room."

And he wasn't even sure why. He wanted to impress her, maybe. He wanted to be the guy who made her smile. He wanted her to think good things about him.

The streetlight illuminated the sidewalk in a golden glow, and he could smell woodsmoke on the air—probably from some fireplaces on this chilly evening. Hope hitched her shoulders up as a breeze pushed her hair away from her face.

"How much longer are you here?" she asked.

"Another week, I think. I have a few more things to straighten up, and then I can head back and sign a contract with a construction company."

She nodded, then dropped her gaze. It didn't sound like long, he knew. It didn't feel like long, either.

"And then I'll be back from time to time to supervise construction," he said.

"That'll be nice. You'll know where to find me."

"You don't have to wait for me to come to town, you know," he said. "We can talk on the phone. I'm old-fashioned that way."

She nodded. "That would be nice."

Was she actually agreeing to this? He'd told himself he wouldn't ask for more—it wasn't really fair—but he'd done it anyway. Maybe they could be friends—close friends. Maybe he could keep her in his life without crossing those lines.

"Seeing you here again, stumbling into your shop, it was the happiest surprise I've had in a really long time," he admitted. "I know you don't remember me, but I remember you very well. You set the bar when you married Pete, you know."

"Me?" She looked like she almost didn't believe him.

"Yes, you." He shrugged. "I saw what my friend found with you, and I told myself I wasn't getting married until I found a woman like you. You're the whole package."

"I'm also pregnant, and grieving, and trying to figure things out—"

"I know," he murmured. "I'm not asking anything of you. I'm just letting you know that you're the one to beat."

Hope's eyes glittered as a smile touched her lips. The wind picked up, ruffling her hair, and he stepped a little closer so that her belly pressed up against him. He moved a little to block the breeze, and her hair stilled. There—success. He could still feel the chill at his back, and discovered just how close he was to her. She looked up at him, her eyes luminous, and suddenly all his rational thinking got swallowed up in the thundering of his own heartbeat. Whatever his reasoning had been to hold back, he couldn't quite remember, and all he could think about was how perfectly she'd fit into his arms, and how pretty her lips were. Her lips parted, and before he thought better of it, he leaned closer, and when he felt her lean in, just a little bit, Curtis dropped his head down and caught her lips with his.

He could feel her belly pressed against his coat, their breath mingling in the crisp autumn air. His own heartbeat thundered in his ears. This was both perfect and foolhardy—that logical reasoning was still floating around somewhere beyond him—but he could feel something inside him cracking open, something soft and hopeful and not easily sealed back up again.

She was the first one to pull back, and he looked down at those lips he'd just kissed. Everything inside him said to kiss her again, but she took a step back, and he reined it in.

"Wow," she breathed.

"Yeah..."

That kiss had scared him a little. He hadn't planned it, and it had done something to him...

"I should get to bed," she said.

He nodded. "I need to get my daughter back, too."

They were both silent for a beat, and he wasn't sure what he could say or do that would make that kiss seem casual. He'd just told her he wasn't asking anything of her, hadn't he?

He needed some time alone to think it over, to see what had happened when he'd kissed her, and figure out if he could stuff everything back inside him again.

"I'll see you tomorrow?" he asked softly.

She nodded. "Good night, Curtis."

"Good night."

He stood on the sidewalk until Hope had let herself in through the side door that led up to her apartment, and that chilly wind swept around him, cooling his skin and blowing away that cloud of bliss. When that door swung solidly shut, he exhaled a sigh and headed back to his SUV. He was feeling more for her than was smart. She wasn't his to protect.

There it was. That was the logic that had escaped him.

Curtis got back into the driver's seat and looked over his shoulder at his daughter asleep in her car seat. Her long lashes brushed her cheeks, and her lips were pouted in a little bow. He started the engine again and pulled away from the curb. Time to get his daughter home and into bed. If there was one thing he'd learned, it was that a good night's sleep left a clearer head.

And right now, Curtis's head was all muddled up with Hope's sweet smile, the intoxicating scent of her perfume, and her kiss.

He'd kissed her! Was he going to regret that come morning?

THE NEXT DAY, it wasn't regret exactly, but he was a little worried about what Hope would say when he dropped Lucy off. He stood in the motel room window, drinking a cup of mediocre coffee, his mind trailing off toward his time with Hope last night. Lucy was in front of a plastic bowl of cereal, picking pieces out with her fingers instead of her spoon.

Kissing her had uncovered a whole lot of feelings he didn't have a right to. It made him want to kiss her again, to make plans to see her, to figure something out where he could ensure he was the guy dating her and not some other guy from town. One kiss and he was feeling territorial. That wasn't okay.

Hope was fragile right now. She was like a magnet for him, but she needed stability. He wasn't planning on staying in this town. He couldn't offer her that. And on top of it all, his sister would always be in the picture, which complicated matters. No matter what else Lynn was going through, she hadn't stopped yearning for a relationship with her daughter.

"It's a O!" Lucy announced, holding up a Cheerio. "See, Daddy? It's a O!"

Sesame Street was paying off, it seemed. He shot her a smile.

"O like octopus," he said.

"Odd-o-pus," she said as she pushed more Cheerios into her mouth.

"Come on, Lucy," he said. "Let's use a spoon."

It was time to stop thinking about that kiss and start being a dad again. He picked up her spoon and handed it to her.

"You need help?" he asked.

"No…" Lucy shot him an exasperated look and plunged her spoon into the milk.

He'd grab a cloth. They'd get some cereal into her, and then he'd bring her over to the antiques shop…and he'd find out if he'd seriously crossed a line with that kiss when he saw how Hope looked at him.

WHEN HE GOT to Amish Antiques, Hope greeted them with a smile at the side door that led up to her apartment.

"Faith is going to man the shop this morning," Hope said. "I thought I'd take Lucy upstairs. We can do some baking together and I'll make her a nice lunch."

So normal. A wholesome thing to do with a morning, but she wasn't meeting his gaze, either, and her cheeks flushed. Nope, they were not going back to normal, and maybe that was good. Because he was only faking it anyway.

"Hope, last night—" He wasn't sure what to say.

"I know," she said. "I had a lot of thinking to do last night."

"About…me?"

"Yeah." She smiled faintly. "And about me, and Peter, and if it's okay for me to be kissing Peter's friend."

"And?" he asked.

"And… I don't know. I mean, Peter trusted you. He trusted me."

As if they'd been fooling around behind her husband's back. He'd never do that—ever. And he was pretty certain that she wouldn't, either.

"You aren't cheating on him, you know," he said.

"Sometimes it feels that way, though. Even though I know it's not true."

"So I made things weird?"

"The kiss was mutual," she said, finally looking up to meet his gaze. He was relieved to hear that. She'd kissed him, too, but it was good she remembered it that way.

"Fine, did *we* make things weird?" he asked, casting her a smile to soften it.

"Maybe. If I had my life together a little more, if I weren't seven months pregnant, if I hadn't lost my husband a few months ago…if you weren't his good friend…" She looked up at him as if she were begging him to understand. "You're fun, and handsome, and kind and…" She sighed. "I really like you—more than is safe for me at the moment."

"It's okay," he said. "I feel the same way. I have a pretty complicated life right now, and you need stability. And what I'm feeling is…not convenient, I guess. Given half a chance, I could fall for you."

He was teetering on the edge as it was, but that wasn't her problem. It was his.

Hope blinked at him. "Really?"

"It's under control," he said. Mostly.

"We'd better be careful, then."

"Okay," he agreed. "We'll be more careful."

"And maybe we don't kiss each other again. We keep it to a firm handshake."

He reached out his hand and took hers. "Okay."

It wasn't exactly a firm handshake, but he did give her hand a squeeze. She blushed.

"You're not even trying, Curtis."

"You have no idea how hard I'm trying," he said, and he let go of her hand. "I'll behave myself, Hope. No more kissing you. You'll see."

"Okay." Was that some fleeting disappointment he saw in her eyes? But he couldn't start second-guessing things. They did need to keep this under control.

"I need to go look over Jespersen Street once more," he said. "As always, if Lucy needs me, or…you do…"

"We'll be fine," Hope said. "If I can't comfort this sweet little girl, I don't deserve to be in the childcare business, do I?"

"All right," he said. "Fair enough."

"See you later." Her gaze was more guarded now when it met his, and he missed her earlier warmth and ease with him. But he understood.

"See you later," he replied.

Lucy happily bounced up the stairs at Hope's side, and he turned for the door. Back to business.

Curtis drove exactly one street over to Jespersen Street and parked along the curb. In his mind's eye he could see the completed brick row houses, the broad sidewalk and the informative signs set up along it that would give some history of the Amish and of Apfelkuchen. There would be a common area in the back with benches, a fountain, maybe even a functional kitchen garden that someone could be hired to tend to once a week. If he could make a big enough profit, he could funnel that back into the community by hiring a part-time gardener and maybe even a tour guide of his own.

A new vacation spot for city-dwelling Pennsylvanians would be welcome, especially with how busy the other Amish centers had become. Apfelkuchen really did have a lot to offer.

Curtis pulled out a ring of keys that he'd been given at the contract signing, and he pushed open his vehicle door and hopped out. Jespersen Street had a whole new chapter now, and he was glad to be part of it.

The first shop used to be the flower store. He tried three keys before he landed on the right one to unlock the rusty padlock. The door squeaked when he pushed it open. It was dim inside, the windows having been boarded up, and he left the door open for some light. The tiled floor was clean, except for a few dried leaves and what looked like a mouse nest in one corner. The service counter was covered in a thick layer of dust. There was a half roll of paper used to package up flowers left on the counter, also covered in dust.

The lady who ran this shop had been kind. His grandmother had lived with cancer for three years before she succumbed to it. And whenever they'd stopped by the florist, the Amish woman who ran the place had given Curtis and Lynn a flower to bring back to their grandmother.

Now you give that to your mammi, she'd say.

He and Lynn used to make deals—if he got to carry the flower to Grandma, then Lynn got to choose the ice cream flavor when they stopped by Beiler Dairy Ice Cream and bought a tub for after supper. If she got to carry the flower to Grandma, then he'd get to lick the beaters when Grandma whipped cream to go on top of pie.

They'd argue over who would carry that flower in the truck, and when he got his turn, he'd guarded that flower with his life. Sometimes it was a rose and others a carnation. Grandma had always responded with surprise and delight and put the flower into a vase right away and placed it on the sill of the window that was over the kitchen sink.

He smiled at the memory. Certainly she hadn't been so terribly surprised, but she knew that it made Curtis and Lynn happy to get a good reaction out of her, much like his exaggerated delight when Lucy brought him some little gift—a stone, a leaf—that she found when they went on a walk. Maybe as a dad he understood better.

Then Grandma died, when he was twelve and Lynn was fourteen. Lynn had always been pretty tough, but she'd been more crushed than anyone expected. She'd worn a necklace from Grandma's sparse jewelry collection ever after.

Maybe Curtis should have let her hold the flower more often.

He exited the shop and relocked the padlock. Jespersen Street. It wasn't about making money for money's sake. Not about getting rich. It was about investing in the community. He wanted this venture to help build up the entire town. He wanted the people here to see more security and stability because of it. This wasn't a vanity project. He really did want to help.

The tourist trap was a good idea on a financial level, but he wasn't getting a lot of support for it from the Amish community. They were worried, and his confidence about all the good things that more business would bring to the town weren't helping as much as he'd hoped. He was right—he was almost sure of it—but he wasn't going to sway people's opinions.

He stood on the cracked sidewalk.

"But the bishop could," he said out loud.

Maybe that was his way forward. Because once upon a time, Jespersen Street had been busy, and beautiful, and full of neighbors who cared about each other. It could be that way again—if everyone could just flourish together.

CHAPTER TWENTY-ONE

LUCY HAD A very nice morning for a toddler. Hope streamed some kids' music for her while they baked. Lucy had a snack and played with her doll, and she pulled all the pans out of a lower cupboard and spread them over the kitchen floor. She was currently sitting at the kitchen table with a coloring page in front of her, drawing with big, long, hard, satisfying streaks of crayon.

Hope was doing her best not to think about Curtis. She couldn't blame him for that kiss! He'd leaned in, and she'd leaned back. She wasn't some innocent, after all. She'd been married, and she knew when a man was trying to kiss her.

And it had been…very nice. Her heart had nearly beaten out of her chest, and his lips had reminded her of what it had felt like to be loved. That feeling was intoxicating, and she realized how very lonely she'd been for affection like that.

Which had sparked the guilt next.

She shouldn't be longing for love—not yet. It felt like a betrayal to Peter's memory. And she shouldn't be longing for anything with Curtis! It would be so much easier if he were someone else. But he was Peter's good friend, and he was tied up with Peter in her thoughts. Curtis would have been in her life with Peter, and he'd known her husband incredibly well. He might have even known Peter better than Hope had—he'd certainly known him for longer.

Here Curtis was offering support, and kindness, and affection. He was handsome, too. If he had never known Peter this might be easier, but as it was, whenever she looked at Curtis, she was reminded in some part of her mind that he'd loved Peter, too.

And she wasn't sure if that was a good thing or not.

The baby inside her seemed to tumble, and she felt him go round. She rubbed a hand over her belly. Were her chaotic feelings affecting him? She hoped not. She certainly couldn't allow romantic instability to affect her son as he grew up. Catherine might think she should deal with such things using a prenup, but Hope wasn't sure she could do that. She might take a different route, focusing on her child and her business and leaving off romance entirely.

"What are you up to in there?" she asked softly.

"What?" Lucy asked from her spot at the table.

"Oh, it's nothing," Hope said. She ran her hand over her belly. She loved being pregnant—the feeling of her baby's movements in their shared space. She was looking forward to his birth now, but she'd miss this pregnant closeness, too.

"TV?" Lucy asked, dropping her crayon. It rolled off the table and hit the floor. Hope looked down at it, wondering how awkward it would be to get down there again after she'd just cleaned up the pans.

"Why don't we pick up the crayons," Hope said. "Can you reach that one?"

Lucy enjoyed being helpful, and she crawled down to pick up the crayon and hand it up to Hope. Lucy had been getting a lot of screen time, and Hope wasn't sure that was a good thing for a small, growing brain. If she could distract her away from it, that would be better. At least for a while.

"Do you want to go downstairs?" Hope asked, pitching her voice to make it sound exciting.

"Yeah! Downstairs!"

Success. "Okay, let's see what Faith is doing. Maybe we'll find Smokey."

Hope grabbed her keys and opened the door. Lucy came dancing through.

"But you have to hold my hand, okay?" Hope said.

Hope came down the stairs, Lucy clinging to two of her fingers as they made their way slowly down the steep staircase toward the store.

When they got to the bottom of the stairs,

Lucy let go of Hope's fingers and bounced into the store. It smelled faintly of the dried lavender that Faith had been stuffing into little pouches. Sunlight was filtering in through the front window, and the shop was warm. But the coziness of the shop didn't match her sister's stressed-out stance—shoulders hitched up and her expression grim. Faith stood by the front counter with Sarah Yoder, and both women looked up as Lucy and Hope came in.

"Hope, I was about to call you down," Faith said.

"What's going on?" Hope asked. Sarah's eyes were reddened and her face was blotchy from crying. "Oh my goodness, Sarah! What's wrong?"

"Eddie's in trouble," Sarah said.

"With the law?" It was the first thing to pop into Hope's head.

"No, with the bishop and the elders." That was almost worse for the Amish, but at least he wasn't being arrested or something. Her blood pressure came down a notch.

Hope led Lucy over to a folded quilt they'd been using for her to play on and got her settled with her doll. Smokey appeared from out of nowhere, ambling in Lucy's direction as if it had been his plan to saunter by all along, and he flopped down in a little pool of sunlight close to the toddler, but not quite within reach.

"What did Eddie do?" Hope asked.

"The Beilers—you were at the corn roast when we were raising money to help them," Sarah said. "They're struggling through no fault of their own, just that milk and cream prices have dropped and expenses have risen, and it's been hard for them."

"I know they needed some electrical work done—" Hope started, and then she froze. "Oh no..." She could see where this was going. "He didn't..."

"He did," Sarah said, sniffling. "Eddie did the electrical work for them, free of charge, because he knew how to do it. Well, he fixed the main outlet they needed for the soft serve machine. It didn't take much."

"He'd asked Trent for a few supplies," Faith said weakly. "I was there when he asked, and even I didn't think anything of it!"

"Good Amish men don't *do* electrical work," Sarah said, wiping a tear from her cheek. "At least not in our community. And now the bishop and elders are questioning if Eddie even has what it takes to be Amish! That's been the worry all along!"

"They think that he won't stick with it?" Hope asked.

"They think that he's in love with me, but that it won't be enough for him to follow the Plain way for the rest of his life." Sarah looked down at her sodden tissue.

"Do you think he can?" Faith asked softly.

Sarah was silent.

"You don't?" Faith pressed. "After all this, you think maybe he won't want to live Amish?"

"It's hard." Sarah looked up pleadingly. "He's given up his truck, his job as an electrician, his *English* life! He's had to learn how to do things the Amish way, which is just harder. His mom and dad told him straight that they think he'll regret all this." She swallowed hard. "We don't have shortcuts or conveniences. And add to that the language! He's doing his best to learn, but when people are chatting in a room, he doesn't understand anything unless I translate for him."

"And you think it's not worth it for him?" Hope asked.

"I'm afraid that now that he's in trouble, it will be the last straw," Sarah said. "He thought he was helping. He's done everything they've asked of him. Everything! They never thought he would! They thought he'd drop it. And he's trying so hard to learn *Deutche*. But now after all his effort, he's in trouble with the church leaders."

"Hold on now," Hope said. "He made a mistake. But honestly, it came from the goodness of his heart. He wanted to help them. He was trying to do the right thing. Is he really in that much trouble?"

"If he was *English*, it would have been the right thing," Sarah said. "But not if he's Amish. The rules are different for us. The standards are different. My father is afraid that the bishop and elders will see it as proof that he doesn't have what it takes, after all. He doesn't understand our reasoning, or how we think."

"And what happens then?" Hope asked. "In the worst-case scenario, if they decide he won't stay Amish, then what?"

"Then they won't let me marry him." Her lips wobbled.

His family was pushing for him to stop this. Her family was pretty sure he would give up…and Hope didn't like how the poor guy was being pressured from all directions. Love was rare enough without two good people being held away from each other, no matter how well-meaning the community.

"Technically, sweetie, you can marry him anytime you like," Hope said softly. "You're an adult—you don't need anyone's permission to marry a man in the state of Pennsylvania."

And she meant it. If those two wanted to get married, they could take their buggy and go make it happen.

"If we aren't married Amish, they won't accept our marriage." Sarah shook her head. "And I'd be shunned for going against their decision. The only way we can get married and be Amish together is if we do it properly."

"And if you get married and…don't stay Amish?" Hope asked.

"I'd definitely be shunned. I'd lose contact with my parents, my siblings, my aunts and uncles, friends, everyone. I'd be dead to them."

A very dear price to pay. Hope knew that the only way to be reinstated with the church again would be to come back and live Amish once more. And if she'd married an Englisher who wouldn't be living Amish, that was an impossibility. A catch-22.

"So what happens now?" Faith asked.

"He'll have to talk to the bishop and the elders. I don't know what they'll discuss. That would be private. And they'll decide what to do."

Hope exchanged a look with her sister. The Amish life looked idyllic from the outside, but maintaining their unique, Plain way of living could be a challenge, and the leadership was very strict because of it. And yet, Bishop Moses was a kind man. He'd have some empathy for a young couple in love, wouldn't he?

The outside door opened, the bell tinkling, and Lucy jumped to her feet. Hope was already darting toward the toddler when Lucy cried out, "Daddy!"

Curtis bent down and gathered his daughter in his arms as she flew toward him.

"Hey, there," he said. "Are you having fun?"

Sarah wrapped her black shawl closer around herself. "I'd better go. I need to finish running errands. My *mamm* is expecting me."

"See you later, Sarah," Faith said, and Hope gave her a fluttering wave.

The bell tinkled again as Sarah disappeared onto the street. Curtis looked over his shoulder the way she'd gone.

"Is she okay?" he asked.

"Lots of romantic drama," Hope said.

"Eddie told me he'd messed up," Curtis said. "Is it that bad?"

"Afraid so."

Curtis put his daughter back down, and she crouched to pet the cat as Hope gave him a quick rundown of what had happened.

"I had a thought, but hearing about what happened with Eddie and Sarah, I think I'm on the right track. I wanted to run it by you first, though," Curtis said.

"Of course," Hope said.

"I can't make this project work without Amish support, and I'm not getting it. Eddie told me he'd fixed the Beilers' electrical problem and what a big kerfuffle that caused. But Eddie thinks, if he'd talked to the bishop first, that might not have been such a big misstep. The bishop might even have made an exception."

"If not an exception, he could have at least have told him not to do it," Hope replied.

"Thinking about Eddie's situation, I think I understand how the Amish work just a little bit better."

"Does that change things for you?" she asked.

"Well, I think I need to sit down with the bishop to talk about my building plan one more time. I know I spoke with him at the corn roast, but I was talking to him like a fellow businessman. That wasn't the right thing to do. I'd like another chance to talk to him alone. If I can show him the benefit of this plan, and discuss some safe-guards, if the bishop saw the benefit, then the rest of the community would probably follow his lead, right?"

"Probably," Hope agreed.

Lucy got up and ambled around behind her father. She put her hands behind her back as she looked at something on a shelf.

"The problem is," Curtis said, "I don't know how to go about asking for a second meeting. Would Faith's in-laws be willing to help with that?"

"I could talk to them," Hope said. "I can't promise they'll think it's a good idea, but I can go by this evening and ask."

There was a faint tinkle of the bell and Hope looked up just in time to see a little blond head vanishing out the partially opened door—opened just wide enough for a tiny girl to slip through, and leaving the bell rocking. Hope's heart thudded to a stop.

Just past the front window, she saw a little crop of blond curls zipping past.

Lucy had made an escape!

CHAPTER TWENTY-TWO

CURTIS SAW HOPE'S face pale, and he turned to look in the direction she was staring. All he saw was the cat lying in a patch of sunlight on the floor.

"Lucy!" Hope dashed for the door, and that was when it hit him. Lucy was gone. His heart stuttered to a stop.

Hope was already outside, and she pointed up the street. "I saw her head this way from the window, but I don't see her now."

"Lucy!" Curtis called.

"Lucy!" Hope echoed.

He waited for a heartbeat to see if her smiling face would pop out from behind something, but nothing happened. Faith appeared in the door.

"She ran off?" Faith asked, breathless.

"Yeah, I saw her out the window," Hope said. "Faith, stay here in case she comes back."

"I'll stay right here and keep an eye out. Maybe I'll spot her," Faith said.

"You're sure she went this way?" he asked, turning toward Hope.

"Positive." She met his gaze and held it firmly. "Let's look."

But there was no sign of Lucy. A horse and buggy came down the road toward them, and a car passed in the opposite direction. Both made his pulse speed up. If Lucy dashed in front of a vehicle…

"You take this side of the street—" Curtis pointed up the street "—and I'll go the other side."

"Okay!" Hope set off at a fast walk, her head swiveling this way and that, and Curtis jogged across the street looking in both directions. How far could a toddler have gotten? But she was fast and fearless, and he knew better than to underestimate his daughter.

Curtis jogged up the street, looking into the alleys between buildings. He stopped and shaded his eyes when he thought he saw a flash of pink. It was only a bag.

A short whoop of a siren pulled his attention back to the road. A Pennsylvania State Police cruiser had pulled to a stop, and a young trooper with a mustache rolled down his window.

"Sir, are you okay?"

"I'm looking for my daughter," Curtis said. "She's two years old, blond hair, pink sweater, black leggings. She just took off. I don't think she could have gotten far, but if you'd keep your eyes peeled, I'd really appreciate it."

His anxiety was mounting with every minute

he didn't spot Lucy. Anything could happen to little girls—anything—and his fears were building.

"I'll go in the opposite direction," the trooper said. "Let me radio in to the other local troopers—just to be on the safe side."

"Thank you!" Curtis said. "I appreciate it."

He crossed a street. He was now a block away from the antiques shop. How on earth had Lucy disappeared so quickly? And what kind of father was he? Hope had noticed his daughter was missing before he did, and he'd been in the store, too! He was Lucy's father—he was the one who was supposed to have a sixth sense for where she was. And he normally did! He could see her making a break for it out of the corner of his eye, or he'd hear that patter of little running shoes, and he'd reach out and snatch her up before she made it too far.

But this was the second time in a week that she'd gotten away from him. He'd been distracted…and this time, he'd been distracted with Hope. That wasn't her fault—it was his! Was Lucy getting sneakier, or was he losing that sixth sense he'd been relying on?

"Lucy!" he called. "Lucy!"

Across the street, Hope was calling his daughter's name, too. He looked at Hope just as she turned toward him, another buggy clopping past between them.

"She's here somewhere!" Hope called. "Look inside shops—she came into ours, remember?"

"Good idea!" he called back.

He headed back the way he'd come and poked his head into the first shop—a craft supply store that doubled as some extra freezer space for Amish families. There were three big deep freezers along one wall with a sign above written in both Pennsylvania Dutch and in English that said they worked on the honor system and customers should only take food from their own bag.

Curtis scanned the store—Lucy wasn't there.

"Can I help you?" a stout older woman asked. He could tell she wasn't Amish because her dress had a printed pattern, and she wore a handkerchief over her hair. But he could see some similarities. Maybe she was Old Order Mennonite, or Hutterite.

"I'm looking for my two-year-old daughter—" And he gave the pertinent information.

"Sorry, she didn't come in here." She gave him an apologetic look. "You know what—I'll help you search."

She grabbed a shawl from under the front counter and wrapped it around herself as she headed for the door.

"Thank you!" he said gratefully.

They exited the shop together. She didn't bother locking up or anything, just walked away at a brisk pace and hurried to the next store, poking her head in the door. He carried on to the one after and did the same. Had anyone seen a two-year-old girl?

With state police keeping an eye out and this lady pitching in, they had a better chance of finding her. And when they did, he was going to feel like a fool, and maybe even like a bad father. But at least she'd be safe.

"Curtis!" Hope shouted, and he turned to see Hope standing at the street corner, Lucy in her arms. Curtis felt tears of relief stinging his eyes, and he blinked them back.

"Oh, thank God..." he breathed.

She was fine. She was safe. He had to mentally repeat that to himself. He turned around and waved to the older woman who'd just come out of a shop.

"We found her!" he said. "Thank you so much!"

"Oh, good for you!" she said with a grandmotherly smile. "Tell your wife not to feel bad about this. All of mine were escape artists at that age, too!"

His wife— Right. Hope looked very much like the mother in this family, even though she wasn't. But he realized he liked the sound of that a lot—he'd be proud to claim Hope as his, but explaining that they weren't married would take too long, so he just shot the older woman a grateful smile.

He looked both ways before jogging across the street. Hope waited for him on the sidewalk, Lucy perched on the side of her belly in a way he'd seen other pregnant women carry their toddlers before. When he reached the opposite curb, he pulled Lucy into his arms, giving her a long squeeze.

"Thank you, Hope," he breathed. Holding Lucy tight with one arm, he slid the other around Hope's shoulders. Before he could think better of it, he pressed a kiss against her warm temple. Her hair smelled of roses, and he realized as he pulled back that he might have crossed a line there. But she didn't move away from him.

"That was a year off your life, I'll bet," she said.

"You better believe it." Then he looked at his daughter. "Lucy, you can't just run away. That's very dangerous. Do you understand?"

"Oh, Daddy." Lucy gave him a coy smile.

"No, don't you try and charm me," he said seriously. "Lucy, you can't run away!"

Lucy reached up and booped his nose with one finger, and he had to restrain his frustration. Lucy didn't understand, did she? At all! So all he could do was tighten up his supervision with her.

"Where was she?" Curtis asked, turning back to Hope.

"She was hiding behind that flower planter," Hope said. "I just happened to see her curls above the top of it—she thought it was a game."

Curtis shut his eyes and pressed his lips together.

"It's okay, Curtis." Hope put a gentle hand on his arm. "We found her."

He liked the sound of that *we*.

"Yeah…we found her. Thanks to you, Hope. I really appreciate it."

"Of course." She smiled up at him, and he slid his arm around her shoulder again. The state police cruiser came back up the road, and Curtis had to let go of Hope to wave at it. The cruiser slowed and the window came down.

"I found her!" Curtis said. "This is Lucy, my daughter. Lucy, this a nice police trooper who was helping us look for you."

"Hi, Lucy," the trooper said, smiling at her. "If you ever get lost, you find someone dressed like me, okay?"

Lucy nodded shyly.

"Thank you so much," Curtis said.

"Just glad she's safe," the trooper replied. "Have a good day, folks."

Hope waved as he eased away, the window going back up. The trooper had thought they were a family, too, it seemed, and Curtis didn't mind that. It would be really nice to have someone else keeping an eye on things with him. It would be nice to have someone to love in a different way…

"Oh, by the way, do you know that lady who runs the craft store?" Curtis asked.

Hope shook her head. "Not personally. I recognize her from my high school years—she's run that shop for a long time—but we don't know each other."

"Ah. That makes sense."

"Why?" she asked.

"She thinks—" He cast her an embarrassed look. "She thinks we're married. You might need to set her straight."

"Why does she think that?"

"She jumped to a conclusion and I was too stressed out to say anything."

Hope laughed, and he was glad she was finding the humor in the whole thing, because he hadn't been sure how she'd feel about that. But he'd take laughter over irritation.

"If she brings it up, I'll let her know," Hope said.

As they walked back toward the store, Faith waved from the doorway when she spotted them and then disappeared back inside. His pulse was coming back down to a normal rhythm again, and he looked into his little girl's happy face.

He loved her so much. Maybe it was a good sign that Lucy thought the whole world was friendly and loving, because that was all she'd ever known. He'd done a good job of protecting her so far.

He took Hope's hand and gave it a relieved squeeze.

"You doing okay?" Hope asked with a sympathetic smile.

"Getting there," he said. Holding her hand made the world feel a little more balanced than it really was. And his blood pressure would come down eventually.

CHAPTER TWENTY-THREE

THAT AFTERNOON, HOPE got into her car to drive out to the Yoder farm, but before she turned the key, she took a moment to just sit behind the wheel. This was the first instance of quiet and calm since her morning shower, and she leaned her head back against the headrest, enjoying the peace.

This morning had been an emotional roller coaster, with Lucy taking off followed by the relief and that warm, special closeness she and Curtis had shared on the walk back to the shop. He'd kissed her temple. Even remembering the gentle press of his lips against her skin put a flutter in her stomach that had nothing to do with the baby.

Curtis had promised not to kiss her again, but surely that didn't count, did it? What did that tender little kiss mean? Anything? The man had been relieved to find his toddler, but things had been building between them, and now everything felt liked it was supercharged. She wasn't imagining the attraction between them. That was very real.

Despite herself, Hope had found herself wondering what "more" would look like with Curtis. But Apfelkuchen was like a cocoon. They were insulated from the rest of Curtis's life…from Lucy's mother, who would always be a part of her life, too, and from the stress of Curtis's other business projects and how much she guessed he traveled for work. Here in Apfelkuchen, Curtis wasn't the big shot he was in the city.

This wasn't a real representation of what life with Curtis would look like if they took things further. He was another wealthy man who needed to work incredibly hard to maintain that income. He was a lot like Peter. He'd been good friends with her late husband, after all. And she knew what that kind of marriage was like. Would it have gotten easier with time? Maybe, but there would have been challenges that she'd never have to meet if she was with a man on her own level. A regular Joe.

Except, financially speaking, she wasn't so regular anymore, was she?

"I don't know why I'm even thinking about this," she murmured aloud, rubbing her hands over her face.

Hope turned the key and started the car. Whatever she was feeling for Curtis, she needed to get it under control. Because Catherine was probably right about the prenups and caution.

The drive out to the Yoders' place was a peaceful one. The sun was high and warm, and once she got out to the Amish farms, she could see lots of straw hats and colorful dresses as families made the most of a beautiful day. Three little girls were raking leaves in their front yard, and another few minutes down the road, two teenage boys were chopping wood, the crack of the splitting logs echoing across the hills. There were more buggies than usual out on the roads—people out and about—and Hope drove slower as a result.

Amish Country was soothing. Somehow it jogged her brain into a calmer, more patient mode just being among her Amish neighbors. They never worried about things like prenups, or a woman having too much money to be able to trust a man's intentions. But she knew they had their own worries. Like Sarah, wanting to marry a man who might never be acceptable to the community. Everyone had their problems.

When she arrived at the Yoder farm, she saw Mary in the front yard pulling some brown, dried plants out of her flower garden and tossing them into a wheelbarrow. She rose when she saw the car and waved when she recognized Hope.

Hope parked next to the house, and when she got out of the car, Mary pulled off her gloves and stepped free of the garden dirt.

"Hello, hello!" Mary called. "What a treat! How are you doing?"

"I'm good!" Hope gave Mary a squeeze when

the older woman came up to hug her. "How are you?"

"It's a beautiful day for getting some outdoor work done," Mary said. "Isn't the sun wonderful?"

"It is," Hope said.

"Are you all right?" Mary examined her face for a moment. "Come inside. You look like you could use some pie."

Did Hope looked as uncertain as she felt? She hoped not, but she wasn't going to argue with it, either. Mary clomped up the steps and kicked her dirty shoes off on the outside step.

"Never mind yours," Mary said. "Come in and get comfortable. You look like you need to talk."

"I'm okay," Hope said. "Really."

"Ah." Mary nodded. "It's that *Englisher* fellow with the building project, isn't it? Has he declared himself?"

"What?" she asked weakly.

"Has he said he loves you and wants to marry you?" Mary qualified. "That's normally the next step after a confusing amount of time together and a whirlwind of emotions, you know."

"It's not like that with us," Hope said. "We know where it stands."

"Hmm." Mary didn't look convinced.

They talked for a few minutes about pregnancy and all the changes and sensations that came with it. It was nice to chat with another mom who had been through it—several times for Mary Yoder. But then the conversation turned to Sarah and Eddie.

"What's happening with them?" Hope asked. "I've been hearing that Eddie's in trouble with church leadership?"

"It's been tough." Mary sighed. "We knew that becoming Amish would be difficult for Eddie, but it's more than language and following the rules. It's learning to submit to authority—in our case, the bishop and elders. *Englishers* aren't used to allowing someone else to tell them what to do, or deciding if they are living appropriately or not. *Englishers*—" Mary stopped and her face colored. "I'm sorry, Hope. I don't mean to offend."

"You're right, though," Hope agreed. "We're used to deciding for ourselves what is right and proper."

"That's the biggest challenge ahead of Eddie," Mary said. "You see, we believe in authority, and we submit to the decisions and direction given to us. And I can see that it's not easy for him."

"It wouldn't be easy for me, either. Honestly, Mary, I think his heart was in the right place."

"So do I," Mary said. "But that means nothing in the face of the bishop's decision. It's not about my opinion, or yours, or even Eddie's. This is about something bigger—it's about authority and community."

"You can't speak for him?" Hope asked.

"We've tried. My husband went to talk to the bishop and elders last night. They thanked him for his input, and now we wait."

"How stressful," Hope murmured.

"Yes," Mary agreed. "But it's our way. This is how decisions are made, and have been for hundreds of years. One situation, one strong opinion—none of it is reason enough to flout the tradition that has maintained our community through generations. So we wait, and we submit."

They were silent for a moment, then Mary jumped to her feet.

"Pie!" she said. "I'm sorry, Hope. I can't believe I'm so scattered."

Mary set about bringing some cherry pie to the table along with two pretty china plates and forks. When they'd both been dished up generous slices of pie, Mary sat back down again.

"The reason I came," Hope said, "was actually to ask your opinion about something for Curtis."

"Oh?"

"Curtis thinks it might be good for him to sit down with the bishop and discuss his plans to bring in more tourists. He's trying to respect your community's ways and talk with Bishop Moses directly and respectfully. But he wanted me to ask you if that's a good idea or not."

Mary was silent for a moment. "Is he going to try to convince the bishop of his way of seeing things?"

"Maybe a little. He does think this would be good for the town, but he isn't willing to go ahead with it if the Amish community isn't on board."

"That's something," Mary admitted. "Far be it from me to tell a man who he's allowed to talk to."

"But do you think it's a good idea?" Hope asked. "That's what he wants to know."

Mary frowned in thought, then nodded. "The bishop is a careful, measured man. He takes our community's future very seriously, and he also protects our traditions. We all have our fears, but if the bishop sees value in what Curtis is suggesting, he'd then bring it to the elders and they'd all discuss it together. If all of them think it's worthy, they'd bring it to the community, and we'd get to have our say. It's his best chance. He should just go visit him," Mary said. "Here. I'll draw you a map. Do you know where the skating pond is?"

After Mary had drawn a simple map with landmarks, she handed it over to Hope.

"What about you?" Mary asked. "Do you think that bringing in tourists is good for the town?"

"It's good for our store," Hope said. "I'll admit to that. More tourists looking to buy Amish goods helps us a great deal. But I'm not willing to sacrifice your comfort and way of life for our gain, either."

"I appreciate that," Mary said with a gentle smile. "You are a good friend."

"What about you?" Hope asked. "Do you think it's a good idea?"

"I normally wouldn't say," Mary said. "It's not my decision to make, after all. But if the leadership decided to go ahead with it and find some solutions to people's worries, then I have half a mind to open up our home as a bed-and-breakfast. I'd enjoy the extra company, and telling *Englishers* about our way of life. Besides, the extra income would be awfully helpful around here." Her face pinked. "Especially if our daughter is getting married."

Maybe Curtis had more support for his idea than he thought. And maybe Eddie did, too.

Outside, Hope could hear raised voices—Sarah and Eddie by the sound of it—and Mary's eyes widened, her face flushing with embarrassment.

"Those two..." Mary went to the window and gave a rap with a knuckle against the glass. The voices went silent. "It's been stressful, to say the least. I'm sorry."

"Stress does that to the best of us," Hope said quietly. "They love each other, and they have to sort through this. Sometimes that's a tense process. That's normal. They're human."

"I know they are, but they don't need to air the fact in front of company, do they?" she said and she pressed her hands against her cheeks, then let them drop. "I'm sorry, Hope. I don't think I'm looking very good today, either. Here I am chattering like a jay when I'm better off keeping quiet."

This was the most human she'd ever seen the Yoders before. They always seemed so perfectly put together, so loving and supportive and ideal. It was almost a relief to see some frayed edges at long last.

"You're a regular family," Hope said. "I hope that doesn't offend you, but you're just like the rest of us." She smiled gently. She wasn't sure if that was a comfort to Mary or not, but it was the truth.

"I should let you get back to your day," Hope said, rising to her feet. It looked like Sarah could use a little advice from her mother right now. "Thank you for the visit, and for the pie."

"Come by anytime," Mary said. "I mean it."

Hope gave Mary a squeeze, and she headed for the door. Outside, Eddie and Sarah were talking, expressions tense and arms folded. Hope really did want them to work it out. She knew from experience that sometimes a great love came with some conflict. She and Peter had butted heads a few times, too.

The young people stopped when they saw Hope, and Eddie murmured something to Sarah. She nodded.

"Hi, Hope," Eddie said. "I wonder if I could get a ride into town."

"Oh! Uh, sure," Hope said, and she looked toward Sarah to see what she thought of this. Sarah just gave Hope a wan smile. "Where can I drop you off?"

"At my parents' place, if you don't mind." That didn't sound good, and he seemed to catch her look of mild alarm. "My dad needs help with the roof. It's a bit leaky. He'll give me a ride back when we're done."

Hope gave Mary another hug.

"I'll try and talk to him," Hope whispered.

Eddie and Sarah exchanged an unreadable look, then Eddie walked to the passenger side of her car and got in. When Hope pulled out of the drive and headed down the road, she glanced in Eddie's direction. He looked somber.

"I heard about the drama with the Beilers," Hope said. "I'm sorry it's tough right now."

"Thanks."

"I know how much Sarah loves you," Hope added.

He was silent. Was this going to be the end of it? Eddie and Sarah's shocking engagement coming to naught because no one would support them?

"Eddie, she loves you," Hope pressed. "Are you giving up?"

"It's not that I don't want to see this through—it's that I'm not sure the Amish will let me in. I'm set up to fail, it seems. I can do my best and try my hardest, and there's always some unseen test I'm failing."

And Sarah had already laid out all she had to lose if she defied the community rules and married him anyway.

"I wish I knew how to encourage you, Eddie," she said. "I know this is your life, but I hope you and Sarah can find a way to have that life together that you want so badly."

"My parents think I'm giving too much and getting too little back," he said.

"Do you think that's true?" she asked cautiously.

"Sometimes it feels that way," he agreed. "I'm not blind to it. But an Amish wife devotes her whole life to her husband and kids. If Sarah marries me, there's no divorce for her, you know. If a couple splits up—and it doesn't happen often for them—there is no remarriage. There are no second chances at finding the right person. So yeah, I'm the one doing all the changing and adjusting right now. But she's got to be able to trust the rest of her life to me. There's no exit if I don't live up to my promises."

Eddie looked over at her, and she saw maturity beyond his years shining in those eyes. Eddie knew what marriage was better than most young people did when they took those vows with romantic ideals dancing through their hearts.

Had she understood all that when she'd married Peter? Probably not.

"Besides," Eddie said. "When you get married, you're marrying more than the girl. You're marrying the whole family. I remember how my uncle used to always come asking for money, and how that affected my parents. And when my grandmother got sick, she moved in with us. If you think you're only marrying one person, you're being naive anyway."

"That's true," she agreed. "A lot of people don't understand it."

"I don't want to marry a girl who could turn her back on her parents and everyone she loved," he added. "I'll figure it out. But today, I've got to help my own family with some stuff. Because when we get married, I also come with a whole pile of people, right? And she'll have to learn how to bond with them, too. And right now, they're so against this wedding that I'm not sure how I'll get them all in the same room again."

He was certainly wiser than his years.

"If it helps you at all, when I talked to Mary just now, she was supportive of you joining the Amish community and marrying her daughter. You've got her in your corner if nothing else."

"I do?" He looked over, surprised.

"Yeah, you do."

"I didn't realize that…" Eddie was silent for a moment, and then he said softly, "I just hope they don't change their minds about letting us get married."

Marriage wasn't the ending point of a story—it was just the beginning. That was when the hardest work started, when a couple had to learn how to live together, and lean toward each other, and prioritize each other, and meet each other's needs. It was about growing together over weeks, months and years. It was about finding out how "we" do things, and learning how to find that identity together, while still having an individual identity, too.

And along with all that came two families with different backgrounds, different expectations and different sets of advice.

For no logical reason, she was suddenly reminded of little Lucy and her biological mother, who struggled with addiction. Some families had bigger stresses than others.

"I think you have a good heart, Eddie," Hope said.

For whatever it was worth.

CHAPTER TWENTY-FOUR

CURTIS SQUATTED IN front of two granite gravestones. Bernard and Maura Jespersen. The dates of their births and deaths recorded. He'd been here for both funerals—and so had Lynn. She'd been inebriated for both of them, too.

The Apfelkuchen graveyard was located outside of town on a rural road. They'd planted some trees to bracket in the little graveyard away from the rolling hills and endless sky.

Lucy sat next to him, looking curiously at the gravestones. She traced the letters with her fingers.

"S," Lucy said. "That's an S."

"That's right, Lucy," he said. "That's an S."

And right now at two, almost three, that was a huge accomplishment to recognize an S. But when she got older, she'd see more in this place. Not just a letter, but a name. She'd see her family name all over this graveyard—Jespersens buried here for generations. She'd see Jespersen Street and whatever Curtis had made of it. She'd see her family's history and her father's best efforts to preserve it for her.

He'd come back looking for something that he wasn't sure he would ever find. Everything here was a reminder of the past—sometimes so far in the past that he hadn't even been part of it. That turned into history, and ancestry, and it was supposed to fill a part of his heart that had been achingly empty all these years. But it didn't.

What would Grandpa have wanted him to do? He'd been quite adamant that the town needed to survive, but what if the town didn't want his help in doing that? Who was Curtis to them anyway? He was just an outsider who wanted to build on their streets. He was just a man with money who wanted to spend some of it here.

When Curtis had visited as a kid, he'd been looking for somewhere where things made sense—where right was right and wrong was wrong. He'd wanted some clear lines, some expectations.

But life had gotten muddier over the years. Every time he tried to do the right thing, his life got more complicated. Lucy had needed a home and he'd been convinced that taking her in had been the right choice. But to Samantha, he'd been the bad guy—the one who had put his sister's baby ahead of their relationship. Coming out here to try and build a moneymaking business in this dwindling little town, he was convinced he could make a difference—the kind his grandfather would appreciate. And he was the bad guy again, because the Amish community didn't want what he was offering.

No matter how many times he tried to do the right thing, he found his life getting more difficult. Was that just a matter of growing up?

"It's a flower!" Lucy called out delightedly, plucking a wilted rose off a gravestone farther on.

"No, Lucy, put that back!" Curtis said.

He sighed. It wasn't a terrific idea to take a toddler to a graveyard, but what was he supposed to do? He was a dad now, and this was what parents did. He'd never been the dad of a toddler until now, and he and Lucy were taking on new firsts with every step. He didn't know what he was doing, but Lucy would never know that. His parents hadn't been any wiser when raising him and Lynn than he was with Lucy. Parents just did their best and tried to appear like they knew what they were doing for the sake of their children.

"It's a flower, Daddy!" Lucy said with a bright smile. "For me?"

"Not for you," Curtis said, taking the rose out of her grip. "Let's go put it back. It belongs over there."

He put the rose back down in the vase beside the grave, and his gaze moved over the inscription. He didn't know the lady who was buried here, but underneath the birth and death dates were the words *Gone but not forgotten. You gave us roots.*

Roots. That was what he longed for—somewhere to belong. But he wasn't going to be able to buy his way into Apfelkuchen. He hadn't grown up here. He'd grown up in a subdivision in the city. His family was known for their laundromats.

But always, deep inside him, Curtis had thought that he really belonged on that farm with his grandfather, away from the chaos at home with his older sister's drug problems, and away from the constant busyness of the laundromat business—bags of change, the jangle of the coin-rolling machine... Funny how the real locals didn't much care about poetic adolescent notions of who he "really" was.

Curtis might be a Jespersen, but he wasn't really one of the people in Apfelkuchen. A street with his family name on it didn't mean much. His grandfather was gone, and life marched on. You couldn't choose your family.

Curtis might have felt closest to his grandfather, but he couldn't deny his sister, either. Lynn might make his life incredibly difficult, and she might do much worse to herself, but she'd always be his sister. And he couldn't deny his dad with dementia. Or his mom, who refused to see Lynn's addiction and still insisted that she was just going through a phase. These flawed, struggling people were all his, whether he wanted it or not.

"Come on, Lucy," he said. "Time to go back now."

But Lucy was his, too, and she was untarnished by all the chaos that had created her. She was innocent and loved, and well protected. Maybe that would have to be his purpose—not forcing roots into rock-hard soil but nurturing this little life instead.

Lucy could do better than her mother had, and Curtis could give her the support to get there.

Generation upon generation upon generation of Jespersens… Maybe this newest generation who bore their name could be the best of them.

THAT NIGHT, AFTER Lucy was asleep, Curtis lay on the queen-size bed watching some news on his phone with his headphones on. A call appeared on-screen, and he paused the video. It was Nanny Judy. She was back from her trip to see her daughter and she was ready to help him out again, if he needed her.

"Do you want me to come to Apfelkuchen, sir?" she asked. "I can easily meet you there and take over childcare duties with Lucy again."

He'd been leaning on Hope. He hadn't meant to, but he had been. And he was starting to rely on her emotionally, too. He was slipping into some dangerous territory with her, and he knew it.

"You know, Judy, that would be great," he said.

"I appreciate that. Are you sure it isn't too much for you?"

"Not at all. I'm rejuvenated. And I miss Lucy."

He smiled. "Thank you. I'll reimburse you for travel expenses, as always, and if you could make it out here tomorrow, that would be perfect."

"I'll be there, sir."

Nanny Judy could always be counted on. She was professional and excellent at her job. He could stop worrying with Judy on the job…but he'd see a whole lot less of Hope.

It wasn't what he wanted, but it was probably what he needed.

It was time to get back to normal and embrace his real life, not live in fantasies.

His life wasn't so bad. He had a daughter he adored, he made good money and he could provide. It could be a whole lot worse.

CHAPTER TWENTY-FIVE

THE NEXT MORNING, Hope squatted next to a jogging stroller, strapping Lucy into it. This might be one of their last outings together, and Hope was going to miss this little girl. She wanted to take Lucy out for a long walk, but she didn't trust her not to make a run for it. At this point in her pregnancy, Hope wasn't going to be able to give a good enough chase. So borrowing Trent and Faith's jogging stroller, which Tyke had outgrown, seemed like a good solution.

"Are we gonna see leafs?" Lucy asked hopefully.

"Yes, we'll go see the leaves. They're so pretty," Hope said, standing up again with some effort. "And we'll go to the Amish market. Maybe we'll even get a treat!"

"A treat?" Lucy's eyes widened. "A treat?"

Maybe she shouldn't have said that so early. She'd mostly just been thinking out loud. There were all sorts of delicious things to eat at the Amish market. Soft pretzels, ice cream, hot dogs, hard candy sticks, homemade marshmallows, hand pies…the list was long. But toddlers had no concept of waiting for a treat.

"Here—" Faith passed her a package of fruit gummies with a knowing little smile.

"Thanks," Hope chuckled. "That's a newbie mistake, isn't it?"

"Yup." Faith shot her a grin. "Enjoy your walk. It seems pretty slow this morning anyway. I'm going to be packaging up those online orders."

They'd only had two street-side customers since opening, and only one had purchased anything. But several orders had come in overnight—the online shop was making up the difference.

"We're gonna see leafs!" Lucy announced from her seat in the stroller, and Hope pulled a thick shawl closer around her shoulders. She would need to buy a maternity winter coat soon, which would involve a trip into the city. There wasn't anywhere to buy maternity wear in Apfelkuchen.

The bell tinkled overhead as Hope headed out the front door. It was an oddly freeing feeling, heading out with the stroller into fresh, morning air. She and her sisters had been working hard these last few months, starting up the shop. Faith had remarried Trent, and she now had a little boy to raise with her husband. Elaine was teaching the second grade, and she was a passionate teacher. Hope had lost Peter, and she was adjusting to her pregnancy and her widowhood. They were all so busy that just taking a morning to walk to the Amish market felt almost surreal.

It felt good to get moving, though. Once she got to the market, there were a few places she could sit and rest her feet before heading back again. It was only four blocks to the pavilion where the Amish market set up, the Amish stalls serving local customers three days a week.

The walk was a pleasant one. The sky was blue, and she spotted some geese flying south in a lopsided V. Several buggies passed her, horses clopping in a cheerful rhythm, and Lucy squealed about "horsies" and called out hellos. An Amish teenager leaned over and waved at her, which only encouraged Lucy to holler at more buggies.

This was the kind of morning that set a part of her heart free again—a piece that had been so bound up with grief. Was this what healing felt like—one piece at a time? The thing was, her marriage to Peter had taught her about the depth of love and the sacrifices that came with it. If it weren't for Peter, she wouldn't be the woman she was, and she wouldn't be able to love as deeply as she did today.

She smiled down at the happy toddler. Peter would always be a part of her foundation. That wouldn't change.

When Hope got to the pavilion, she pushed the stroller inside and headed for the tables by the food stalls. A few were already open, but the soft pretzels and the ice cream stall were both closed still. Hope sank down on a seat and pulled the stroller around so she could face Lucy.

"I need a rest," Hope told the toddler. "Do you want some Goldfish crackers?"

She pulled out a ziplock bag of crackers and Lucy's eyes lit up at the snack. Hope took a few out and held them out in her palm so Lucy could take them one at a time. As Lucy ate her crackers, the baby inside her started to push and jab, as if he knew he was missing out on something fun. She gave her belly a little rub.

Apfelkuchen was a beautiful place to raise a family, and her son would enjoy trips to the Amish market one day. He'd get to see the horses and buggies and go to school with the same kids from kindergarten all the way up to twelfth grade. In a town this size, people knew each other if they grew up here.

Across the food court, Hope spotted a familiar face—it was Sarah Yoder, who was helping set up at the soft pretzel stall. Hope started to smile a hello, but then she saw Sarah's face. Her eyes were red and her face was splotchy, and Hope's heart dropped in sympathy. She was crying still? Or crying again?

Sarah spotted Hope at the same time, and after a brief conversation with the woman working with her, Sarah crossed the food court and sank into the seat next to Hope.

"Sarah, you look terrible!" Hope said, then winced. "I'm sorry. But you look like you've been crying. Are you all right?"

Sarah's eyes welled with tears. "No, nothing is all right! The bishop came to see us last night. He wanted to talk to me and Eddie together, but Eddie is helping his family right now, and I didn't want to wait a few days to hear what he wanted to say."

"And?" Hope pressed.

"He won't give us permission to get married," Sarah said. "He doesn't think that Eddie will be ready to join the faith, and he doesn't think Eddie would stay Amish even if he was allowed to."

"Oh, Sarah..." Hope reached out and took the younger woman's hand.

"I don't know what to do..." Sarah's chin trembled.

"What do your parents say?" Hope asked.

"They say that if the bishop and elders don't think it will work, then I should trust their wisdom and find an Amish man."

"But you don't want to."

"No! I love Eddie! And everyone is against us now. My parents think I have to obey the bishop, and the bishop thinks that Eddie won't make a good Amish husband. He thinks he's protecting me from a heartbreaking future. Everyone thinks they know better than I do!"

Lucy looked up at them, her eyes wide, and Hope leaned down and held out the whole bag of Goldfish crackers.

"Do you want the whole bag, Lucy?" Hope asked.

Lucy nodded and held out her hands. When Hope passed the bag over, she plunged her hand into the bag and rammed a handful of Goldfish into her mouth, crackers falling into the stroller and onto the ground around her. That should keep her occupied.

"And I can't even reach Eddie! He'll be back tomorrow, but I can't even talk to him until then! What am I supposed to do?"

"You could go see him at his parents' place," Hope suggested.

"I don't think they want to see me," she whispered.

"Who cares?" Hope said. "This is your life, Sarah. Everyone seems to want to have a say about what you do and who you love. But you're the one who's going to cry yourself to sleep. Who cares if his parents are in a bad mood? Go talk to him."

"I think I will," Sarah said, considering. "But… ultimately, if the bishop says I can't marry him, then it's over."

Hope pressed her lips together, biting back some

words that wouldn't be terribly helpful. Sarah was Amish and intended to stay that way. Hope's advice wouldn't be supportive of that right now.

"If it were you, Hope," Sarah said earnestly, "what would you do?"

"I don't think your family would like it if I told you what I'd do," Hope said. "But then, I wasn't raised Amish, and I have a bit of a rebellious streak that your family wouldn't like one bit."

"You'd go *English*," Sarah whispered.

"I'm already English, so it doesn't scare me."

"Would you walk away from your parents and your sisters, and your little nephew?" Sarah asked.

As angry as Hope was at the unfairness of Sarah's situation, imagining walking away from Elaine and Faith, from her parents, from her extended family… They were why she'd come back to Apfelkuchen. She had Peter's family in her life still, but would Catherine have been enough to replace her own family? With Peter's death, Hope had come home to her parents…she hadn't turned to Catherine for that comfort.

Would she have been willing to write off everyone she loved to marry Peter?

"I don't think it's a fair request for the bishop to ask you to choose between your family and the man you want to marry," Hope said. "That's cruel."

"Maybe it is," Sarah replied. "But that's my choice right now."

Her family or Eddie. The man she loved or her faith and her community. It was an impossible choice.

"Treat?" Lucy asked hopefully, her face covered in Goldfish crumbs.

"You haven't forgotten, have you?" Hope asked.

"I can get her a miniature pretzel if you want," Sarah said.

"Sure," Hope said, but she fixed her friend with a direct look. "Sarah, I want you to know that if you do choose Eddie, you'll have us. I know we're a poor substitute for your family, but we'd do our best."

Sarah nodded. "*Danke.* But first, I have to talk to Eddie."

"Do you know where his family lives?" Hope asked.

Sarah nodded. "I do. But when I go tell him what the bishop said, everyone is going to want to know my choice. Especially Eddie. And I don't know what to tell him."

Poor Sarah. How was a woman supposed to make that kind of choice?

"Whatever you choose, I'll support you," Hope said.

And Hope could only be grateful she wasn't faced with that kind of heartbreaking decision. For all of her community's hopes for Sarah's future, the bishop was taking a chance in trying to sever this relationship. Hearts were more fragile than anyone realized. If they made Sarah give up Eddie, she might not ever get over him completely, and she might not marry at all.

Did they know what they were doing?

CHAPTER TWENTY-SIX

CURTIS SAT AT an empty intersection, the little hand-drawn map to the bishop's home in front of him. It showed a circle indicating an old silo, and in front of him was the huge old silo that he remembered from driving the pickup truck with his grandfather—long before he could legally drive. But Grandpa had insisted that there were no cops out there and a boy needed to know how to handle a vehicle.

The map didn't have any proper directions indicated. Just an X drawn about halfway down one of the roads, and an arrow with the word *lake*. What was Bishop Moses's last name? He didn't even know that much. He was Bishop Moses—no one had indicated a last name. None of them needed it.

"Okay…" he muttered, turning the map. If the silo was on that side of the road, then… He did a mental approximation and then signaled a left turn. He was pretty sure this was the right direction. Out here, if you got completely lost, you could ask someone and they'd point you in the right direction. But Curtis felt some manly pride at work, and he preferred not to ask, if humanly possible. That was very un-Amish of him, and he knew it.

He drove down the gravel road slowly, Amish farmland rolling out on either side. He spotted one drive and slowed. There was no way to know if it was the right one. All he knew was that according to the map, this was the right side of the road. He'd have to give it a try.

He signaled and turned in.

The farm was large by Amish standards. There appeared to be two barns and three large chicken coops. A small orchard with yellow and green leaves mingled together stretched out on one side of the house. He parked in front of a hitching post and leaned forward to get a better view of the property. Most of the apples appeared to have been harvested from the orchard, but he spotted a few red apples at the tops of the trees—too high to be picked, it seemed.

Chickens bok-bok-bokked to each other from a large enclosure, and when Curtis hopped out of his SUV, he heard the squeak of a screen door. An older Amish woman stood in the doorway, a cautious look on her face. Her dress was dark gray, and she wore a white apron over it. Her *kapp* was a shade whiter than her hair.

"Hi, my name is Curtis Jespersen, and I'm looking for Bishop Moses. Am I in the right spot?"

The woman silently regarded him for a moment, then reached up and grabbed a short rope attached to a bell and gave it a good hard yank. The bell clanged loudly.

"He'll come," she said. "Would you like to come inside and get some coffee? I just put some on."

"Thanks," Curtis said. "I appreciate that."

He went up the steps and followed the older woman into the house. She appeared to be canning applesauce—a peeler was attached to one side of the table, a tall pile of apple peelings sitting on a newspaper bed next to it.

"You look busy," he said.

"It's the time of year for it," she replied, then eyed him speculatively. "We don't get *Englishers* looking for the bishop too often."

There was a question between the lines there, but she wouldn't ask it outright. Amish women didn't ask after men's business. And he guessed that people's business with the bishop was usually private in nature.

"I wanted your husband's opinion about some buildings in the area," Curtis said.

"Ah." She looked pleased that he'd shared that much. "I'm sure he'll be happy to help."

She poured a cup of coffee and set it down on the end of the table closest to him. Then she fetched a pitcher of cream and a bowl of sugar. He gave her a smile of thanks and doctored up his coffee to his liking. When he dropped Lucy off this morning, Nanny Judy not having arrived yet, Hope had told him about her conversation with Sarah. It was done—the bishop had nixed her wedding to Eddie. He wasn't sure what that said about his chances today.

The sound of boots on the step saved Curtis from small talk, and when and older man came inside, he cast Curtis a surprised look.

"Curtis Jespersen, nice to see you again so soon," Bishop Moses said.

Curtis stepped forward and shook his hand. "Hello, Bishop. I'm sorry to pull you away from your work, but I was told that the best way to talk to you was to just stop by. I hope that's all right."

"It's no problem at all," the bishop replied, and he bent to take off his boots. "What can I do for you?"

"I came for advice, sir," Curtis said.

"No 'sir' necessary," the bishop said with an indulgent smile. "In our community we are all equal. No one higher than another."

Except the bishop was obviously respected a whole lot more than any other farmer around here. His word held weight.

"Come into my office with me," the older man said, and he led the way, sock-footed, down the hall. Curtis followed him, idly wondering if he was supposed to take off his shoes, too, but it was too late for that now.

The bishop led him into a small office. There was a desk to one side with a large antique-looking Bible sitting in the center of it. One bookcase held maybe thirty or forty books in it, most of which looked to be quite old hardbacks. The shelf was beautifully made, and he stopped to appreciate the workmanship. Two chairs were arranged in front of the desk, and the bishop sat in one of them instead of taking his place behind the desk. He gestured to the other for Curtis.

"Have a seat."

Curtis looked down at the well-made chair. It was simple but solid. These days with mass-produced furniture, chairs just fell apart after a while. This one didn't look like that was possible.

Curtis sat opposite the Amish man, who regarded him an open, frank expression, and Curtis found himself feeling a little self-conscious, probably thc direct opposite effect the bishop was hoping to encourage.

"Well, sir—" Curtis cleared his throat. "Bishop, I should say."

"Moses is fine."

"Moses," Curtis said with a nod. "I appreciate the time you took with me at the corn roast. It was illuminating, being able to talk with the community about my building plans on Jespersen Street in town."

"I'm glad."

"I realize that the community is still unsure of me and my intentions. My hopes to bring tourist money into Apfelkuchen won't do a whole lot of good if we don't have support from both the Amish and the English people in the area, if we don't make sure the whole community feels the idea is safe. So I wanted to discuss it with you and hear your thoughts."

"You wanted to convince me," Moses said.

"I'm hoping to convince you," he admitted with a small smile. "But I need to understand what you need. The thing is, I'm not trying to make a big profit here. This is for the town. I visited my grandfather every summer growing up, and he and I were very close. My grandfather was worried about the town dwindling away. He wanted it to last. He wanted to bring jobs in, and money. I'm pretty good at looking at a business and seeing how to grow it. I don't mean that to be boastful. We all have something we're good at, and that is mine. But I wanted to use the inheritance my grandfather left me for this."

"Tell me about your grandfather," Moses said.

"Oh… Well, he was a good man. He farmed, worked hard and was faithful to my grandmother for fifty years of marriage until she passed away. He never married again, but he did have a girlfriend for a few years. They used to meet for breakfast in town a few times a week."

Curtis wasn't sure why he was sharing that, but Moses had asked an unexpected question.

"Did he mention me?" Moses asked.

"You?" Curtis raised his eyebrows. "No, not specifically. Did you know him?"

"We all knew Bernie Jespersen," Moses replied. "He was a good friend to the Amish. One year, there was a big oil company that was coming through, looking to do some fracking. We all stood firm—not on our land. Your grandfather stood firm with us, even though it would have made him some handy cash."

"Really..." he murmured.

"He employed my nephew one winter, too, when he needed work to support his wife and *kinner*," Moses said. "Bernie contributed to more than one barn raising, too."

"He told me about a barn raising once," Curtis said. "I hadn't realized he'd worked with you. I thought he'd just watched it."

"No, Curtis, he worked."

That brought a surge of pride. That was Grandpa Jespersen—surprising people with his integrity, even after his death.

"Your grandfather was indeed a good man."

"He didn't want this town to die," Curtis said. "He was always concerned about that. He talked about it a lot. He could see families moving away, going closer to the city for work, and it concerned him, because he understood. People need employment, and they have to follow the jobs."

Moses met his gaze thoughtfully. "How much do you stand to make by bringing in tourists?"

"Enough to grow the business."

"And your profit?"

"I'll never recover the investment money, if that's what you're asking, but it'll make enough to keep itself afloat and continue to grow."

"You really do just want to help," Moses said quietly.

"Yes, that's what I'm trying to do. The truth is, this town needs money—a regular influx of people willing to spend their hard-earned dollars at the stores and shops around town. Tourists do just that, and you must know the enthusiasm Englishers have for your culture."

"I do."

"You have a whole generation of young Amish people who will need employment," Curtis went on. "With tourists coming here, looking for Amish experiences, that's a whole lot of opportunity for new businesses. I'm thinking buggy tours, restaurants, a gift shop… I'm sure some motivated young businesspeople could come up with some really creative ideas that don't cross the boundaries of your faith."

Moses nodded slowly. "That is true. But what about you?"

"What about me?"

"Don't you have any other ideas besides this one?"

Curtis blinked. "I've invested quite a bit into this idea already."

"I realize that," Moses said. "But you're a father, and you've already acknowledged that not everything comes down to money and income. We don't want curious *Englishers* coming to take pictures of our children. We don't want people with bad intentions discovering a vulnerable Amish community to prey upon. And we don't want to offer up our lifestyle as entertainment for people getting away from the city for a week. We've discussed it at length."

Curtis sighed. These were some of the points the deacon and some of the other men had brought up last night. It looked like his building plan was dead in the water, because without a cooperative Amish community willing to show visitors the beauty of their lifestyle, there was no point in building any short-term rentals.

"Are there any safeguards we could put up to put your fears to rest?" Curtis asked.

They talked through it, with Curtis attempting to find solutions. Moses admitted that a few of them might work, but he wasn't convinced. They still had a lot of reservations. This plan only succeeded with tourists coming with goodwill and respect, and while Moses believed in the good of humanity, he didn't trust it. That was an important distinction. They were going in circles, and Curtis could see the writing on the wall. This wasn't a solution that the Amish would embrace.

Finally Curtis said, "All right. I don't want to badger you when I can see you don't like the idea, Moses."

"I appreciate you wanting to talk it out," the older man replied. "And I appreciate your respect of our community and way of life. I see some of Bernie in you."

That was a high compliment, indeed, and it soothed some of the sting.

"Can I ask you something?" Moses asked.

"Sure."

"What were you hoping to discover here?"

Curtis shrugged. "A solution. A way forward for my building plan."

"More than that, though," Moses pressed. "You're an *Englisher* who came to Apfelkuchen in search of something—something you are missing in your own life. That's why you want to offer it to others."

Curtis was silent. Was that true? He certainly wouldn't be renting a place for a week of Amish adventure. Curtis could see what worked on a money level. He could see what would sell—call it a gift, but he was seldom wrong. That was what he'd had in common with Pete.

"I'm not sure what you mean," he confessed.

"What would you gain by building your tourist experience?" Moses asked. "For you, personally."

"Roots," Curtis admitted. "I suppose that's what it comes down to. I wanted to keep this place afloat so that I can bring my daughter back here when she's older and show her where her great-grandfather lived, where I visited as a boy. Where her mother—" He swallowed. "Lucy is my sister's daughter, and I adopted her. My sister, Lynn, was happy when she visited here. She was…a better version of herself at my grandfather's home. Maybe I want to preserve some of that."

Moses nodded sympathetically. "Roots are a good thing. The deeper the roots, the less life's gales can bend you."

"Yeah. I agree there," he said. "I want Lucy to have roots. I need to give her something that is more lasting than cash. And I want this town to last."

For Jespersen Street. For Beiler Dairy and the Yoder farm. For the Amish Antiques Shop.

"Your intentions are pure," Moses said softly. "You're a good father."

"Thanks." At least Moses could see that much.

"I'm about to give you some very un-Amish advice, young man. If you'd like to hear it."

"I would."

Moses put his palms on his thighs and looked down at his dirt-stained fingernails in silence for a moment, and when he started to speak, his Pennsylvania Dutch accent was even stronger than before, as if the act of concentration brought him closer to his mother tongue.

"We put our roots down in the very soil where our parents put down theirs, and our grandparents, and their grandparents... But roots don't have to sink down into the same soil. Sometimes a seed can travel on the wind for quite some time before it finds a suitable place to put down roots. It's the roots that matter, Curtis, not the precise soil. If you want roots—why, plant yourself and grow."

He raised his gaze to meet Curtis's, and that weathered face was filled with both respect and understanding. Moses was a father, too, and Curtis wondered if he'd encouraged his own children to stay here. He'd encourage young families to stay with their community, with their people, wouldn't he? But not Curtis. Was this a kind way of saying that they didn't need him around here?

"I'll probably take your advice on that," he said. He wouldn't have much choice. Would it be enough to know that he'd tried?

Curtis pushed himself to his feet. "I'm looking to rent out my grandfather's farm, too. If you know of any families in need of it, maybe you could put them in touch with me."

"That's kind of you to think of us," Moses said. "There is always a young family looking to farm."

Curtis pulled a card out of his pocket. "My contact information is there."

He had a feeling that his grandfather would approve—at least he was giving something back to the people here. And that farm needed a loving couple, some rambunctious kids and a farmer who knew how to make the most of that land.

As Curtis headed for the door, he realized with a sinking certainty that the farm did not need him, just as this town didn't need him. Maybe the bishop was right about a seed traveling in the wind.

CHAPTER TWENTY-SEVEN

HOPE SMOOTHED HER hand over Lucy's silky curls. The toddler lay on a pile of quilts, Smokey curled up at her back. She'd decided it was nap time early today, and she'd been sound asleep now for—she checked her watch—forty-five minutes.

Faith was arranging a new shelf of used books, but she'd stopped at an embossed hardcover and was turning it over in her hands.

"I can't believe the bishop is making Eddie and Sarah break up," Hope said. Ever since her talk with Sarah, she'd been carrying around this grief. It wasn't her problem or her heartbreak, but it was unfair all the same, and Sarah was a friend.

"He's not making them break up, though," Faith said. "He's just not giving them an Amish wedding."

"It amounts to the same thing," Hope replied.

"Unless she just marries him," Faith replied. "Would it hurt? Of course! But she loves him, and he's willing to become Amish. Maybe with time, the bishop would relent and let them join the community together."

"That's a risk."

"Worth it, though, I think," Faith replied.

"Will Sarah be able to do it? She's young. She's never lived away from her parents. I mean, something that we think is no big deal at our age is almost unimaginable for a much younger woman."

"That's true." Faith turned the book over in her hands once more, then looked at Hope. "I know they have rules to keep and all that, and I can respect that. I know it takes a lot to maintain a distinct and separate culture in the middle of America, but this is cruel. It really is."

The bell tinkled, and both sisters looked up to see Curtis. Right behind him was a gray-haired woman who looked to be about twenty years older than Curtis, dressed in jeans, running shoes and a windbreaker. She scanned the shop with an efficient gaze, and when she spotted Lucy on the quilts, her expression melted into something more tender. So this was Nanny Judy.

"Hi," Hope said, and Curtis returned her smile. "Lucy's asleep."

The little girl stirred then, and opened her eyes. She blinked a couple of times, and then a smile broke over her little features.

"Nanny Judy!" she said, and she scrambled to her feet and ran toward the older woman.

"This is Judy Flemming," Curtis said.

Judy squatted down and gathered Lucy up in her arms.

"Are you having fun?" Judy asked her.

"Uh-huh! There's a kitty!"

"I see that." Smokey roused himself and slunk away. "Is that a new dolly?"

Judy talked to Lucy in a cheerful tone, and Lucy looked completely delighted to be reunited with her. Hope felt an unexpected pang of sadness. Of course, Lucy had a nanny. Hope knew that already. And maybe it was her tangle of emotions over Sarah and Eddie's situation, but she felt it like an unexpected stab.

Curtis came over to where Hope stood, and she noticed a different air about him this afternoon. He was quieter, a little more reserved. Judy's arrival seemed to have changed things.

"Hey," he said quietly.

Hope's attention was still fixed on Judy and Lucy together. "Hey." She glanced toward Curtis, and found his gaze locked on her.

"She's been Lucy's nanny since she was born," Curtis said. "She's ready to retire from full-time childcare, but she says she won't leave me in the lurch. She wants to make sure that Lucy gets into school before she steps back."

"She loves her," Hope said softly.

"Yeah. Judy is great."

"I think I'm just emotional," Hope said. "It's

been a morning. How did your talk with the bishop go?"

"He was very polite and humble, and very clear on where they stand. The Amish don't want tourists."

She had expected as much. They'd made their position clear, but all the same she could feel the change in Curtis—that energy of his had faded. Was this what he was like when he was disappointed?

"I'm sorry," she said.

"It's okay. I tried. That's all I could do."

They were silent for a beat, and Hope sighed. "All it took was one morning for everything to fall apart, huh?"

"Are you glad there won't be tourists?" he asked.

"No. I'd warmed up to your idea."

"Thanks for that." He smiled sadly. "I'm sorry about your friend and her electrician."

"Thanks. They're young and sweet. I just hoped they could be happy together."

Curtis caught her hand and for a moment he looked down at her fingers. "Care to take a walk with me? Judy will keep an eye on Lucy."

He still had half his mind on the parenting details. But when she met his gaze, she saw something deeper there, something less settled. Curtis wasn't okay, and she had a sense that he needed her right now—someone to talk it out with.

"Sure," Hope replied.

"Thanks." He gave her fingers a squeeze, and then released her.

Curtis stopped to say a few words to Judy, then he gave his daughter a kiss on the top of her head. Lucy wasn't one bit concerned at his departure, and she gave him a sweet little "'Bye, Daddy!"

Hope looked over at Faith. "I'll be back in a few minutes?"

"Of course. I'll see you later," Faith said, but there was a mild worry in her gaze that belied her casual words. She seemed to sense the change in the air, too.

Hope tugged her shawl around her shoulders and she and Curtis slipped out of the shop together and into the brisk autumn air. With the farewell tinkle of that bell, Hope sucked in a deep breath.

"You're upset," Hope said.

"I am…a bit." Curtis caught her hand again. "But I'll be okay."

"Did the bishop give you any other reasons for his decision?" Hope asked.

"Nothing new. The same reasons we've heard so far. The same concerns. I understand it, I suppose. The money it would bring into the community wasn't enough to offset the risks for them. He said he was friends with my grandfather, which was why he was willing to sit down with me at all, I imagine."

They started down the sidewalk together. The afternoon had warmed up considerably, and the sun felt warm and comforting, seeping in through Hope's shawl. Curtis's hand was warm and confident, despite that stormy look in his eyes, and she allowed herself the brief comfort of leaning into his strong arm.

"So what will you do?" she asked.

"I'll halt all plans for construction," he said.

As easy as that? She knew he'd already sunk a good amount of money into building plans. He'd also put his heart into the project. He'd really wanted to see it succeed. Backing down couldn't be easy for a man who was used to finding a way forward.

"That's decent of you," she said.

"I'm not here to push my agenda on anyone," he said. "If they don't want my business plan, I won't keep moving with it. My grandfather would understand."

"I'm sure he would," she said. "You did your best, Curtis. And I'm sorry they weren't willing to find solutions. It would have put us on the map."

"Thanks." He heaved a sigh. "I wanted to leave something here for Lucy—something that could last and connect her to some family history. But it won't be a rental property."

She wasn't sure how she felt about Curtis giving up. Had the bishop really succeeded in chasing him out?

He shot her a smile and pivoted them at the corner and they headed south.

"Judy looks like she's really good with Lucy," Hope said.

"She is. She knows Lucy really well, and she's been there from just about day one. I had to hire someone to help me out, and she came well recommended."

"You live in a different world than I do," she said.

"Do I? You've got Pete's estate," he said. "You could hire a nanny when your son arrives, you know."

She'd never considered that. But the fact was that she didn't have Peter to continue making that income, so his life insurance and their estate had to take care of her their son for quite some time. She'd open her day care, and she'd find a way to raise her son with integrity and a good work ethic. The money had to be budgeted.

"What I mean is, in my circles—with my family and friends—we don't have nannies. Faith runs the antiques shop, and Trent is an electrician. They drop Tyke off at an in-home day care. People don't have nannies in Apfelkuchen. They have day care, and they have jobs. But more than that, I love kids, and I want to open my own day care. I want to take care of my son myself."

Curtis looked down her, and he looked like he was holding himself back from saying something.

"What?" she said.

"You could be more comfortable."

"I am comfortable enough. Curtis, I can't spend like Pete is still here making the money he made. I have to be realistic."

"You could let someone else take care of you."

And that was the temptation, wasn't it? Just lean into this good man's arms and let him take over?

"I'll manage," she said tightly.

He sighed. "I live in a five-bedroom home in a little gated community outside Pittsburgh. There's a park for the kids, and nannies pitch in as much as the parents need them to. I have a cleaning company that comes in once a week, a landscaping company that takes care of the yard, and a great big kitchen that I stand in the middle of by myself every single morning drinking a coffee. I keep a house that size because one of these days my parents will agree to come live with me, but they haven't yet. Do you know what I'm missing there?"

Hope held her breath.

"A woman to share it with," he said. "I was always a little envious of Pete."

Curtis tugged her to a stop as they reached Jespersen Street—those boarded-up shops giving an air of melancholy to an otherwise bright autumn day. But there was one building that was like a ray of sunshine in the midst of the decay—the old schoolhouse. It was half a block from where they stood, and the faded siding was badly in need of more white paint. The bell in the steeple above was stable enough, but it looked rusted and in need of some work, too.

"You're a well-off man, good-looking, sweet—" She forced the words out. "You could find a woman very easily, Curtis."

So easily. He was everything a woman could possibly want. He was sweet, a loving and devoted dad, a confident businessman, and he was successful, too. He could fill a woman's heart right to the brim… If he wanted, he could have a lineup hoping to get his attention.

"I don't want just any woman," he said. "It turns out, I'm kind of hard to please."

"You should do something about that," she said earnestly. "You don't need to do any of this alone, you know."

He chuckled and tipped her chin up with one finger. "Hope…"

Curtis met her gaze meaningfully, and she looked up at him, her breath bated. And suddenly what he was trying to say sank in. He wanted *her*… Her pulse sped up, and he tugged her in close, her belly pressed up against him, and even the baby stilled inside her. Then Curtis lowered his lips over hers. His breath was warm and soft, and her heart thrummed in response to him. His kiss was slow and filled with yearning, and when he pulled back, she blinked up at him, breathless.

"I didn't bring you here to ask you this, but… I think this could work."

"You and me?" she whispered.

"Yeah. You and me. What do you think? Could you let me take care of you?"

CHAPTER TWENTY-EIGHT

CURTIS HADN'T MEANT to say any of that, but standing with her on this street that bore his family's name, he knew what he wanted to bring with him from Apfelkuchen. Her. He knew she could take care of herself and her son admirably, but he wanted to help. He wanted her to be able to look at him and know that he made her life happier, that he contributed to that beautiful smile that could pour into a room like sunlight.

"Curtis…" He could hear it in her voice. She was going to say no, and he wanted to explain himself first.

"I didn't mean for this to happen," he said. "I saw you again, and… I don't know. You were Pete's wife before, and I would never have let myself feel anything more for you. I do not cross those lines. But now…" He dug around inside himself for the words. "Hope, you're amazing. I know I won't be the only man to tell you this, but I mean it from my heart. You are the real thing. You've got depth and compassion, you're smart and beautiful. You have me completely captivated, and the thought of just driving out of town and leaving you behind—" It hurt like a punch to the gut. That was what it felt like. It felt wrong.

"Is that what you're planning?" she asked. "You're still going to leave?"

"They don't want my business plan, Hope."

"I knew you had to leave eventually," she said. "I didn't expect it to feel like this."

"Like what?"

"Like a breakup." She smiled faintly. "I'm sorry if that sounds silly. I just mean that this feels like a rather final goodbye."

"It doesn't have to be. Could you see yourself making a life with me and Lucy in Pittsburgh? We could always come back here to visit."

Now he'd said it—put it right out there—and he held his breath, waiting for her answer. Because this was the question that mattered most—could she see herself with him?

"You have your life, Curtis, and I have mine," she said softly. "I don't know what mine will look like, but I do know that I can't swim with the sharks. I need something quieter, more peaceful. I love the life I'm making here, standing on my own two feet. I've let a man take care of me, and it wasn't the right fit for me. You need to build things—so do I! I need to put something together that I can be proud of. I need to do a few things on my own, because I'm not happy just being kept."

"So that's it?" he asked. "You don't want to see me again?"

"I didn't say that." She sucked in a wavering breath. "Of course I want to see you again! I'm going to miss you so much. I shouldn't admit to that. I should try to play this cool, but it's the truth. I've…gotten attached."

"Good." That felt like success. "Me, too."

"But this—" she spread her arms "—isn't your life. This isn't your rhythm. This is a break from your regular routine. But for me, this is my home."

She'd put down roots. Did people know how precious that was—that stability that came with a root system, an extended family, a history in one place?

"And you don't want to share mine," he said. That was what it came down to. She didn't want the life he'd built in Pittsburgh.

"It's not that…it's—" Her eyes skipped over him, over Jespersen Street, over the schoolhouse… Then her gaze came back to him. "Marriage was harder than I thought. You know, women in my position think they've hit the jackpot if they fall in love with an affluent man. The comfort, the lifestyle, the lack of worry over the regular stuff everyone else worries about constantly—it feels like this massive gift. And it is. But it comes with challenges, too."

"What don't you like about it?" he asked.

"Maintaining a lifestyle like that takes a certain

amount of focus and a specific set of priorities," she said. "Work comes first. It has to. I understand it, but…on an emotional level, it took a toll on me. And we women are supposed to be grateful for all of it. We don't worry about paying for medical things—it's simply taken care of. We don't have to tire ourselves out with the kids because we can hire help. We don't have to scrape and save for a new vehicle—it might end up being a birthday present. And if we say we're lonely, people tell us to stop complaining, we have it so good. But, Curtis, I was lonely. Deeply, deeply lonely."

Blast it, Pete! Why couldn't you have listened to her?

"I'm not Pete," he said quietly.

"No, but marriage was harder than I thought." She slowly shook her head. "That's something you learn after having been married. I always thought that after marriage it would be easy—you just love each other and build a life." She shrugged. "But it's difficult to go about loving each other in ways that are meaningful for both of you, and building a life that works for two completely different people. I loved him with all my heart, but we had so much trouble getting on the same page and understanding each other. Supporting each other's priorities and needs. Getting married isn't the end—it's the start! And it wasn't what I expected. I thought marrying a man with Peter's ability to provide would make my life easier. But it was harder in all sorts of ways I never anticipated. Now… I just need to put together a life for my son—my kind of life. With ordinary people who run shops and work regular jobs and raise their kids to the do the same. That's the world I know how to navigate."

Seeing Judy had spooked her—he'd noticed that. Maybe having a nanny around the house wasn't a treat for her. Maybe it was intimidating. Heck, he'd grown up middle-class. He'd never had a nanny. And it was true that he lived in a different world than she did right now, but she wasn't naive. She knew the difference—she'd seen it all with Pete.

Am I the naive one here?

Because now she was nervous of that world Pete had introduced her to, and she knew better than anyone that money couldn't solve every problem. In fact, it created a few, too. Here was this sweet, beautiful woman turning him down because his life was too much like her first husband's. And he'd also bring along with him all the unpredictability of Lynn's life. She hadn't even mentioned Lynn, but he knew what he brought to the table… Samantha hadn't been able to handle it, but what about Hope? Maybe he was trying to offer Hope a solution to Samantha's complaints. Apparently, he had some of his own baggage.

He looked past her toward the schoolhouse. This historic building was why he'd taken her out there, after all, and he hadn't changed his mind about it. Even if she'd never be his.

"Then let me help make that sweet, regular life a reality for you here," he said.

"You don't have to—"

He caught her hand again.

"I brought you here to tell that I'm going to restore the schoolhouse for you and make sure it's suitable for your day care."

"Really?" She looked up at him, confusion in her eyes. "Why would you do that?"

He swallowed hard. "I want you to have that touch of history. I'll pay for it, and I'm not going to charge you a lease. If you ever want to move to another building, I'll charge the next people who use it. That'll be my gift to Apfelkuchen—a fantastic day care run by the kindest woman I know."

Tears misted her eyes, and her chin trembled.

"I don't know what I'll do with the rest of this street, though," he said. "I guess that's a problem for another day."

Hope stood up on her tiptoes and pressed a chaste kiss against his cheek. Her belly brushed against his coat, and he had to hold himself back from gathering her up into his arms. He was going to have to drive out of town and leave her behind—and it was going to be the hardest thing he ever did.

He knew exactly why Pete had fallen for her so quickly—it was the same reason he had. Hope was that special combination of integrity and beauty that was so hard to find. She was the kind of woman a man could trust with his life, if only he was lucky enough to secure her heart.

Maybe it was timing. Maybe she'd never want what he had to offer…and he had to respect her values, how she wanted to raise her son. Her roots.

"You deserve that peace and quiet," he said softly.

"And you deserve someone who can appreciate the life you offer," she said. "I'm so sorry, Curtis." Her voice broke then and she took a step away from him. "I need to get back…"

He nodded, not trusting his words, and she headed back up the street at a quick pace, her head down. He swallowed hard against a lump in his throat. And then he turned back to Jespersen Street. That old schoolhouse was a beautiful historic building, and Hope would bring life back into it again…

But the rest of the street—those sagging and gutted buildings—were where his own history lay. In his mind's eye, he could see his grandfather walking along the sidewalk, two skinny kids in tow. These were the streets where Curtis has seen what it looked like when people put down roots, for better or for worse. This street had shown him a community of people who had helped each other out in times of need.

And it was going to stay empty, occupied by

the ghosts of friends and neighbors who'd done their best.

Maybe there was some small part of him that hoped that if he could rebuild Jespersen Street, then miracles could happen, and recovery was possible, and Lynn would be able to pull out of the nightmare of addiction and put her life back together again.

A cat slid out of a broken window of the old flower shop and dropped stealthily to the ground.

Give your mammi this flower for me, Curtis. And tell her I say hi.

Grandma needed one last flower on her grave. Grandpa needed one last apology for not getting it right. He'd have to leave Lynn to her own battles, and maybe it was time to let go and find somewhere else to put down those roots.

Lucy's future had to come before his regrets.

CHAPTER TWENTY-NINE

WHEN HOPE CAME back into the shop, she was doing her best to hold everything together, but her heart felt like it was about to break in two. She should not be feeling this way! Not so soon after losing Peter, not for someone who had been Peter's friend.

But her feelings had changed so quickly in a very short period of time. She just wasn't brave enough to act on them, to accept the life he offered. Catherine had warned her about prenups and lawyers, and Hope didn't have it in her. She'd rather build her life alone than deal with contracts and nannies, lifestyle pressures and work always coming first.

The door swung shut behind her, and she looked around the shop to find that Judy and Lucy were already gone. It was just as well. Lucy wasn't her little girl, even though Hope had fallen in love with her. Judy was Lucy's nanny, and Hope getting attached to Curtis's little girl was foolish on her part anyway. A tear leaked down Hope's cheek and she dashed it away with the back of her hand. Faith looked up in surprise from the box of books she was unpacking.

"I've got another one that looks like it's worth something—" Faith started, and then stopped short. "Hope? You okay?"

"Yup. I'm fine." She started toward the door that head up to her apartment, but her sister was faster and intercepted her.

"What happened?"

"He wanted to take me to the city and take care of me."

"Wow… Okay, this reaction doesn't seem right. What's going on?"

"It would never work, Faith," Hope said. "It's only been a few months since Peter died. And I'm not ready to jump back into marriage. I know you and Trent have just slid into this wonderful honeymoon period this time around, but I was always feeling frustrated, and unheard, and… Marriage wasn't easy for me."

Faith met her gaze sadly. "You and Peter would have gotten there."

"I like to think so." She shrugged her shoulders weakly. "Or maybe our entire marriage would have been like that—loving each other so much, but also never quite getting onto the same page."

"You can't know that," Faith said. "And Curtis isn't Peter."

"I think it's better that I put my life together on my own, have my baby and figure myself out."

"Without Curtis."

Hope's eyes welled with tears, and she nodded, not trusting herself to words.

"Sweetie, if you need to rest, then you rest," Faith said, putting an arm around her. "You don't have to do anything you don't want to. And if you just want to focus on your baby, you should do that. This baby is your miracle, and he's going to be so loved."

That was the right answer, but somehow it didn't feel as comforting as it should. Because Curtis was a wonderful man and she was going to miss him more than she'd thought.

THAT EVENING, HOPE'S family descended upon her upstairs apartment. Her parents came with a box of baby things that had belonged to Hope when she was born. Her sisters arrived with food—Elaine brought some Chinese takeout, and Faith brought cheesecake. Trent and Tyke stayed home to give the sisters and their parents the night together.

"You're going to be a mom," her mother said softly. "I could argue that you already are. It makes things different, Hope. You don't look at the world in the same way, or at marriage. Your goals shift when this little bundle arrives and needs you in ways no one has ever needed you before."

"Am I foolish for turning down a good man?" Hope asked, tears in her eyes.

"No, you're brave," her mother replied. "Listen to your heart. You'll know the right thing to do, even if it hurts right now."

Her father opened the boxed cheesecake. It was from Martha's Amish Bakery. Their cheesecake was delicious. He carefully began to slice it, and he dished up the first portion for Hope.

"Cheesecake helps," her father said. "And, Hope? I'm proud of you."

"You've got us," Faith said. "You are never going to be on your own, okay?"

And Hope knew that she wouldn't, but deep in her heart, she was still thinking about Curtis's slow smile and strong arms, and Lucy's headful of bouncing blond curls. In order to choose a quiet life in Apfelkuchen, she had to let go of a very good man and a very sweet little girl.

And that was just going to hurt.

CHAPTER THIRTY

THE NEXT DAY, Curtis sat in Peachy Diner at the far end of Main Street, a burger and fries in front him, but he wasn't hungry. Judy had taken Lucy back to the motel for her nap time, and Lucy was mad she couldn't go nap at the antiques shop with Smokey. She'd gotten attached. So had he. Curtis couldn't shake the feeling that he wasn't done here.

He wished he was. Now that Hope had handed back his heart, he wanted to get out of town, back to the city, back to somewhere he felt like a success again. But the bishop was right that he'd come to Apfelkuchen for a reason. His grandfather would have wanted him to find a way forward with this town, not give up and leave. There was still a dilapidated row of shops on a street that bore the family name.

He couldn't help but think about his experiences with his grandfather on the farm—lessons learned, wisdom acquired. There was one time with a bottle-fed calf when Curtis had been struggling to get the calf to use the bottle. *Find a way, Curtis. All I'd be doing is heading out there and trying something just to see if it would work. It might work, or I might have to try something else. You just keep trying stuff until something works. Now, go on.*

Grandpa had formed him more than the old man had probably realized. So had his father—the man who'd built up a whole laundromat empire to support his family. One quarter at a time. Neither man would give him a pass, and today of all days, he wished he could talk to his grandpa, even rail at him and tell him that he was wrong—that sometimes there wasn't a solution. That sometimes you did everything you could and a community just didn't want what you offered.

Sometimes the woman you fell for wouldn't feel the same way. Apfelkuchen didn't want his offerings, and neither did Hope.

Peachy Diner had an array of cuckoo clocks—different sizes, different ornaments. But on the hour, every hour, those clocks all went off at once and tiny birds came bursting out of those little wooden doors with the cuckoo sound.

"Can I get you anything else?" the Amish waitress asked. She wore a blue dress with a Peachy Diner apron on top. Her hair was pulled back in a bun and covered by a white *kapp*. She didn't look more than sixteen or seventeen.

"No, thanks," Curtis said. "Wait—"

The girl turned back.

"Who makes these clocks?" he asked. "I'm just curious. They're beautifully done."

"Jeb Zook," she said. "He owns this place now, and he's made clocks for years. His *daet* made them, too, but he's since passed on, so Jeb's the last one making them."

Another craftsman who was doing some beautiful work in the background somewhere.

"Does he sell them?" Curtis asked.

"*Yah.* You can buy one off the wall, if you want. The prices are on the back of them. He'll put up a new one if someone buys one."

"So Jeb makes clocks. I've seen a lot of locally made furniture," Curtis said. "There are a lot of local craftsmen who are incredibly talented."

"I guess." The girl squinted at him. "I mean… people need furniture, right?"

People did need furniture. And a business that tended to do well in other Amish communities was carpentry shops. Englishers loved Amish-made furniture. It was high-quality and built to last—something regular furniture stores couldn't boast anymore. Jespersen Street couldn't just molder away. Something would have to be built there, and if not row houses…

The front door opened and Eddie came inside. Curtis was surprised to see that he was still dressed Amish. Had he heard the news yet about the bishop's decision? Eddie's gaze landed on Curtis, and he looked deeply sad. Yeah, he'd heard. Curtis lifted his hand in greeting, and Eddie came over to his table.

"Have a seat," Curtis said.

Eddie pulled out the chair and sank into it. He met Curtis's gaze with an empty look of his own.

"I heard," Curtis said.

"Yeah."

The men sat in silence for a moment. Sometimes a guy didn't have to say anything more. They both knew what this was. They both knew how it felt.

"I had my heart handed to me, too, so I get it," Curtis said.

"Hope?"

"Was it that obvious?" Curtis asked.

"Yeah, you weren't hiding anything," Eddie replied. "I'm sorry. She looked happy with you."

That was somewhat reassuring, but it hadn't been enough. He would have worked hard to make her happy. But his life wasn't the one she wanted. She'd been through too much. She just wanted something ordinary, and ironically, that was one thing he couldn't provide.

"It looks like the Amish community doesn't want any touristy sort of business here in Apfelkuchen, either," Curtis said. "I don't know... I really wanted to do something for the town—something to help build it up."

"I would have gotten behind those tourist rentals," Eddie said. "But I'm not Amish, I guess."

"What do you need here in town?" Curtis asked. "You, personally."

"I need a job," Eddie said.

"Are you going back to electrical work?"

He shook his head. "You're going to think I'm stupid, but I'm not done trying for Sarah yet. I need a job that would abide by the Amish *Ordnung* and that I'd be good at, because I'm a terrible farmer."

Curtis shook his head. "You are one determined man."

"Yes, I am." Eddie rubbed his hands over his face. "But Sarah isn't convinced they'll ever change their minds. She hasn't broken up with me, but she's crying like it's over, if you know what I mean."

Yeah, he knew what that felt like. He and Hope had never been a couple—but this sure felt like a breakup.

"How are you with carpentry?" Curtis asked.

"Oh, I don't know. I've designed a few chicken coops in my day and built a shelf or two. I'm better with the numbers side, actually."

Curtis stilled, the young man's words sinking in. "Yeah?"

"Not that it helps me much on the farm, but I took a few college business classes. I was going to use them for running my own electrical company eventually."

"How many Amish guys could use some extra work?"

"I mean…" Eddie frowned at the apparent change in topic. "A lot of the younger guys. Working on their fathers' farms, they need income of their own."

"And of them, how many are decent with woodworking? Because I've seen some real talent around here."

"They all make their own furniture. Some are better at it than others."

An idea was spinning in Curtis's head—a business that would work with the Amish *Ordnung* in these parts and would bring in customers but not tourists.

"I have a street with my name on it that is filled with condemned shops," Curtis said. "I'm going to restore the old schoolhouse, but I can't leave a street of dilapidated buildings."

Eddie eyed him uncertainly.

"What if we rounded up some of these guys who are good with woodworking, and we started an Amish furniture company? People could come out here to buy pieces in person, and we could probably ship pieces out to furniture stores in the city, too. We could build up a loyal clientele."

"We?" Eddie asked, but there was light in his eyes that Curtis recognized.

Curtis kept talking out his idea. “I don’t have to rezone anything if I’m putting a new business on that street. I can demolish the old buildings and start putting in one big showroom and workshop…”

That would be pretty simple to put together. It would be cheaper than the row houses and a simpler build.

“But you said we?” Eddie pressed.

“I’d need a manager,” Curtis said. “If you were planning to run your own business and you like working on the numbers side…plus, you know the community, you’d know who to hire…”

“Are you serious?”

“I am.” Curtis shot him a grin. “If I can get this off the ground, will you be my manager?”

“Just like that?” Eddie asked.

“You’ve got experience on both sides of the fence—that’s valuable to me,” Curtis said. “Plus, you’re determined. Nothing gets you down. You look for solutions even when you don’t see any. That’s the kind of man I want running my business. So yeah, just like that. If I can get this off the ground, will you be my manager?”

“Yes, sir.” Eddie held out his hand. “And I’ll shake on it.”

In these parts, a handshake was binding, and that suited Curtis just fine. He took Eddie’s hand and gave it a firm shake.

"Thank you," Curtis said. "I think this one can work. I really do."

It was Amish-sanctioned work, it didn't include bringing tourists into town and it would bring business into Apfelkuchen—slowly and steadily. If Amish men needed work, he could provide that, and more steadily employed men in this area would make for a stronger economy and a stronger Amish community. It wouldn't be a surge of money, but it would bring steady growth. And it would still benefit the other businesses, with people who came for furniture also stopping in for antiques and ice cream and other supplies. Plus, when locals made more money, they spent more in local shops, too.

Curtis's phone rang. It was Lynn. He sighed.

"I'd better take this call," he said. "Give me the number at your closest phone shanty, and I'll be in touch, okay?"

Eddie went in search of a pen and paper, and Curtis picked up the call.

"Hi, Lynn," he said.

"Hey, Curtis." She sounded different this time. Quiet. Sadder. She didn't sound so manic. She was no longer in withdrawal.

"You okay?" he asked.

"For now," she said. "I went to the hospital for help. They got me some methadone."

"Good. I'm glad you're doing better." Withdrawal was agony, and he knew it. But she'd never get off the drugs if she didn't get past the hard part, either.

"Lucy's birthday is coming up," she said.

"Yeah." He hesitated. "Will you be there?"

"I want to, but then I thought… It wouldn't be good for her to see me like this."

"We can find a way."

"I think I have found one. Not for this birthday, but maybe for her next one," Lynn said. "Curtis, it costs a lot, but I want to go to rehab. I've been thinking about my life, and what I'm doing to myself. One of these days I'll die on the street if I don't change something."

"And you're ready for rehab?" he asked, his pulse speeding up, but he was afraid to get his hopes up about this.

"Yeah. I can't keep missing out on her life."

"Are you really sure?"

"I know I'm asking a lot of you, but yes. I can pay you back sometime. It would take me a while to scrape up the money, but once I'm clean I'll get a job and I can save, and—"

"I'll pay for it," Curtis cut in. "Lynn, this is great. You don't have to pay me back. I'll pay for it."

"I'm going to try and kick the drugs," she said, her voice shaking. "For Lucy."

"Lynn, Lucy is just fine," Curtis said softly. "She's happy and loved and growing so quickly. You don't have to worry about her. And don't even do it for me, or Mom and Dad. Do it for yourself. Do it because you deserve a better life."

"I'm not sure I deserve anything," she said, her voice choked.

"Yes, you do. You deserve happiness, and peace, and confidence, and safety. You can get over this, Lynn. You can. I'll pay for it, and I just want you to work on this for yourself, okay?"

"I'll do my best."

Curtis took down the information for the hospital so they could transfer him along to the rehab facility. She was trying—that was a really good step!

There was hope in the strangest of places. Maybe one day he could bring Lucy back to Apfelkuchen and show her a town that her great-grandfather had loved and that her dad had invested in. He could show her the graves of her ancestors and the streets named after them. But most importantly, he could show her people who worked together despite their differences and who made a better life for everyone.

No one left behind.

Not even Lynn.

CHAPTER THIRTY-ONE

HOPE WENT UPSTAIRS to her apartment while Faith closed up the shop that night. She just needed some quiet time to herself to try and process everything.

She looked down at her phone, then tossed it onto the couch irritably.

She missed Curtis already. How many times had she been waiting on a call from Peter, missing him so much… This heartbreak felt too familiar—missing Curtis and wishing he'd call her, even though she'd told him clearly that it wouldn't work.

This was the very tangle of emotion she'd been trying to avoid! She wiped a tear off her cheek. She never should have let herself fall for Curtis. It had been foolhardy. She was getting over her husband's death, and she was in no emotional state to be starting over with someone new!

Obviously. Right? Wasn't that clear by how quickly she'd fallen for Curtis? Would she have had more of a shield up if she'd met Curtis a year from now?

Hope ran a hand over her belly. She'd been growing. Her maternity top was filled out now—more so than a couple of weeks ago. Strange how things could change so slowly that a woman didn't notice it happening. Like a pregnancy…like falling for a guy she had no business falling for.

She stopped at a framed photo from her and Peter's wedding. Her makeup had been impeccable, and that veil had been a frothy miracle of lace. They both looked so happy, and Peter had been looking down at her adoringly. Hope touched the glass over Peter's face tenderly.

She didn't wish away a moment of their union, though. Not a single second of it, even their struggles. And in the midst of that struggle to understand each other, their little boy had been conceived. Somehow, this baby inside her was a truer representation of their love for each other than anything else.

Downstairs, she thought heard Elaine's voice. Hope went over to the window and looked down. There was Elaine's hatchback parked out front.

Hope wasn't in the mood for a sisterly gab session, though. She needed to get her emotions sorted out—put Curtis behind her in some rational way that would let her stop missing him like this.

But Curtis was being benevolent and kind. He

was going to renovate the schoolhouse for her so she could use it for her childcare business. She would have the very things she'd wanted before Curtis had stepped into her life two weeks ago. He was making it all possible and then…walking away. Like she'd asked him to.

This was supposed to make her feel better! She rubbed her hands over her face. What she wanted was for Curtis to come back and give her some magical solution that would let them be together without the tough parts. Maybe she wanted him to come back and tell her that he'd stay by her side, bring her breakfast every morning and be her best friend so she'd never have to actually lose him.

But that wasn't fair to him, either.

Footsteps echoed in the stairwell, and then there was a tap on her door. Her sisters had come up. She sighed and opened the door.

"I've got doughnuts from the Amish bakery," Elaine said before Hope could get a word out, and she came inside holding a box in front of her. Faith was behind, and she cast Hope an apologetic look.

"Sorry, Hope," Faith said. "I know you said you wanted a quiet evening, but Elaine insisted on coming up."

"Darn right, I insisted," Elaine retorted. "You don't get to suffer alone when you've got sisters. That's how this works."

Elaine deposited the box on the kitchen table

and then peeled off her coat and tossed it over the back of a kitchen chair. They were coming to her rescue, just like they had when Peter died. Just like they had with boyfriends of yore. This was what sisters did—they bickered in the good times and pulled together when they needed each other most.

"Elaine, I'm okay," Hope said. "It doesn't count after two weeks!"

"What doesn't count?" Elaine asked. "Falling in love? How long did it take you with Peter? Because I remember you telling us after first meeting him that he was the kind of guy you'd want to marry."

"Quit being logical," Hope grumbled, and Faith laughed.

"I don't care if this is reasonable, or rational, or not. You get to be sad," Faith said.

"And you get to have doughnuts." Elaine came out with a plump, honey-glazed doughnut on a plate. She held it out for Hope, and she accepted it with a small smile.

"And you get our company for the night," Faith added.

"What about Trent and Tyke?" Hope asked.

"Trent understands."

Hope took a bite of doughnut—it really was delicious. The baby seemed to like the shot of sugar, too, because he wriggled inside her. They moved to the living room and Hope sank into the recliner, her sisters opposite her on the couch.

"Okay...lay it out," Faith said. "You've had some time to think and process. Tell us where you're at."

So Hope did. She explained how sweet Curtis had been, how insightful, how fun and strong. He was kind and protective, everything a woman could want in a man. But he was also work-driven, clearly spent time on the road, relied on nannies and cleaners because he was so busy. And felt the need to take care of her...something that had become a prison for her in the past. Hope had married a man just like that, and she was afraid of letting herself need another man the same way. Maybe if she'd needed Peter less, she could have been happier!

"And Curtis's life is complicated," Hope said. "He has obligations in Pittsburgh. His parents are out there, and so is his sister. She needs his help, and he needs to be able to be there for his family. I would never ask him to give all of that up. But I don't think I can live that life all over again."

"And you're tired," Faith said softly.

"So tired." Tears welled in Hope's eyes. "I just want to put together a life for me and my baby and do it while not missing a man."

"I wish I could fix it for you," Elaine said softly.

"Me, too," Faith said.

Elaine went back to the kitchen and came back

with the box of doughnuts. Hope licked her fingers from the doughnut she'd just finished and plucked a fresh one from the box.

"I talked to Tim today after school when he was picking up Oliver," Elaine said. "Marriage being tough—that's what reminded me of it. He was talking about when he and Matilda got married."

"The wedding he didn't invite you to," Hope said.

"Yes." Elaine shot her a rueful look. "But that's not the point. He and Matilda were both cops, and apparently that's a pretty terrible mix."

"Is it?" Faith asked.

Elaine nodded. "They both worked shifts, so they could go three days without sleeping in the same bed together. They both had the pressure of police work, and the trauma that comes with seeing some of that tough stuff cops see every day in their job. Cops have a really high divorce rate, like twice as high as the average person."

"The pressure, I guess," Hope said.

The sisters nodded.

"Anyway, he was talking about all those challenges. I mean, they had Oliver right away, too, so Matilda's parents were helping out with childcare, and Tim and Matilda were both working different shifts, and Matilda wanted to just quit and be a stay-at-home mom, but cops don't make much."

"So how did they make it work?" Hope asked.

"He said he realized that life would be hard

being married to another cop, or it could be hard in different ways without her. But he loved her, and she loved him, and they figured they'd rather face the difficulties together than apart."

"Pick your poison, so to speak," Faith said quietly. "It'll be hard regardless."

"Yeah..."

Hope leaned her head back against the chair. *Pick your poison...* It didn't sound like very inspiring marital advice, but it had worked for Tim and Matilda. Could that apply to her and Curtis? Could she even make a relationship work with him, one that would have some of the same issues as her marriage? One that might be harder now that she knew she wanted more independence and agency, that she didn't like having a partner who traveled so much. One where they'd have to navigate difficult family situations with Lucy, with her baby...with future children they might have together. It might be hard as she and Curtis figured each other out and found out how to stay close... Then again, it would be hard to raise her baby alone without that strong shoulder to lean into. Two hard scenarios. But one of those challenges had Curtis at her side. Her heart skipped a beat.

Was that the answer?

Her sisters had turned the discussion to Tim and his son, though.

"How's Oliver doing?" Faith asked, turning to Elaine.

"The talk with the counselor helped a lot. He was struggling with his mom's death, and he was just really angry. He missed her. Nothing was the same without his mom," Elaine said.

Tears misted Hope's eyes. No, nothing was the same after someone you loved died, was it? But life wasn't easy, either. There was no guarantee it would be simpler if she let Curtis go. That was the thought that was hovering in the back of her mind.

"I got Oliver helping his friend Cameron with reading. Cameron has been struggling a lot, and I think Oliver was just trying to be like his friend. So I got Cameron to read to Oliver, and they're both doing better. It turns out his dad was right—Oliver is a very good reader. He was just trying to fit in."

"Maybe Oliver just needed a little extra love," Hope said.

"It never hurts," Elaine said. "Even children who come from incredibly loving homes need love when they're away from it, you know?"

Hope nodded. "You're a good teacher, Elaine."

"Thanks." Elaine shot her a smile.

What about Lucy? She would have her own struggles as she grew up. Her family life would be complicated. She'd have questions about why her family was different from her friends'. She had Nanny Judy for now, but she wouldn't stay working in childcare forever. Lucy had a dad who adored her, and extended family. But what about a stepmom who could step in and offer all that love, support and stability that her biological mom couldn't give? Sometimes that extra bit of love could make all the difference.

And who would give it to her? Did Hope want another woman stepping in to be Lucy's mom? Did she want another woman holding Curtis's heart?

Pick your poison.

CHAPTER THIRTY-TWO

DAYLIGHT WAS HELPFUL for boosting a mood. Curtis got Lucy up, and Judy tapped on the door and started her shift a bit early. She helped Lucy get washed and dressed while Curtis packed up their toiletries.

"We're going home?" Lucy asked.

"Yes, we're going back home," Judy said. "Let me wash your face. Look at me."

"Will we go to our park?"

"We'll have to, won't we?"

"Will you get me a cookie?"

Judy always got Lucy a single cookie from a bakery up the road from the park. Lucy looked forward to it more than playing.

"I always get you a cookie… Okay, let's brush your teeth."

"I'm getting a cookie!"

"You're getting your teeth brushed," Judy chuckled.

Curtis listened to Lucy chatter to her nanny, and he wondered if this was enough for now. He was doing his best. He was raising her with love and stability. He was helping his sister get herself off the drugs—as much as he could, at least. But would it all be enough for Lucy once she was grown and she looked back on her childhood?

When Lucy and Judy were finished in the bathroom, Judy started sorting Lucy's clothes into piles—laundry to wash and clothes that were still clean.

"So you're finished here in Apfelkuchen?" Judy's hands seemed to work independently from the rest of her, because she had an eye on Lucy, too, and Curtis was still confident that she was listening to him.

"Yeah," he replied. "I don't need to apply for any rezoning for Jespersen Street if I'm putting in a workshop there. It's less money to build, too."

"I have an Amish-made rocking chair at home," Judy said. "Once I slow down, I intend to use it, too."

Curtis smiled wanly. "I hate thinking about you changing careers, Judy."

"You need a wife, Curtis," she said frankly. "You need a woman who will pitch in with you and raise Lucy, have more kids, make plans for your future together… That's what you need, you know."

"I know," he admitted.

"Oh?" Judy shot him a smile. "I didn't expect

you to agree. I've said that a hundred times. What changed?"

Hope was what had changed. He'd met the woman who made all that seem possible for just a little while. And she was wonderful. She was the perfect woman—warm, kind, smart, beautiful… Plus there was some unnameable quality that was just her.

"Maybe I'm just seeing the light," he said.

"What's her name?" Judy didn't look up this time. She put a pile of little dresses into the suitcase. He could choose not to answer that—that was his right. Or he could make a joke about how Judy was worse than his mother when it came to setting him up. But somehow he couldn't bring himself to deflect her.

"Her name is Hope."

"That's appropriate." Judy looked up then. "Wait, I met a Hope yesterday…"

"You did."

"So why are we leaving?" Her eyebrows went up.

"Uh—" He sighed. "It won't work. The situation—" He glanced toward his daughter. He couldn't say too much in front of her. She might look like she was playing with her dolly, but he had no doubt that she was tuned in to their conversation. "—my situation is a complicated one, and she just lost her husband a few months ago."

"That's difficult." Judy nodded. "But is there no solution you two can work out?"

"I tried," he said. "Maybe it's the timing. Maybe it's just that I come with a lot more baggage because of my breakup with Sam. I seem to be trying to provide Hope with the life that I think Sam might have agreed to. It's not smart on my part. Hope wants something completely different."

"And what you want, and what she wants…is there any crossover?" Judy asked.

"A lot, but not enough."

Judy sighed. "I'm sorry, Curtis. You're a very good man, and I'd love to attend your wedding when you find the right one."

"Speaking of which, I need to pay her for the childcare she provided while you were away," Curtis said. She'd told him to just put the money toward the food bank, but he'd let her do that if she didn't want to keep it. Besides, he wanted an excuse to see her again.

"Maybe bring flowers," Judy said with a little smile. "They help."

What was most helpful right now was just constant, kind, professional Judy helping him out with his daughter and wanting the best for him.

He shot her a grateful look. "I don't know what I'd do without you, Judy. Really."

"You'd get married is what you'd do," Judy said,

rolling her eyes, and then she bent down to look at the dolly Lucy held up for her inspection.

A future with Hope was impossible…wasn't it? Or was there a solution here that he couldn't see? He was a man who solved problems. He found a way. He built bridges or tore down obstructions. But a woman's heart wasn't quite so easy to solve. Whatever Hope had chosen, he would still bring in a team to restore that old schoolhouse for her. He'd make sure it was ready for when she wanted to start her business. Apfelkuchen would be better for it, but so would he. At least he could give her something.

And yet, Curtis still felt like the ground had crumbled out from beneath his feet. Because no matter what he added to this town, he wouldn't have Hope. And this wouldn't be home, either. He'd have to let go of that boyhood fantasy.

Curtis's phone rang, and he looked down at an unfamiliar number.

"Curtis Jespersen."

"Hi, it's Eddie. I'm calling from the phone shanty." The young man's voice sounded different. Cheerier. Brighter. Something had improved for him.

"Right. Hi, Eddie. I didn't expect to hear from you so soon. Did you find some other guys who want to work in carpentry?"

"Not yet. Sorry about that, but I was focused on some other stuff. I talked to the bishop."

"Oh, yeah?"

Curtis bent down and caught Lucy as she made a mad dash past him.

"I wanted to talk to him about your job offer. I was hoping it might change things, honestly. I pointed out it would be a good, solid Amish job that would allow me to support a family."

"Did it change anything for him?"

"Well, the job offer itself was helpful, but the thing that made the difference was that I asked him for permission."

"Oh…" That would have been hard to do for a regular guy just looking for a job to support himself. Asking permission. It didn't seem to him that a man should have to ask someone else permission to earn a living.

"The thing I've learned about living Amish is that you have to respect authority," Eddie went on. "And the bishop is our authority here. I asked if I'd have his permission to take the job and work it. That's what changed things."

Curtis huffed out a breath. "Wow. Really?"

"Yeah. He said that it sounded like a good solution to him, and he appreciated me asking for his guidance. He said I was showing the change in attitude that he needed to see. When I fixed the electrical issue for the Beilers, I was going rogue, doing stuff on my own. But he said he needed to see me submitting to the community, putting aside my own ideas and accepting a new way. So…he gave me his blessing."

"To work for me?" Curtis asked. Because that was good news. He needed a quality manager he could count on, and he had a feeling Eddie was the guy.

"Yep. And I have his blessing to marry Sarah."

Curtis grinned. "Congratulations, Eddie. I'm happy for you."

"Thanks," Eddie said. "I owe it to you, Curtis. I'm a terrible farmer—there is no getting around it, and no one was going to ignore it. But you're giving me a job where I can actually be good at the work. I can hold my head up and provide for my wife. So thank you. Really. I'll be loyal and hardworking. You'll never regret giving me a chance."

"I'm happy to have helped," Curtis replied.

They talked a bit more about how Curtis would contact Eddie and some of the prep work he could start on—and bc paid for—while they got ready to demolish the old building and put in a new foundation. They could do that much before the ground froze.

As he ended the call, he pursed his lips in thought. Even Eddie had taken an impossible situation and found a way forward. Eddie loved Sarah, and Sarah loved Eddie. That was enough for an industrious guy to work with.

What could he offer Hope that would relieve

some of her fears? What could he do to show her that he was going to put her and their children first? It needed to be a solution for Hope, not one based on his past baggage.

There had to be something…

CHAPTER THIRTY-THREE

HOPE FELT LIKE a shell of herself. She'd been up too late last night picking her poison, so to speak. Could she really walk away from Apfelkuchen and go back to a life in Pittsburgh? Was it just a matter of standing up for her own needs, or would Curtis be different there?

That was a worry—and she'd been trying to look at it rationally when she finally fell asleep around three in the morning.

So this morning, she was bleary and exhausted, and she was browsing through the sales page for their website. The bell above the door tinkled as a browsing customer left.

"Faith, that antique poetry book sold," Hope said. "A flour sifter, too. And we have seven people with items in their carts."

Any further chatter evaporated on her tongue as she looked up. The customer hadn't left… someone had arrived. The older woman was still going through some embroidered items, her attention absorbed in her shopping, and Curtis stood there in the middle of the store, his tired, heartbroken gaze fixed on her.

He'd come to say goodbye.

Faith slipped away, and Curtis crossed the store and stopped in front of her.

"Hey," he said quietly.

"Hi." Her throat suddenly tightened.

"I was about to head back to Pittsburgh," he said. "And I couldn't leave without seeing you once more. I've been thinking about things, and before you answer me, I just need to say it all, okay?"

"Okay." She turned toward him.

"I love you," he said, and with those three words, it was like the whole shop melted away.

"You do?"

"You think I ask a woman to move to a new city without loving her?" he asked with a small smile. "Hope, I love you. That's the foundation of all of this. I've probably been halfway in love with you for longer than I should have been, but there it is. I'm in love with you. As in… I'm not going to get over you. If I don't find a way to make things work between us, I'm going to just go on loving you for the rest of my life, and that is going to seriously mess up my ability to move on."

Hope smiled faintly. "Yeah, I know that feeling."

She came out from behind the counter, and

Curtis touched her cheek and then bent down and kissed her gently.

"Did you know that the bishop finally gave his blessing to Eddie and Sarah?" he asked.

"No! When?"

"Yeah, Eddie called me this morning. His willingness to seek guidance from the bishop made the difference. And my job offer didn't hurt. He'll be able to support her. But that guy is willing to completely change his way of thinking and all his priorities just to get a chance at forever with the woman he loves. And I'm inspired."

Eddie and Sarah—they'd found a way… It was a relief to hear that. If anyone deserved to just love each other for the rest of their lives, it was those two.

"That's such good news but…wait, a job offer?"

"I'm getting to that," he said with a smile. "But first, I need to say… I can't change my sister's struggle with addiction or how that might complicate my life and Lucy's…and anyone else who shares our life."

Hope bit her lip but didn't interrupt him.

"She's asked me to pay for her to go to rehab, though, so that's hopeful. But even if she gets off the drugs, she's always going to have to keep working the steps to say clean. And I can't change that, Hope. I can't."

"That's great for her," Hope said. "And I would

never ask you to change your relationship with her. I know families can be messy."

He caught her hand and he ran his thumb over the tops of her fingers gently. She could feel the pleading in his touch.

"There are a few things I can change, though. You've found a lot of meaning and happiness here in Apfelkuchen. With your sisters, your family. With your plans for a day care. With people who are present for you. In Pittsburgh, you weren't happy. That's a fact. You've already tried that life, and you don't like it. I think we've both been assuming that me making money—traveling for work, putting my job first, running in that kind of social circle—that that's got to be the priority. But I'm a resourceful guy. If Eddie can change careers, I can change my center of operations. I can keep doing what I do—I can even open another local business or two if we can think of something that's bound to work. I'll sell my house in Pittsburgh, and I'll relocate."

"You'd—" Hope frowned, trying to take it all in. "You'd move here? For me?"

"Hope, I'll live in that apartment above the store with you, if that's what you want," he said with a small smile. "And when you're ready, we can build our own house where we can raise our kids, and have a few more, if you want. And your day care—that's a priority, too."

"Can you do that?" she asked. "Can you really

just relocate to this little town in the middle of nowhere?"

"Sure," he said. "If I make a bit less money, I guess I'll have to get my hands dirty and figure out something local. And I'm not so far away from my parents or sister that I can't be there for them. That's where the job offer comes in. I have a new idea for Jespersen Street that will fit this community better. You're right—there is something about this place that just begs for roots. And I want to put mine down right next to yours. I want you to be Lucy's mom, and I want be your little boy's dad. I came here looking for some sense of home, and I didn't find what I thought I would. Instead I found you."

"Curtis…" Her words choked off and she looked up into his gentle eyes. Would he really give up his whole lifestyle for her? Would he risk it all for a home with her in Apfelkuchen?

Curtis bent down and pecked her lips. "I love you…and that's all I've got. I just love you."

"I love you, too!" she said.

"Okay, so… I'm not asking you to date me. I'm asking you to marry me," he said. "Call me old-fashioned, but I'm going to need you to make an honest man of me, Hope Taylor."

Hope started to laugh, and she nodded. "Yes."

"Yes?"

"Yes, I want to be Lucy's mom, and you'll be my son's daddy, and…and…" Really, it all came down to one thing that suddenly didn't feel scary anymore. "I'll marry you."

Curtis gathered her up into his arms, and his lips covered hers in a kiss that seemed to seal the two of them together. It felt like a promise, and as she leaned into his embrace, she could see a wonderful life rolling out ahead of them. Her baby boy would have a dad who loved him, too, and a big sister who was going to be so thrilled to have him to cuddle. She'd have a husband to enjoy all these firsts with, and she'd be the woman to stand by his side and fill his heart.

When he finally pulled back, he whispered, "Judy and Lucy are waiting at the park. What do you say we go tell them first?"

"Tell who what first?" Faith exploded from across the room. "Come on, you two! I'm not blind. Did you just get engaged?"

"Yeah, we did," Hope said, and her sister swooped in with a laugh of delight and put her arms around both of them. The customer looked up from her shopping in surprise.

"Oh, I'm thrilled!" Faith exclaimed. "I've got to call Elaine. Do you have wedding plans yet? No, of course not. That's too soon. Okay, go and enjoy. Celebrate. Buy a ring! I'm texting Elaine!"

Hope had to laugh as her sister pulled out her phone. Elaine would be in class, but she'd have a doozy of a text waiting for her. When she saw it, Hope had no doubt that the happy family celebrating would begin, and Curtis would be pulled right into the heart of the Fairchild clan.

"Let's go tell Lucy," Hope said. "Do you think she'll be happy?"

"Lucy is going to be thrilled," Curtis said. "And, fair warning? So is Nanny Judy."

They headed for the door, the bell overhead tinkling merrily as they headed out into the autumn breeze hand in hand.

Somehow, Hope could feel it all coming together as they walked along the sunny sidewalk. It was like she could feel the beat of his heart through his strong, warm grip, and suddenly she wasn't scared of the challenges they'd most certainly face, because they'd be facing them together.

EPILOGUE

ON A COLD November morning with snowflakes pirouetting through the air, Hope stood in the vestibule of the Presbyterian church. Being as pregnant as she was, she'd suggested they just go to the judge and get married quietly, but Curtis had insisted that he wanted their friends and family there to see their vows, and now that the time had come, she was glad she'd agreed.

She wore an empire-waist gown with lace sleeves and a tulle skirt, and a single blue ribbon going around the waistline. It was her "something blue," but it was also for her baby boy, who was due in December. Curtis was excited about the baby. He was embracing fatherhood again with enthusiasm.

Elaine was on Lucy duty for the wedding day, and she'd helped the toddler down the aisle as the flower girl and was currently holding her at the front of the church as Hope waited for the organ music to begin.

"You look beautiful, sweetheart," her father

said, casting her a misty smile. "I wasn't sure I'd get to walk you down the aisle again, but Curtis is a good man."

"He really is," she agreed.

Curtis had put his house in the city on the market and he was moving into the apartment above the antiques shop just as he'd promised. There were two bedrooms, so they'd have enough space for now with Lucy and the baby coming. There was time to find the right piece of land and build their own home.

"Now, you're absolutely sure about this?" her father asked with a teasing little smile.

The organ music started then, swelling up to the traditional wedding march.

"Positive, Dad," she said, and she slipped her hand into the crook of his arm.

Their friends and family waited in those pews beyond. Mary and Albrecht had come, as had Sarah and Eddie. Mom, Faith and Trent were in the front row, Tyke dressed in a tiny suit that made him look absolutely adorable.

"Okay," Hope breathed. "I'm ready."

The doors swung open, and they stepped into the aisle. Curtis stood at the front of the church, his eyes glued to Hope as they slowly walked down the aisle.

This was it…her second chance at happiness, love, commitment and all the joys that came with joining her life with the man she loved. And the best part? Not a single prenuptial agreement had been signed between them.

When she'd asked if he wanted one, Curtis had laughed. "Not me. If you feel like you want one, I'll sign whatever you want, but I was raised by a man who was in the laundromat business. What's mine is yours, babe. Take me to the cleaners if you must, but I'm here to stay."

And then he'd laughed at his little pun.

His dad jokes were already second to none.

It was almost like she could feel the first roots sinking down around them. This was the start of a family.

* * * * *

Don't miss the next book
in Patricia Johns's
An Amish Antiques Shop Romance
miniseries, coming December 2026
from Harlequin Heartwarming